W9-ARM-341

"You!" Chesterton gasped.

Dandre struggled to warm her smile, to say something that would reassure the gentleman before her, whatever it was he needed reassurance of. But before she could say anything, Mrs. Redding was hailing them from across the stream, and Mr. Redding was already splashing his horse across, pulling Mr. Chesterton's horse behind him.

Chesterton glanced over his shoulder, then turned and leaned toward the young woman again.

"You must not say anything to my sister or Mr. Redding," he whispered urgently. "I beseech you not to tell them what you know."

Dandre looked at the gentleman, nearly dumbfounded. Not only did she not know what it was she knew that she must not tell the Reddings, but Mr. Chesterton did not sound as if he were beseeching her. Rather his words sounded like a command— *and* a warning....

Dear Reader,

Harlequin Historicals would like to introduce you to a new concept. Big books! Beginning with October, we will be publishing one longer title a month with books that will include everything from popular reprints to originals from your favorite authors.

Our first longer title, *The Bargain*, by Veronica Sattler is a sexy historical set during the Regency period. It's the story of Lord Brett Westmont and Ashleigh Sinclair, two people who are thrown together in a series of compromising positions, only to fall madly in love.

In *Tapestry*, by author Sally Cheney, heroine Dandre Collin discovers that the rough mill worker who rescues her from a runaway carriage is really her uncle's aristocratic neighbor.

An ex-masterspy grows bored with his forced retirement and winds up creating more mischief than he can handle by taking a wife in *The Gilded Lion*, a sensual tale from Kit Gardner.

Finally, author Louisa Rawlings returns to France as the setting for *Scarlet Woman*, an intriguing story of murder and revenge.

We hope you enjoy all four of this month's titles.

And next month, be on the lookout for the long awaited reissue of *Pieces of Sky* by Marianne Willman, the unforgettable story of a spinster who marries the cruel Abner Slade but finds true love in the arms of Roger Le Beau, her husband's sworn enemy.

Sincerely,

Tracy Farrell
Senior Editor

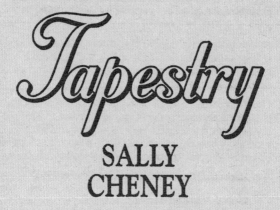

Tapestry

SALLY CHENEY

Harlequin Books

TORONTO • NEW YORK • LONDON
AMSTERDAM • PARIS • SYDNEY • HAMBURG
STOCKHOLM • ATHENS • TOKYO • MILAN
MADRID • WARSAW • BUDAPEST • AUCKLAND

If you purchased this book without a cover you should be aware that this book is stolen property. It was reported as "unsold and destroyed" to the publisher, and neither the author nor the publisher has received any payment for this "stripped book."

Harlequin Historicals first edition October 1993

ISBN 0-373-28792-5

TAPESTRY

Copyright © 1993 by Sally Cheney.
All rights reserved. Except for use in any review, the reproduction or utilization of this work in whole or in part in any form by any electronic, mechanical or other means, now known or hereafter invented, including xerography, photocopying and recording, or in any information storage or retrieval system, is forbidden without the permission of the publisher, Harlequin Historicals, 300 E. 42nd St., New York, N.Y. 10017

All the characters in this book have no existence outside the imagination of the author and have no relation whatsoever to anyone bearing the same name or names. They are not even distantly inspired by any individual known or unknown to the author, and all incidents are pure invention.

®: Trademark registered in the United States Patent and Trademark Office and in other countries.

Printed in the U.S.A.

Books by Sally Cheney

Harlequin Historicals

Game of Hearts #36
Thief in the Night #112
Tender Journey #148
Tapestry #192

SALLY CHENEY

was a bookstore owner before coming to her first love—writing. She has traveled extensively in the United States, but is happiest with the peaceful rural life in her home state of Idaho. When she is not writing, she is active in community affairs and enjoys cooking and gardening.

Every author owes particular thanks to a special librarian. Mine goes to Mona Henner for her relentless pursuit of the information I need.

Prologue

The night air was moist and clinging, reminding one rather of the white of an egg. The year was still new and travelers were well advised to bundle up warmly and ride in closed carriages.

The fine gentleman on horseback was commencing to wish he had hired one of the commercial coaches for this trip. His cheeks were stinging; the air was damp and had penetrated the material of his trouser legs; the knee he had twisted when he was a child throbbed.

Although he had been through Manchester to Oldham before, his last visit to this part of the country had been years ago and he was not familiar enough with the countryside to know exactly how near to his destination he was. Now the moist, heavy cold was sinking through the thick wool of his cloak, and he hoped he was very near his journey's end.

He was concentrating more on his discomforts than he was on the unfamiliar roadway and he did not see the small form scurrying along the shoulder of the road. He felt his leg brush against something soft, knocking it down. His horse snorted and shied away.

"Ow!"

Even in the confusion of his surprise and the sudden effort it took to calm his steed and bring it under control once more, the gentleman recognized the cry to be that of a child.

As quickly as possible he jumped from his horse's back and ran to the side of the road. He almost stumbled over the child, who was struggling to his feet, but drew up short when he detected the movement and avoided another collision.

"Are you injured?" he asked with concern, though he did not believe the child had been struck with enough force to break any bones.

"Don't hurt me!" the youngster wailed, shying away from the hand the man extended.

"I am not going to hurt you," the man said, his voice soothing, his hand still trying to reach the little stranger.

At last his fingers touched a shoulder and then closed around a very thin arm. His eyes had at last adjusted themselves, and as he pulled the child to him, he was able to see that it was a mere slip of a boy.

"Don't send me back!" the boy wailed.

"I will not. Do not worry. Good heavens!" the horseman exclaimed. "What are you doing out here dressed like that?"

"It's all I had . . . what I had on. It's all we're allowed."

The apparel that so appalled the man was a thin, short-sleeved shirt and a pair of ragged pantaloons. The child, who had hardly an inch of insulating flesh covering his bones, was unprotected from the cold by any outer garment.

"All you are 'allowed'? What do you mean?"

"To keep us from running they lock our cloaks away. So you have to run when you can, with what's on your back." The boy twisted and winced at the grip of the man. "Oh, let me go! They'll catch me if I don't get further away."

"Who will catch you? From what are you running?" The man kept his hands around the boy's arms, though it was like trying to hold an eel as the child squirmed in his grasp.

"The overlooker. The mill. Oh, mister, *please!* They'll beat me if they catch me."

"I will not allow..." the gentleman started, but suddenly a look of hopeless, helpless dismay suffused the child's face.

"Well, Danny." A voice as heavy and cold as the wintry night air sounded behind the gentleman's shoulder. He was kneeling in front of the child and had to look up and over his shoulder to see the speaker.

It was a moonless night, but the darkness surrounding the man behind him seemed almost to be generated from within.

"I'll take 'im off your hands now, and Mr. Braid thanks you, sir."

The gentleman did not offer to release the child, but with a gesture that was surprisingly swift and strong, the newcomer reached out and grabbed the child's arm away from him. Before the gentleman could do anything to prevent it, the other man pulled the resisting child to him and, putting his arm around the boy's middle, raised him from the ground and rested the kicking, clawing little bundle against his hip as carelessly as if the boy were a sack of flour.

"I say there," the gentleman protested, rising to his feet. "What do you mean by forcibly taking that child? This is England, you know. There are laws here." He took a step forward but was stopped by the glimmer of a knife in the man's free hand.

"You're right there, there are laws. And one of those laws says a mill owner is entitled to the work he pays for."

"Are you telling me this child is paid to work in one of those mills?" the man asked, a note of disbelief in his voice. Why the boy was six, perhaps seven years old!

"I'm telling you the *boy* was paid for. As long as he's at the mill he gets food and clothes. And if he runs away he gets brought back and taught a lesson."

"But he is—" the gentleman started.

"Like I said, I thank ye for stoppin' the lad, and now I'll thank you to get back up on your horse and ride away and let me do the job *I'm* paid for."

The man waved the knife in front of him as he backed away toward his own horse.

The child had never stopped resisting, but now, when he saw his only chance of succor about to vanish, he redoubled his efforts. He might have been a mouse trying to free itself from a steel trap.

"Oh, mister, help me! He'll lay the strap on me!" the boy sobbed.

The entreated gentleman could not stand and do nothing while the helpless child was so cruelly taken. He stepped forward. The other man sliced through the air dangerously with the blade. The gentleman tried to knock the arm and the weapon away so he could grapple with the abductor. For his troubles he sustained an ugly gash across the back of his hand. In surprised pain he stopped and stepped back. The other man took advantage of the momentary pause to drop the child and deliver a full-handed slap to his face.

The little boy fell down, not knocked unconscious but dazed by the heavy blow.

The gentleman, recovered, rushed forward, but the child's captor was now free of encumbrances. He crouched and threatened the would-be rescuer with his knife, weaving it back and forth in front of him, a nasty smile raising one corner of his mouth.

"So you think to take the boy from me? You'll have to get by my blade first. And I should advise you that this blade demands a heavy toll."

He lunged forward, but the gentleman sidestepped him. He had meant to turn swiftly and catch the other man before he could get the knife in front of him again, but the cloak he wore was heavy with moisture and made him ungainly. It wrapped itself around his legs, and when he tried to kick the weight of the material away, he stumbled and fell to his knee.

The man with the knife was on him in a moment. He raised the blade, but a motion behind the gentleman caught his eye.

The child was attempting to crawl away. Impatiently the assailant drew back his fist, which was curled around the handle of the knife, and struck the man beneath him on the jaw. The gentleman's head slammed into the hard dirt of the road and immediately his muscles relaxed in unconsciousness.

Then, before the boy had even pushed himself to his feet, his captor had his arm, like a tentacle, around him again, lifting him from the ground.

"No! Help!"

"Shut up, Danny," the man snarled into the boy's ear. "Nobody can hear you now, so if you ever want to work again, don't make any more trouble for me."

The child did *not* want to go back to the mill to work, but he was able to deduce that his alternative was taking his captor's blade between his own ribs.

Forlornly he looked behind him at the gentleman crumpled and still on the ground. His struggles weakened and he gulped back his sobs.

The man pulled himself onto his horse and rode swiftly away, back toward Manchester.

Ten minutes later the gentleman who had knocked the child down and frustrated his flight moaned and stirred under the layers of soggy wool. He pushed the treacherous cloth from in front of his face and sat up. Gently he moved his jaw back and forth. It hurt, but it was not broken.

The boy was gone and so was the man with the knife. Doubtless they had left together. The gentleman shook his head and stood up. He looked around for his own horse and was relieved to see it standing docilely by the side of the road.

As he climbed astride his animal again, he tried to remember the name his assailant had mentioned.

Bard? Boyd?

Braid!

"Mr. Braid thanks you," the villain had said.

The wail of the frightened child still rang in his ears.
Something ought to be done....

Chapter One

With a start, Dandre Collins pulled herself up and opened her green eyes very wide, willing them, however unsuccessfully, to stay open.

The pretty young woman in the coach car had been forcing herself to remain awake the whole ride from Coventry to Manchester. Not because she had never traveled from Coventry to Manchester before. She had been going back and forth for most of her life, and the passing scenery used to be perfectly bucolic and quite dull. But in recent years, solid, imposing factories had started to appear all around Manchester, and then a year ago the Liverpool and Manchester Railway line had opened. This was Dandre's first ride on the Manchester railway, having previously traveled by coach the entire trip, and what had developed over the years into a chance for several hours of uninterrupted sleep had suddenly become an adventure again.

But the ride *was* long, and by the time the train reached the crowded Manchester station Dandre was very tired, feeling the aches of travel and generally cranky. When at last the wheels stopped turning and the train came to a complete stop, it was in a state of disorientation that the young woman stumbled from the car and down the two or three steps from the train onto the solid, unmoving ground.

She stood swaying uncertainly for a moment, experiencing some of the residual motion sensation sailors encounter when they try to walk on land with their sea legs. At last she started forward, beginning to feel foolish just standing there, but as it turned out, she had been a little premature in her initiative.

"Watch out!"

An arm shot through the cloud of steam and encircled her waist. Dandre was pulled into the close embrace of a great lout of a fellow, a filthy workman. His face towered above hers, and as she was held so close to his person, Dandre was only immediately aware that his neck was streaked with grease and grime and he had a hairy chest, as revealed by the loosened buttons of his collar and the gaping vee of his shirt which exposed a fair amount of that chest.

Dandre's traveling ensemble included a veiled hat, which very properly protected a lady's anonymity in the public depot, but at the moment she was grateful the thin gauze of material that covered her face also hid the bright pink that suffused her cheeks at the stranger's familiarity.

"I beg your pardon!" she cried, placing her hands against his chest as she tried to push herself away and regain her equilibrium.

The establishment of the young woman's balance seemed also to be the aim of the workman, but they were striving for that goal at cross purposes. Every time Dandre pulled away the man crushed her to him more tightly, endeavoring to back the two of them off the crowded passenger lane that fronted the recently arrived train.

Even in the shock and confusion of the moment, Dandre was aware of two very distinct physical sensations. The first was the flutter of her skirts and the swirl of air around her ankles as the wheels of a swiftly moving carriage skimmed past her.

The second sensation was the tension and solid strength of the muscles in the arm around her, the chest in front of her and in the man's thighs, which were indecently and intimately pressed against her own—discounting, of course, his trousers, her dress, the length of his coat and several layers of her petticoats.

The carriage that had very nearly run her down, that had rustled her skirts as the man pulled her from its path, had not left both of them completely unscathed. Dandre was uninjured, but a jagged bit of metal protruding from the carriage door, no doubt attached to the folding steps, caught the flesh at the back of the man's hand, the hand that held her so tightly against him, despite her efforts to free herself and fling her person once again into harm's way.

The metal bit snagged the skin of his hand, leaving a long, bloody gash along the back of it and a few inches up his arm.

"Damnation!" the fellow roared in agony, but even then he did not release her, making sure she was safe and steady on her feet, well out of the traffic, before he finally withdrew his arm.

Only then did he clasp his hand to his chest and stomp his feet, though he did not follow his initial curse with a stream of profanities, which he would very much like to have done, as Dandre could tell from the grimace on his face.

Separated at last by a few feet, Dandre could finally see more of the man than a dirty neck and a hairy chest. He was tall and appeared to be broad shouldered and big, dressed as he was in a black, bulky coat and baggy trousers made of coarse homespun. The parts of his body that were not covered by the heavy fabric were covered by grime and oil.

His hair was black and tangled, and his face, like his neck, was streaked with dirt, with black patches of oil on his cheeks like dabs of sooty rouge.

When the man released her he left smudges of his dirt all across the light fawn-colored material of her traveling coat, and a clear outline of his hand stood in stark relief square on the back of her coat, where he had pressed her to him.

Ignoring the smudges, not even clearly aware of them, Dandre stepped toward the man.

"Thank you," she said, and then, "I might have been injured."

"You would have been killed," the man snarled, but more from pain than anger. She hoped.

All things considered, she actually admired his restraint and self-control and, ignoring his growl, took another step toward him. Her hand in its pearly white glove was extended solicitously.

"Can I help you?" she asked.

The fellow shook his head. He pulled a handkerchief from the pocket of his jacket. The handkerchief was, predictably, gray and dirty. He wrapped the square of material around his hand and over the blood seeping through the torn flesh.

"You really ought to have that looked to," she advised seriously. She put her fingertips against his hand and its clumsy bandage, not seeming to notice the spots of dirt and oil or the scarlet traces of blood that clung to her glove at the contact.

He barked a harsh laugh but did not withdraw his hand or push hers away.

"I shall do that very thing, m'lady." He smiled wearily. "'Ave it looked to proper like, cleaned and bandaged neat as a pin. With a fine recommendation from a subscriber such as yourself, I can just go see Dr. Fisher in the infirmary and 'ave my every care soothed away by one of his magic potions, now can't I? Soon as 'e tends to the poor little mites that 'ave been brought in all bloodied and torn limb from limb." He spoke angrily, but glancing at the girl he saw the hurt and confused droop of her lips and assumed a gentler tone.

"It's all right, miss. Nothin' but a scratch, really. It bein' the end of the week it's only half day tomorrow, and since the mill owners all call themselves Christian men, don't you know, they won't work us on the Lord's day. Eases their consciences for driving us like dumb animals the rest of the week." He laughed his hoarse laugh again, smoothing the rough edges of his bray a little, and then did drop his arm away from the gentle pressure of her fingers.

"Very well," Dandre said, once again confused and embarrassed, this time by his rejection of her compassion.

"You mustn't worry, girl. I suppose I will survive a little cut on my hand. What about you, though? You're not hurt?"

"Not at all."

At last they faced each other squarely. Until that moment his eyes had been darting around the busy thoroughfare or tightened against his pain, and Dandre's eyes, startled out of focus, had been avoiding the boldness of his glance. But finally the fellow looked directly at her, trying to see through the haze of material across her face to the hints of green fire that were her eyes. And Dandre was frankly amazed by what she saw in the man's eyes. Under his black brows and surrounded by long, dark lashes, his eyes were a clear blue, full of interest and intelligence, humor, keen wit, deep understanding.

Always before Dandre had clumped common laborers, like this man, into a dull, faceless mob who went about their necessary tasks with slight interest and even slighter intellect.

"I do seem to have dropped my things, though...when you grabbed me...that is, when you pulled me from harm's way," she told him, stuttering and halting, embarrassed by the flush of genuine attraction she felt for this man and his black brows and blue eyes. *This* would never do.

"Is that them there?" he asked.

Dandre was relieved to turn her eyes in the direction he indicated. Directions, actually. Her carpetbag and umbrella had flown to opposite destinations when she dropped them. Now one was twenty feet to the right of them, and the other, the umbrella, was ten feet to the left. But that distance was steadily increasing as passersby stumbled against the bag and kicked the umbrella along in front of them.

She took a step toward her receding umbrella but turned back to tender one final word of appreciation.

"I do thank you," she said. "You have been most kind. I believe I can manage for myself now."

A very fine gentleman dressed spotlessly in suit coat and fine twilled trousers, with a brown derby on his head and crisp white spats on his shoes, was hurrying to catch one of the trains rumbling on the rails and slammed into Dandre's shoulder, knocking her off balance as she reached for the umbrella. The gentleman merely glanced distractedly in her direction, then hurried away without even slowing. It was the bandaged hand, wrapped in the dirty handkerchief, that grabbed her arm again, this time her left arm, putting another outline of his hand on that sleeve as he steadied her on her feet.

"I'm not sure of that myself," he said, a smile pulling at his lips despite his injury and impatience. He drew her once again from the mainstream of traffic and planted her firmly next to the platform.

"Now you just stand right here," he said. He held up his index finger in stern warning. "Stay." He spoke like a master to a puppy straining against unfamiliar control, as Dandre was straining against the hand that held her in place.

"My things," she protested.

"I'll get your things," he said. He shook his forefinger beneath her upturned nose in a final caution, then turned and plunged into the thinning crowd.

Dandre watched the tall, black-haired, gray-skinned figure dart in and around the swarm of people, grabbing the carpetbag from between two big coal workers who flanked it and snatching the umbrella just as it was kicked off the walkway toward the tracks.

The man skipped back through the crowd, surprisingly light on his feet, considering his size, the baggage he was carrying, the bulk of his clothing and the weight of the heavy work boots he wore.

"'Ere ye be, miss. Safe and sound and only a mite worse for the wear. Now where is it you're trying to get to?"

"One of those coaches," Dandre said.

The man looked over his shoulder at the line of cabs waiting for the trains on the newly opened Liverpool-Manchester line. He pulled the carpetbag and umbrella back toward him, shaking his head, a sorrowful smile on his lips.

"What is it?" the girl asked. "Are not those coaches for hire?"

"Oh yes, miss. But first you have to get to them."

Now there was no mistaking and no hesitation to his mocking smile.

Dandre felt another wash of pink on her cheeks that she was glad her veil hid. The pink was not only from embarrassment but pique, as well. The fellow had been very helpful, even, she was sure, gallant, in his rough way, but she would not be laughed at or condescended to.

"I can manage myself," she said frostily. She leaned toward him, reaching for her bag, but the hat she wore tipped forward and, grabbing for it, she was thrown off balance. The man gave a warning cry, dropped the bag and umbrella and stopped her fall with one hand against her shoulder and his other hand groping wildly as he himself tripped over the carpetbag and fell heavily to his knees.

Dandre, firmly on her feet once again, secured her hat and then offered her hand to her fallen rescuer.

"Let me help you," she said.

The man shook his head, pushing himself up off the roadway and rubbing his knee.

"No, miss, let *me* help *you*. I beg you."

He picked up the umbrella and the overturned carpetbag and turned toward the coaches, which seemed so far away. He sighed and hitched his load, glancing over his shoulder at the young woman.

"Just follow me. And try not to get into any more trouble than you have to," he warned.

Chapter Two

Dandre Collin had come from Coventry, where she was born and grew up. She lived in a large, comfortable home with her father, James Collin, Esquire, Katey Collin, her mother, two younger sisters, Katherine and Beth, and, only on school holidays now, her brother, Paul.

She studied ancient history and dry literature with her sisters, rode some and walked often, practiced the piano and produced lovely embroidered tea towels and crocheted doilies. She tended the flower garden in the summer and wrote impassioned poetry during the long winter evenings, which she read to her sisters and carefully hid from her mother.

She had always considered her life to be idyllic, but being halfway through her twentieth year, she was beginning to revise that idea and replace the word *idyllic* with *tame*. Definitely tame.

The Collin girls alternated summer visits to their Woodley aunt and uncle in the north, and this was Dandre's summer. Dandre was determined to make it a summer of adventure.

She had begun her visit by nearly getting herself killed in the Manchester train station.

That was not exactly the type of adventure she was looking for this year, and a rude, dirty workman was not the sort of person with whom she was hoping to share her adventure. But it was a start.

The factory hand had hailed a coach for her, lifted her luggage up to the driver and had even given her a hand up into the passenger box. His reward had been a pretty smile, and it was only after the carriage door was closed that she realized with a guilty start that he had probably been expecting a monetary reward. He certainly deserved it.

But the opportunity was gone, and in only a moment the coach rolled away from the grime and chaos of the Manchester terminal and into the pretty, peaceful Lancashire countryside.

Her aunt and uncle, Mr. and Mrs. Woodley, lived outside of Manchester near Oldham, on the way to Huddersfield. It was a trip she had made before, at least once every other year, but always before it had been by coach the whole long, uncomfortable way. With the opening of the train line only the year before, Dandre had been able to board the train at Stoke-on-Trent and ride it all the way into Manchester this time.

That had been a proper beginning to her *summer of adventure.* She relaxed her head against the cushion of the seat and smiled faintly as she finally allowed her lids to sink and cover her eyes. With her eyes closed she saw the man's face before her again, the man who had clutched her to him at the station. She saw his clear, intelligent eyes and was forced to admit they had been very handsome eyes. She smiled again.

Dandre had always been unfortunately prone to mishap, and though the incident at the Manchester terminal might have been serious, it was not completely surprising that it had threatened her. As the coach rolled along the roadway, its wheels only occasionally dropping into a hole or a rut, she determined that she did not need to tell her aunt about the near accident in Manchester. Aunt Bea worried enough about her as it was. And if she did not tell her aunt about her brush with catastrophe, she was certainly not going to say anything about the common workman with gorgeous eyes who had rescued her.

Aunt Beatrice, Mrs. Woodley, was her father's sister, his only sister, and the Woodleys and the Collins often exchanged visits. Dandre's mother, Katey O'Brien Collin, had numerous brothers and sisters, but they were all across the sea in Ireland, and so far only Cousin Edward had attempted the one hundred and seventy miles from Dublin to Coventry and then down to London town to seek his fortune, which he had not as yet found, as evidenced by the regular pleas for five or ten pounds they received from him by way of mail.

Dandre's father, James Collin, was a lawyer, semiretired now, who had, for some reason none of the Collins understood, taken up the study of the violin in midlife. He devoted an hour or two a day to extracting sounds from it: whines, screeches, wails and even occasional notes, though very rarely recognizable melodies. His practice was indulgently tolerated by his family, as had been his short-lived interests in long-horned sheep, semiprecious gems and the prophet Jeremiah in the Bible.

When one considered it, life in the Collin home was really quite interesting. But not adventurous.

Henry Biggins, the Woodley coachman, handyman, serving man and occasionally, though always under protest, formal butler, met the young woman at the Oldham crossing and transported her to the Woodley carriage; her and her umbrella, carpetbag and the large trunk that had made its way from the train to the coach with much less peril than had Dandre.

"Dandre!" Mrs. Woodley waved her kerchief in excitement from the door of the house when Henry pulled the team to a halt.

"Aunt Bea!" Dandre flung the door open and hopped from the carriage, scorning Henry and his stately procurement of the little stepladder.

She flung herself into her aunt's arms and the two of them hugged and kissed fondly.

In a moment, though, Mrs. Woodley held the girl away from her, her eyes opening wide as she noted her niece's dishevelment and saw the dirty marks across the girl's clothing, including the very distinguishable outline of a large hand on either sleeve.

"Good heavens, child! What has happened?"

Dandre glanced down at the mark on her right sleeve and brushed at it, not wiping it away or even dimming the outline, yet somehow managing to transfer a dark smudge to the palm of her glove.

"A fellow in Manchester gave me some assistance," she said.

Her aunt furrowed her brow quizzically, but since Dandre appeared to be perfectly all right and unwilling to say any more about it, she did not press the girl for details.

"Well, come in now, my dear," she said instead. "Your Uncle Peter and I are both eager for news. And, of course, delighted to see you."

Mrs. Woodley pulled her into the little house.

The Woodleys had no children of their own, which, besides making visits from their extended family especially welcome, also allowed them to live comfortably in a tiny little domicile that looked as if it might have come straight from the pages of a fairy tale book.

Downstairs was a small sitting room, dining room, kitchen and pantry, and off the pantry was a small set of rooms for the Bigginses, Henry and his wife, Mildred, who served the Woodleys as housekeeper. There was another little room off the sitting room, approximately the size of a walk-in closet. Mr. Woodley called it his library. Mrs. Woodley called it the morning room, since it did have one window that faced east. It also had a bookcase against the north wall that held a dozen volumes or so, vindicating Uncle Peter's claim.

Upstairs were two bedrooms and another small room that could, in an emergency, serve as another bedroom, if an emergency ever arose. In the twenty-five years of the Woodley marriage, no emergency had.

"Your parents are well?"

"Very well," Dandre answered.

"Kathy and Beth? How do they get along?"

"Fine, I suppose. They both have their heads in the clouds and refuse to take anything seriously, save the neighborhood boys and the style of their hair. But you know what *children* they are."

Dandre spoke scornfully of her sisters, fifteen and eleven, and Mrs. Woodley hid her own smile at her niece's great show of maturity. The length of time it had been since Dandre's primary concerns were neighborhood boys and hairstyles could be measured in months, not years. But Mrs. Woodley did quell her smile as she studied her niece carefully. Dandre had grown since last her aunt had seen her. She held herself with a more erect bearing, and there was a sober light in her eyes, which was new. Her voice was lower, calmer, her green eyes less given to flashing. She seemed not to be as influenced by the red tint of her hair, inherited from her mother and her mother's Irish family, as she was by the reasonably taupe undertones her father had given her.

Mr. Woodley came in from his consultation with Henry and joined the two ladies. The afternoon passed pleasantly. Mildred served supper, and then the evening passed pleasantly. As good-nights were exchanged, Dandre picked up her traveling cloak from the chair where it had lain since she entered the sitting room with her aunt, and Mr. Woodley noticed the dirty marks on either arm.

"What is this?" he asked.

"What? Oh, that. Nothing. Just a brush I had with a mill worker in Manchester."

"Good heavens, child!" Mr. Woodley cried, outrage in his voice as Dandre put the cloak over her arm, displaying the clear outline of a man's hand against the back, which mark Aunt Bea had not even seen before or she would have pressed her own questions. "Were you accosted?"

"No, no." Dandre folded the cloak casually, but so the mark was hidden by the material. "A man just helped me a little at the Manchester station."

"Not a gentleman," Uncle Peter said, directing another disapproving scowl at the smudges of dirt on his niece's coat.

But Dandre was seeing once again the dark figure before her, holding her bundles with a bandaged hand, walking with a slight limp as he escorted her to the coach, and she was forced to smile and shake her head.

"You are wrong, Uncle Peter," she said. "He was very much a gentleman."

It was the beginning of summertime in Lancashire, as indeed it was all over England. Dandre was awakened by two noisy swallows outside her window, chattering and quarreling as they attempted to work together to build their nest. The air was as clear as a goblet of Waterford crystal. Less than ten miles away was the stench and smoke of the Manchester mills, yet here the countryside was like a morning dewdrop.

Dandre stretched, sighed and turned onto her back.

Now another bird had come into the tree outside her window and evidently possession of the limb was being hotly contested.

"Miss Collin, are you awake? Oh, I hope I did not disturb you." It was Mrs. Biggins who opened the door and put her head around the panel.

Dandre smiled.

"Not at all," she said. "I have been listening to them."
She looked toward the window and laughed as one of the
swallows fluttered its wings toward the intruder, startling it
off the limb.

"Mind if I put these linens away?" Now the door was
fully open and Dandre could see that Mrs. Biggins's arms
were piled with sheets, pillowcases and towels. The "spare
bedroom" in the Woodley house was attached to Dandre's
room and served, until an emergency arose, as a linen
closet, which was a function that made full use of the
available space.

"Come in, come in," the girl said, flinging the blankets
back and swinging her legs over the edge of the bed.

Mrs. Biggins bustled into the room. The housekeeper was
short and plump and talkative. She and her husband,
Henry, quarreled merrily almost all the time. They were, in
fact, the perfect personifications of the two sparrows outside Dandre's window.

"It is a distinct pleasure to see you again, Miss Collin. A
distinct pleasure. I know the missus has been anxious for
your visit. And you are here for the summer?"

"A month or two." Dandre smiled in Mrs. Biggins's direction, though that lady had her back toward the girl as
she put her armload away.

"You have arrived in time to take dinner at Timbrey,
anyway. The Woodleys are invited for supper this evening."

"Timbrey? Timbrey is let?"

"Let? La, miss, its owner is back. Mr. Chesterton himself. Young Mr. Chesterton, that is. The old Mr. Chesterton died six or eight winters ago. Timbrey has been empty
since then. But Mr. Chesterton, young Mr. Chesterton, has
seen the world now, been about sowing his wild oats, as
people say. People don't say it aloud, certainly, but Mr.
Biggins says it to me often enough. A body would think it
is not Mr. Chesterton's wild oats he is thinking about but

his own. Or lack of same. And sincere regrets he has about them, too.''

''And he is hosting a dinner party?''

''Mr. Biggins?'' Mildred asked in confusion, having lost the thread of her conversation with Miss Collin in the labyrinth of her asides and commentary. ''Oh, Mr. Chesterton, you mean. No, well, that is, your uncle and aunt—and you, too, I am sure—are invited to dine at Timbrey, but I do not know that it will be a dinner party.'' Mrs. Biggins stopped talking for a moment while she raised one pile of towels in order to put the towels she had brought in with her underneath them. That operation finished, she spoke over her shoulder while patting the towels, and then the sheets next to them, into place. ''The invitation coming from Mr. Chesterton last week, I *assume* he will be there, though I have it from the girls up at Timbrey that he has been away all this week. Goes and comes a good deal. Well, you would expect that, wouldn't you?'' Mrs. Biggins stepped back with hands on her hips to study the restocked shelves in front of her with an approving eye. ''There now.'' She nodded and turned toward Dandre. ''Mrs. Woodley asks if you are coming down to breakfast. Shall I tell her you are awake and will be down directly?''

''Directly.'' Dandre stood encouragingly by her door, hoping that Mrs. Biggins would leave her to get dressed before breakfast became a cold, late lunch.

Mrs. Biggins did leave her alone quickly enough so she was able to get dressed and join her uncle and aunt at the breakfast table.

They exchanged morning greetings and what items of news that might have transpired between their good-nights yesterday and their good-mornings today.

Mrs. Woodley selected one more of Mrs. Biggins's flaky biscuits, choosing the smallest one she could find, since she had already eaten two before Dandre joined them.

"And we are to dine at Timbrey this evening with Mr. Chesterton," Mrs. Woodley said.

"The *young* Mr. Chesterton. Yes, I know," Dandre said, smiling toward the door that led to the kitchen and the sounds of activity in there. "Though I understand he has been away from Timbrey this week and his actual presence at the gathering is in question."

Uncle Peter laughed. "Henry did not have the chance to talk with his wife or your information would have been more current. Mr. Fransen stopped as we were looking to the horses this morning. It seems that while Mr. Chesterton has not arrived yet, he *will* be at Timbrey Hall tonight and has sent final instructions for the dinner. He had a list of purchases his cook was to make, and it just happens that Mr. Chesterton's cook and Mr. Fransen's cook shop at the same stores in Oldham."

"There, you see? We shall be supping with young Mr. Chesterton after all." Mrs. Woodley smiled at her niece.

"What is Mr. Chesterton like?" Dandre asked, understandably interested in someone who owned a lovely old place like Timbrey Hall and was always designated as "young," though that was as much description as she had heard of him so far.

"Well, he is young," Mrs. Woodley reported vaguely.

"I understand he is a pleasant enough fellow," her uncle offered.

"You understand? Then you do not know Mr. Chesterton? You have never met him?"

"He only just opened Timbrey again and has been repairing and refurbishing the hall after its years of disuse," Aunt Bea said defensively.

"The dinner invitation was brought across to us by the Chesterton footman—scandalized poor Henry to see such a duty required of a serving man. Mr. Chesterton himself has been kept very busy. Back and forth to Manchester, once even down to London, I hear. Of course, that is where he left to come to Lancashire. He has many friends in London, I imagine.''

"So you have not met him." Dandre looked from one to the other of the Woodleys for a confirmation of her deduction.

"Not recently," Mrs. Woodley said, still sounding vague.

"What your aunt means but is reluctant to admit is that we were introduced to the elder Mr. Chesterton during one or the other of the family's infrequent summers at Timbrey before the old man passed away, but she cannot remember the boy."

"I remember they had a pretty little daughter. Married now, I believe."

"And I remember a skinny rascal sent from the room in disgrace on one visit, but Mrs. Woodley must not have been with me on that occasion, for she remembers offensive behavior even better than I do, and if she had been there she could no doubt tell you whether it was his sister's ringlet that was pulled or the cat's tail."

"And *he* has inherited Timbrey?" Dandre asked, appalled that such a childish ne'er-do-well should be in possession of so important a piece of property.

"He is a grown man now," her aunt said with a laugh. "Your uncle was speaking of him when he was twelve years old or younger."

"Oh, younger than that, I should say," Mr Woodley said. "The boy would have been sent away to school by the time he was twelve, probably at ten. No, the boy I am remembering was very young, unrecognizable in the man he has become, I am certain."

Dandre pushed her breakfast plate away from her and wiped her lips with the napkin before slipping it back into its ring.

"And what does Mr. Chesterton do?" she asked.

"Do?" Her aunt smiled. "My dear, Mr. Chesterton is very rich. He does not *do* anything."

In the hours before the time of their engagement, Dandre unpacked, went with her aunt through the house, looking at mementos that were familiar and loved, and went with her uncle over the Woodley property, looking at the modern innovations that had been made in the stables, the well, the carriage house and equipment since last she visited.

With her uncle she heard Henry's list of repairs that needed to be made around the house and grounds and his excellent excuses why *he* could not see to them himself and his recommendations for who in the neighborhood could.

She was also interested to hear her uncle's report on the cotton mill in which he shared part interest with a Mr. William Firth. Lancashire, owing to the waterways and the moisture of the climate, was ideal for spinning and the production of textiles. The county, especially around Manchester, was positively thick with cloth mills of one sort or another, cottons, silks and woolens. Every man of means in Lancashire, who in years past might have invested in cattle or grain or even the little cottage industries, now put his money into textiles and realized a healthy return.

"With the new power loom, one man and two children can do the work of twenty. It is a marvelous age we live in, Dandre, my dear," her uncle told her.

"What are they like?" the girl asked.

"They?"

"The mills. The train must have passed twenty on the way into Manchester."

"I am sure it did. Business is booming!" Her uncle smiled broadly and threw back his shoulders. Though he had not answered her question directly, it was clear that what the mills were like was of very small moment, as long as business was doing well.

When Dandre was not talking with her aunt, her uncle or Henry Biggins, Mildred Biggins completely filled up any quiet moments with her chatter, opinions, comments and gossip. It would have taken more than two days to run that reservoir dry. The Bigginses had worked for the Woodleys now for fourteen years, and Mildred showed no signs yet of slowing down.

In a flash the day was gone and Mrs. Woodley was fretting over her preparations and their departure, though dinner was not to be served until eight o'clock.

Dandre, with her reddish hair and greenish eyes, had a wardrobe stocked with autumnal-colored dresses, so that the hanging gowns looked like a leafy tree after the first frost, some leaves orange, some red, some yellow and some few hardy ones green still. Dandre chose a sunny apricot for this evening, Mrs. Woodley was in lavender, Mr. Woodley was uncomfortable in his stiff collar, and Mrs. Biggins was consumed by envy and curiosity as the master and mistress and their niece made preparations to leave.

"What do you think they will eat, Mr. Biggins? And who else do you imagine will be there? Will they dance or play cards afterward? Or will Mr. Chesterton have engaged some sort of entertainment, do you think?"

"I think it is none of your affair, Mrs. Biggins."

But Mrs. Biggins was not to be discouraged, much the same way that a red flag does not discourage a buffalo stampede.

"I wonder what Mr. Chesterton is like—what sort of man he has grown up to be? I remember some of the stories Daisy over at the Timbrey used to tell of him. A hellion. Oh, a boy, right enough, but all boy, as they say. When do you think the Woodleys and Miss Collin will be home, Mr. Biggins?"

Mr. Biggins did not answer his wife but studied his reflection in the mirror and straightened the riding hat on his head.

Timbrey, or Timbrey Hall as it was more formally called, was the ancestral home of the Lancashire Chestertons. It stood in the middle of a lush park two miles from the modest little Woodley home.

The invitation the Chesterton man had brought across to them said dinner would be served at eight o'clock, post meridiem. Mrs. Woodley determined they could arrive at seven forty-five, but no later than 7:50. She left a very narrow window for error, but Henry seemed to understand her anxiety and moderated the speed of the team of horses so that they pulled onto the Timbrey drive at 7:43, which allowed them two to seven minutes to halt, disembark and smooth dresses, trousers and hair before Mr. Woodley raised the heavy knocker on the massive front door.

There were a number of carriages in the drive, and the door, opened by a footman in velvet coat and white wig, released the confusion of a myriad of voices.

"It *is* to be a dinner party," Mrs. Woodley whispered to her niece. There was a note in her voice that was part injury and part flattery. She had expected the Woodleys to be the exclusive guests of Mr. Chesterton, but she was certainly honored—and relieved—to be included in his larger, more distinguished party.

Another wigged footman led them across the receiving hall and into a dazzlingly lighted salon. The flicker of innumerable candles was reflected off glass, crystal and mirrors everywhere Dandre turned her eyes.

The girl recognized the Kimbers, who stood right inside the salon doors, and Mr. and Mrs. Fransen further in the room, but she did not know the Mr. Brewster her aunt identified as the man who had hailed her uncle when they came in. Nor did she know the Misses Humphries.

"Miss Roberta Humphries, Miss Wilhelmina Humphries, this is my niece, Miss Dandre Collin. She is visiting from Coventry."

Dandre murmured her salutations and said what a signal honor it was to meet the Misses Humphries, wondering as she did so how parents knew, when a wee babe was first laid in their arms and they were required to give the child the name by which he would be known all his life, what that tiny bit of humanity would grow up to be like. Miss Roberta and Miss Wilhelmina Humphries looked exactly like a Roberta and a Wilhelmina. They were large-boned, heavy-featured, pasty-faced women, well past their prime, whenever that had been. But Dandre was not a mean-spirited soul and was certainly willing to assume the Misses Humphries had had a prime when they could have been described as—not handsome, no, but "pleasant," perhaps.

"Mrs. Woodley." It was her uncle who claimed his wife's arm and motioned for his niece to join them. "I believe we should exchange introductions with our host, if we are to share in the bounty of his board." He led them toward a group of people standing on the far side of the room.

Dandre did not recognize any of them and Mrs. Woodley softly told her, "I know only Rawley Cooper. That is his wife over with Mrs. Kimber. I wonder which of the others is our host?"

Dandre wondered herself. The older gentleman of the group, identified as Mr. Cooper, she had dismissed as a possibility already. Not only were there streaks of gray in his hair, which were distinguished and not unattractive—nor was that even an indication of advanced years, though people looking at Mr. Cooper would never refer to him as the *young* Mr. Cooper, as she had heard Mr. Chesterton designated several times, but Mr. Cooper was also of such a placid, sober, calm-bordering-on-unconscious mien that Dandre could not imagine him at any time in his entire life being described as a hellion.

There were two younger gentlemen in the grouping, along with an attractive woman. Mrs. Woodley, to herself, called her a "girl," but the unknown female was two or three years older than Dandre and had about her person that air of comfortable security that is indicative of the married state. To Dandre she was a woman.

One of the men was facing Dandre's direction. He had blond hair, which he wore long on the sides and swept across his forehead in an obvious attempt to disguise the fact that the hair on top of his head was beginning to thin and pull itself back, as if it were ashamed to be associated with the unattractive styling. That gentleman did have a spark in his eyes, which were a sharp hazel, and Dandre could well imagine he might once have been a ne'er-do-well. But from the labored combing of his hair she could tell he no longer was, and she sighed softly over how much to heart some men took the notion of maturity.

The third man of the little gathering had his back to her and his dark head bent, listening to something the woman at his side was telling him. He was obviously the tallest gentleman of the three, but when the blond man facing the approaching Woodleys spoke to him, evidently to alert him to the newly arrived guests, and he raised his head, Dandre saw that he was doubtless the tallest man in the room.

He turned toward the girl and her relatives. Merely from the way he moved, the carriage of his shoulders, the smooth flow of his torso and hips, the lifting of his chin and his long, straight nose, the raising of his eyebrows in polite inquiry, Dandre could tell that *this* was Mr. Chesterton. This man was the master of the house.

"Mr. Woodley, I believe?" he said. His voice was low and positively dripping with culture and refinement. "Mrs. Woodley. What a pleasure to meet my neighbors."

"And this is our niece, Miss Dandre Collin, Mr. Chesterton," her uncle said, turning to the girl.

Dandre offered her hand. The gentleman took it and bent soberly above it. He was looking into her eyes with a keen, intelligent gaze. Dandre could easily imagine a fire blazing in those eyes. This gentleman had most definitely been a blood in his day, and she suspected it was still his day.

"Miss Dandre Collin? What an interesting name."

"It is a pleasure to meet you, Mr. Chesterton. Dandre is an old family name. My mother's family is from Ireland and the Irish exchange first and last names freely from one gender to the other through the generations. My grandfather's middle name was Dandre, his mother's maiden name."

"Indeed?" Mr. Chesterton said. He smiled. Dandre smiled. Mr. and Mrs. Woodley, looking on, smiled.

The Woodleys and Dandre stepped back to allow the couple who had arrived just behind them to greet their host.

"Mr. Chesterton? Roger Steward. We met last week over in Bury? This is my wife, Mrs. Steward."

Dandre watched the meeting with an almost avid eye. She did not know Mr. or Mrs. Steward well, though she had seen them before. But her attention was focused on Mr. Chesterton. She was racing backward through her memory trying to recall when she had met this man before. She did not know a Mr. Chesterton. When Mildred Biggins mentioned his name this morning it was the first time she had ever heard it, she was quite certain. She might have seen him at some public place or other in Coventry, she supposed, but she would have thought she would remember even the most casual meeting with this man. And anyway, his face was not really familiar to her, but she *had* looked into those eyes before....

The butler, not wearing a wig but crowned with his own venerable white locks, approached Mr. Chesterton from the side and murmured something in his ear. Mr. Chesterton nodded slightly and directed his next words to the room in general. With the clear resonance of his voice his words could easily be heard from where he stood with his party at the door of the salon.

"Stanis informs me dinner may be served. If you would follow me..."

He took a step that brought him to the side of the young woman of his group, revealing, as he did so, a slight hesitation in his step. A barely noticeable limp. He offered the crook of his elbow to the young lady now at his side and Dandre's attention was riveted on a white rectangle on the back of his hand, secured by a thin gauze wrapping. The dressing was discreet, hardly worth notice, as was the slight length of some sort of scratch not completely covered by the cloth. The cut was cleaned, the bandage spotless and white. *Unlike the first bandage.*

Dandre's eyes flew to the gentleman's face.

The first bandage he had applied himself, in the form of a gray handkerchief pulled from his pocket when a passing carriage cut him. A carriage that would have run her down had she not been yanked out of the way by a dirty, ragged workman.

Chapter Three

"Aunt!" Dandre whispered into Mrs. Woodley's ear. "Aunt, Mr. Chesterton..."

"My dear?" Mr. Woodley said, offering his arm to his wife.

Mrs. Woodley dutifully turned to her husband, interrupting whatever it was Dandre was so excited about.

Mr. Chesterton spoke to the blond-haired man.

"Mr. Redding, will you be so kind as to give Miss Collin your arm?" he asked. He looked behind him to assure himself everyone was prepared and no other damsel was left in distress, unable to find her way through the double doors the two footmen held open to the table visible ten feet away in the next room.

In stately procession the party entered the dining room.

"Miss Collin, did Chesterton say?" Mr. Redding asked politely.

"That is correct," she answered, then smiled. "And I believe our host called you Mr. Redding."

"Jeremy Redding. I am Mr. Chesterton's brother-in-law. The lady on his arm is his sister, my wife."

"Of course. I can see the resemblance now that you mention they are of the same family."

They were at the table now and Mr. Redding held her chair. Dandre found herself seated across from Mrs. Fransen and bracketed on either side by the Misses Humphries, like two heavy bookends. Mr. Redding took the seat next to Wilhelmina and Dandre was sorry to see that. They could ask each other for the salt cellar or how they were enjoying the early summer weather, but Miss Wilhelmina's bosom was too broad an expanse across which to try to exchange her burning questions and his hopefully detailed explanations.

Good heavens! What had Mr. Chesterton been doing in Manchester yesterday, in the guise of a workman? Dandre glanced toward the head of the table, toward the elegant, sophisticated gentleman presiding there.

Surely she was mistaken. The meeting with the workman had been so sudden, the depot a mass of confusion. She was distracted. The two could not possibly be the same man.

Mr. Chesterton raised his head and surprised her as she watched him. He looked into her eyes and smiled politely, at the same time dismissing her.

Dandre dropped her eyes, but irresistibly shook her head. The eyes were the same.

There was no way around it. Their color, their depth, their intensity, even the way they looked at her with interest and awareness, but conveying as they did so that he had something else of real importance with which he was more concerned at the present.

She paid slight attention to what she ate, only becoming interested in what was on her plate when Miss Roberta or Miss Wilhelmina threatened to engage her in a conversation. She had nothing against the Misses Humphries and normally would have gladly listened to their stories of their dog or cook or exotic houseplant. But she was too consumed herself at the moment by this baffling mystery and was not, evidently unlike Mr. Chesterton, able to momentarily redirect her attention to be polite. The meal was doubtless delicious, and she was aware of the sensation of a satisfied appetite when Mr. Chesterton made a quiet inquiry of Mrs. Redding at his side and then pushed back his chair to stand.

The host led the party to yet another brightly lit salon in which a number of small tables were distributed throughout the room. Mr. Fransen and, if she remembered correctly, Mr. Kimber immediately sat at the nearest table, to be joined by Mr. and Mrs. Steward.

Another table of card players was assembling itself and the Misses Humphries implored her to take the fourth hand.

"Not this evening, I believe," she said, and turned quickly, looking for her aunt.

Mrs. Woodley was on a long divan, talking to Mr. Brewster. There was a space at her side, so Dandre sat next to her, waiting for her conversation to end, unable almost to sit still until it did and she could finally ask her questions. But just as Mr. Brewster rose and asked if he could bring either of them a drink or one of the minted chocolates he had seen somewhere in the room, in a final act of frustrating hindrance, Mrs. Redding sat next to her in the small space she had so foolishly left available on her other side.

"So, Miss Collin, you are the niece of Mr. and Mrs. Woodley? How fortunate you could join us this evening."

"Ah, yes," Dandre agreed. She was a more skilled dissembler than she believed herself to be, and it never occurred to Mrs. Redding that Dandre begrudged the interruption, was burning to talk with her aunt and had no desire to attend the pleasant young woman and the polite inquiries of correct society.

"Allow me to introduce myself, if I may be so bold. I am Mrs. Redding, Mr. Chesterton's sister."

"So I understood from your husband."

"Jeremy? Mr. Redding?"

"Your husband was good enough to lend me his arm to supper," Dandre reminded her.

"Of course. Then we have both had the pleasure of making your acquaintance."

"We have all shared the pleasure," Dandre said.

She knew this conversation. She might have written a book on the subject. Next Mrs. Redding would ask how she was enjoying the weather? Was it not pleasant so near the sea? A little cool? Oh? Did she think so? But that was an advantage in the summer, was it not?

The inanities made Dandre want to scream. Instead she smiled. In an attempt to break from the prescribed form she looked about her.

"This is a lovely house," she said. It was not a terribly original remark, but it was not in the least suggestive of the weather. "Are you staying here at Timbrey, or is this a short visit?"

Mrs. Redding laughed. "I am convinced dear Vincent believes he is shackled by a permanent burden in my husband and myself. We do have rooms in London, but my brother is gracious, our time with him is enjoyable, and our visits, I fear, tend to run to six months or better." Mrs. Redding ended her reply as she had begun it, with a laugh.

Dandre smiled, dismayed to feel her aunt stand and move away. Hopelessly she looked around her and then back at the other young woman.

"I am especially taken with some of the art here, and the beautiful furnishings," she said brightly.

"I had forgotten what a fine old place Timbrey is. It has been years since we were here. Not since before Daddy died." Now Mrs. Redding looked around her.

"I thought not," Dandre nodded. "I have visited my aunt and uncle here in Oldham for the past several years and I did not remember ever meeting you. I am sorry."

"That is hardly your fault. Mr. Redding..." The young woman held out her hand to stop her husband as he crossed in front of them. "This is your first visit to Timbrey, is it not?"

"I am afraid it is, my dear," he said.

Mrs. Redding spoke again to Dandre. "I thought not. It has been at least eight years since I was here. Miss Collin was just apologizing for not recalling me. I was neither surprised nor hurt by that, but I knew if she had ever met you she would remember."

Mr. Redding grinned boyishly in embarrassment, then bowed toward the two ladies. Dandre was distressed to see a clump of his hair fall away from his forehead. As he stood he smoothed the hair back into place.

"Jeremy," a voice interrupted them. "Mrs. Brewster is poised at the piano."

"At the piano?"

"I may have mentioned that you have a passable voice and a remarkable memory for song lyrics."

It was Mr. Chesterton who had joined them and now clapped Mr. Redding heavily on the shoulder.

"Well, certainly, with such a fawning recommendation, how could I refuse?" Redding said, then excused himself to the two young women on the couch.

Now Mr. Chesterton stood alone, towering over them. Dandre suddenly became uncomfortably aware that the gentleman was studying her.

"Miss Collin?" He sounded puzzled. "Have we met?"

At last. Her opportunity had come, had presented itself, in fact, on a sliver platter. If she had questions about Mr. Chesterton, his house, his family and a bizarre life-style that took him in rags to Manchester, now was her chance to get the answers to her questions from the wellspring. She inhaled and then looked into the face of the man standing above her.

Slowly she exhaled, allowing the air to escape from her lungs in a soft, even flow.

"I do not believe so, Mr Chesterton. As Mrs. Redding said of her husband, I think I would remember it if we had met before." She smiled at him very prettily.

"I think you are right about that, Miss Collin," he said, returning her smile before he moved away. Mrs. Brewster had experimented with a few chords and she and Mr. Redding seemed to have come to an agreement on the key.

She just could not ask him. Not when he looked at her. Not when he looked at her looking like that. The white starched ruffles of his shirt that pushed against his firm jaw could have been molded from a bank of freshly fallen snow. From where she was sitting she could smell the bracing scent of the fine French soap he used. His hair, with just a touch of natural curl, was combed and smooth and clean. His nails were manicured!

But Dandre had no doubt that this was the man who had pulled her from in front of the carriage at the Manchester station. She could not, however, confront him with that knowledge here in his own stately home. And she realized in despair that she also could not tell her aunt or her uncle about the experience. They would doubtless believe her, or at least believe that *she* believed what she told them, but she did not have the right to call into question the character or the actions of the man who was their gracious host and close neighbor.

As Mr. Chesterton moved from in front of the divan whereon she sat to attend Mrs. Brewster and his brother-in-law in their musical rendition, she sighed in defeat. But at the same time she was forced to smile. Mr. Chesterton was a gentleman in evening clothes at a formal dinner party in his manor house, but he was also a gentleman who, covered with dirt, clad in rags and having just received a painful injury, after a single, startled roar of pain, refrained from cursing in the presence of a lady.

* * *

"Well, what a delightful evening that was," Mrs. Woodley said, interrupting her soft hum to speak. "Do you not agree, Dandre? And Mr. Chesterton." She paused to pull the thread tight in her needlework and sighed heavily. "And what a handsome gentleman."

"Very," Dandre agreed.

Uncle Peter did not contribute anything. A discussion of a handsome man and his characteristics was a topic best left to the ladies' purview.

It was Sunday morning, late morning. Their rising had been tardy because of their postmidnight return from Timbrey Hall the night before. Breakfast was finally over and Mrs. Biggins had cleared away the dishes and retreated to the kitchen. Now the Woodleys and their niece were in the sitting room, where Mrs. Woodley took up her sewing and Mr. Woodley lighted his pipe. He was not a heavy smoker, but he did enjoy a few soothing inhalations of the pungent smoke after breakfast. Dandre sat staring out the window.

Mrs. Woodley glanced in her niece's direction.

"I am afraid you are going to find the Woodley home rather dull this year, Dandre. The stay with us is exciting for a child, but there is little here to occupy a young woman."

"Oh, doubtless I shall be able to find something to do," she said. "One does not need to be busy every moment to enjoy oneself, I suppose."

Mrs. Woodley did not accept her niece's protestations unquestioningly. Despite the young woman's claim, her aunt knew the girl could not remain inert for the entire summer and believe she had enjoyed her visit. Some activity would have to be devised.

She broke her thread and shook out the petticoat she had been mending to inspect her work and the fall of the material.

"Mr. Woodley, I thought I heard either Mr. Redding or Mr. Chesterton say something about going for a ride today?"

"It was Mr. Chesterton, and with ill-disguised relief I am afraid I must admit I refused his kind invitation to join them."

"Oh. Well. That will never do. You must send Henry across with a note—"

It was just that sort of thoughtless demand that worried Henry Biggins when he saw the Timbrey man trotting across the field to them the other morning.

"—and tell him you will be extremely pleased to go riding with them."

"My dear?" Uncle Peter said, very nearly losing his pipe when his jaw dropped open.

"I am aware that *you* have no great desire to go horseback riding anymore, but it would be an excellent opportunity for your niece to associate with younger people and she cannot very well accompany them alone, can she?" Mrs. Woodley's voice was so reasonable, her points so inarguable.

But egads! Woodley's desire to go horseback riding was not just weak, it had shriveled up altogether and left a rather nasty taste behind, as well.

And Mr. Woodley would have said as much, too, if he had not seen the eager light of anticipation in his niece's eyes.

"Riding?" she breathed.

Woodley put his hand to his pipe to cover the grimace. If the girl was going to use that happy, pleading, hopeful tone of voice, he *would* be going horseback riding, he knew.

"Nothing too strenuous, I am sure," his wife was saying. "I think Mrs. Redding said she would join them, so it will be only an easy jaunt around his park. When were they going, dear?"

"Sometime this afternoon," Mr. Woodley said. He really tried not to sound too gloomy, but it would not have mattered anyway. Dandre was so caught up in the idea already she would not have heard a gun blast.

"I do not know that I have brought anything entirely appropriate with me. I have my riding habit, of course—" a young lady with proper social training evidently never left her front door without taking her riding habit with her "—but surely the Chesterton party will expect something more elegant."

"Posh!" Mr. Woodley exploded, not even his pipe able to quell his derision this time. "You put on your skirt and gloves, you ride a horse until both of you are sweaty, then you come home and bathe. Any skirt and gloves at all will be elegant enough for even the most demanding of steeds."

Dandre looked uncertainly between her aunt and uncle, feeling mildly hurt and disappointed, unaware of how valiantly her uncle was striving not to take every bit of enjoyment out of the adventure for his niece.

"What you have brought will be lovely, I am sure," Mrs. Woodley said soothingly. "Now, Mr. Woodley, send Henry this morning, before it gets to be noon and it appears presumptuous of us to expect to be included in an outing of Mr. Chesterton's and his guests on the spur of the moment."

Mrs. Woodley was a woman very much concerned with doing the right thing and doing it at precisely the right moment, as well.

So Mr. Biggins was off, complaining, not completely under his breath, and Mr. Woodley heaved himself up from his comfortable chair to see what his own closet held by way of a riding outfit.

He found something that would do, was meant for riding, had been worn for riding and which even, most remarkably of all, still fit him. It buttoned where it was vital that it button and did not gape open comically at those places—around his stomach, the tails across his back-side—where it was not supposed to.

Henry, for his part, returned with word that "Certainly Mr. Chesterton and the Reddings would be delighted to have Mr. Woodley and his niece join them."

Dandre and her uncle were to meet the Chesterton party at the Timbrey stables at two o'clock that afternoon. Dandre laid out her riding things, carefully brushing them off, mending a small tear in the veil of her hat, cleaning a smudge from the skirt. She went out to Uncle Peter's stable to choose her horse. The choice was limited, but there was one pretty little Arabian mare she had ridden before that she knew she looked very well sitting upon.

Henry had been instructed to clean and oil one of the two ladies' saddles the Woodleys owned and elicited his wife's sympathy and agreement that this little "riding excursion" for Miss Dandre was putting a good many people to considerable trouble. Mrs. Biggins was referring to Mr. Woodley when she clicked her tongue; there was no question to whom Henry was referring.

At twelve-thirty Dandre donned her riding habit, perhaps influenced by her aunt's regard for time or perhaps by Mr. Chesterton's finely molded lips, dark, waving hair, patrician bearing and burning gaze. Dandre made up that description for Mr. Chesterton's gaze herself.

"How do I look, Aunt Bea? These things are so old." She glanced down at the front of her habit forlornly. "The jacket is worn here at the elbow and the skirt has been torn. Oh, I mended it, of course. But you can see the stitches. I tore it riding, not precisely 'to' hounds but after a pack of the silly things one afternoon. Rather, Summer Lady was chasing after the dogs and I was clinging to the reins. She ran through every clump of bushes and brambles she could find, and all things considered—" Dandre held the mended portion of her skirt up and studied it "—that I got off with only a torn skirt and a lost riding cap is rather remarkable." Now she scornfully dropped the material in her hands. "All the same, I shall look frightful."

"Do not be ridiculous, Dandre. Let me see. There." Mrs. Woodley pulled the jacket sleeve so it was straight and critically eyed the skirt. "The skirt looks very well, and if your jacket is worn, you are the only one who knows it."

Dandre plucked discontentedly at her blouse.

"I believe I will change this cream silk for the white cotton," she said doubtfully.

"Perhaps you had better," her aunt said thoughtfully.

"Oh! I knew it was wrong," Dandre wailed.

The silk riding blouse was exchanged for the lighter cotton, which, in turn, was changed for a linen and then changed back to the cotton. Her aunt tried to convince her that such meticulous care was not needed for a casual afternoon ride. And Mildred "oohed" and "ahhed" over everything the girl came out in, which Dandre did not find in the least helpful, although it did bolster her courage.

Finally—*finally*—at one-thirty Uncle Peter said they could leave and a half hour later they joined Mr. Chesterton and Mr. and Mrs. Redding behind Timbrey Hall. Mr. Redding had just assisted his wife onto her horse and was in the process of pulling himself into his own saddle. Mr. Chesterton stood beside a fine bay gelding. His light-colored jodhpurs were exceedingly handsome on his tall frame and Miss Collin nearly blushed as she considered that Mr. Chesterton, as her mother would say, "showed a good leg."

In one smooth, effortless motion, he swung onto the back of his horse and into his saddle. It was a grace that reminded Dandre of the unlikely agility the rough workman had shown as he retrieved her umbrella and carpetbag from between the feet of the milling crowd at the Manchester station.

She smiled.

Mr. Redding inquired if they were all ready.

Mr. Chesterton nodded.

And they were off.

The Timbrey estate was a far-reaching property that included woods and meadows and a brook that undeniably burbled over its rocky bed on the warm summer afternoon.

"Your family is from Coventry, Miss Collin?" Mrs. Redding asked her.

"Yes."

"Lovely part of the country," Mr. Redding said.

"Rather far from the sea, though," Mrs. Redding added.

"I am afraid so," Miss Collin agreed.

"Mr. Chesterton, you have spent some time in Coventry, have you not?" Mr. Redding asked.

"Only as I passed through it on my way to and from London."

They were riding along a saddle trail that widened and narrowed as the trees on the right encroached or retreated from the stream on the left of the trail. Here the lane was so wide as to allow them to ride two or three abreast. Dandre was riding beside Mrs. Redding, who was beside her husband. Behind them rode Mr. Chesterton and Mr. Woodley.

The three in front chatted quite companionably, occasionally able to draw forth a comment from Mr. Chesterton. Uncle Peter Woodley was lost in his own thoughts, dealing primarily with a consideration of how broad this horse's back was and the troubling idea that it seemed to be getting broader with every step the animal took.

Everything was serene, peaceful, bucolic, and then—well, considering the fact that Dandre had always been a quiet, thoughtful girl, even from her earliest childhood, it really was surprising she should have met with so many mishaps in her life.

It was not at all surprising that a carriage had nearly knocked her down at the Manchester train station. Dandre had been slipping, falling and breaking things on a fairly regular basis since she was old enough to walk. When she was nine she fell into a well and broke her arm; when she was nineteen she slipped on a seemingly dry church step and carried the minister, the deacon and Mrs. Pomeroy down the steps with her. In between those two catastrophic events were shards of countless shattered goblets and broken dishes, cut fingers and sprained ankles. Such childhood accidents one could expect if the central actor was a nervous, active, boisterous, flighty, careless girl. But Dandre was none of those things, yet Pastor Dunn still merely nodded at her, hesitating to this day to take her hand after service.

And now, as the little company ambled along the lane, here was another amazing example of Dandre Collin's exceptionally bad luck.

The horsefly originally buzzed around her uncle's head. Woodley absently waved his hand at it, and defying every inherent characteristic of the *Tabanidae* fly family, the creature left Mr. Woodley and his horse and alighted not on Mr. Redding's horse, right in front of Woodley, but, passing several inviting horses' necks and rumps, crossing three airstreams to do so, settled on the rump of Dandre's docile Arabian mare. And it did not just settle there and rest, it immediately bit the unwary animal.

The horse started and jumped, neighed loudly and plunged into the stream and up the bank on the other side.

Though caught off guard, Dandre managed to stay her mount until the horse made its final lunge for dry, sure footing. Dislodged at last, she slipped from her saddle and landed in the brook. It burbled merrily around and across her, causing the folds of her skirts to undulate on its surface. Her hat was askew and the worn elbow of the riding jacket was now torn.

Mr. Chesterton, with all of the grace that Dandre Collin had been denied, was down from his horse and wading through the stream to her rescue while the rest of the party was still reacting to the horse's neigh of surprised pain.

"Are you injured, Miss Collin?" he asked.

"I am shaken but not actually damaged," she said, smiling weakly.

Mr. Chesterton extended his hand and pulled the girl to her feet.

She picked up the heavy folds of her water-soaked skirt and struggled to the bank. But instead of the right bank, where the rest of the party waited, she chose the left bank, where her horse stood alone, looking back in amazement at the spectacle its rider had made of herself.

Mr. Chesterton accompanied the young lady and assisted her up the short incline to stand beside the mare.

Without even stopping to wring out her skirts, Dandre dropped the material so that it flapped coldly against her leg and put her hand solicitously on the horse's mane.

"Are you all right, girl? What is it?" She ran her hand in a calming caress along the mare's neck, cooing softly as she did so. Any idea of her own indignity, her own hurt, her own discomfort, was driven from her in her concern for the animal.

Mr. Chesterton watched the movement of the young woman's gloved hand, admiring its tranquilizing effect on the spooked animal which still quivered slightly. And as his gaze followed that hand, his eyes suddenly opened very wide.

"You!" he gasped.

Dandre heard the recognition in his voice and turned to him with a relieved smile. Now was a perfect opportunity for him to hurriedly explain his dishevelment in Manchester, while they stood alone and apart from the others. No doubt his excuse would be perfectly pedestrian and unremarkable, though she could not imagine any pedestrian explanation that would put the gentleman before her—who "showed a very good leg"—into the guise of a begrimed workman.

But when she faced him the smile on her lips froze and her conspiratorial laugh was aborted. The look on Mr. Chesterton's face did not invite humor, did not suggest a harmless shared joke. The look on Chesterton's pale face was appalled, and only because he was a very self-controlled gentleman was it this side of sheer panic.

Chapter Four

Dandre struggled to warm her smile, to say something that would reassure the agitated gentleman before her, whatever it was he needed reassurance of. But before she could say anything, Mrs. Redding was hailing them from across the stream, and Mr. Redding was already splashing his horse across, pulling Mr. Chesterton's horse behind him.

Chesterton glanced quickly over his shoulder, then turned to the young woman again and leaned toward her.

"You must not say anything to my sister or Mr. Redding," he whispered urgently. "I beseech you not to tell them what you know."

Dandre looked at the gentleman, nearly dumbfounded, certainly in confusion. Not only did she not know what it was she knew that she must not tell the Reddings, but Mr. Chesterton did not sound as if he were beseeching her. Rather his words sounded like a command—and a warning.

Before she could gather her senses and make any sort of a reply, Mr. Redding had urged the two horses up the embankment and was now directly behind Chesterton.

"That was a bit of excitement, what?" he said loudly and cheerfully, the way one jollies a child who has fallen down, hoping to divert tears. He handed the reins of the other horse down to his brother-in-law. "I trust you are uninjured, Miss Collin?"

"Miss Collin is perfectly all right," Mr. Chesterton said. He pulled his horse behind him and gave Dandre another warning look.

"And you, Miss Collin, are you willing to allow my brother's verdict to stand, or do you have a differing opinion on the subject?" Redding asked her.

Dandre managed a weak laugh.

"I am as uninjured as a lady can be who is damp and disheveled," she said.

"I must admit, Miss Collin, that you look better than any other damsel I have seen thrown from her horse."

Dandre ran her soothing hand along her horse's neck again.

"Shaharah did not throw me. You are too much of a lady to do that, are you not?" She spoke in the cooing voice women assume for animals and small children.

Chesterton cleared his throat.

"We must return to Timbrey at once, of course," he announced.

"Oh," Redding said, sounding surprised, as if grasping for the first time that Miss Collin's misadventure might have a detrimental effect on them all.

But Dandre could not devote much attention to Mr. Redding or his disappointment. She was struggling to understand Mr. Chesterton. She was certain that Mr. Redding had not noticed the strange hoarseness in his brother-in-law's voice when he spoke, but Dandre heard it. In studying the man's face, his expression might have been seen as polite concern, hovering on placid indifference. But the set of his jaw, the working of his eyebrows, which he kept pushing apart from a scowl, the fine beading of perspiration on his brow, a brow that Dandre was not certain had ever seen perspiration before, all evinced the fact that Mr. Chesterton's calm expression was a mask.

His perturbation was infectious. Suddenly Dandre did not want Mr. Redding to know that she and Mr. Chesterton had met before any more than Mr. Chesterton did.

"You must do no such thing," she said, carefully fixing her own pleasant mask as she answered Chesterton and then smiled up at the other man. "I will not hear of you quitting your ride here. I will return to the Woodley home with my uncle. He, I know, will be more than willing to end our ride early. Is that not so, Uncle?" she called across the stream to Mr. Woodley.

"Is what not so?" he called back.

"You would be willing to go back with me instead of finishing the ride?"

"Absolutely!" Mr. Woodley called, daring to hope his niece's misfortune meant he would not be trapped atop this animal with the gargantuan girth for the rest of his life.

"You see?" She smiled up at Mr. Redding and then turned to Mr. Chesterton.

"Very well," Chesterton said. He offered her a hand onto her horse.

"But you must allow Mr. Chesterton and myself to look in on you tomorrow, Miss Collin. Sometimes a fall from a horse causes muscle strain of which one is not aware until the next day."

"Mr. Redding..." Dandre began, willing to dismiss his offered courtesy but not really anxious to do so.

"I am not sure..." Chesterton spoke over her half-hearted protest.

"Now, now, old man, it is the least we can do. And whatever business is waiting for you in Manchester on Monday will surely be awaiting you just as stolidly on Tuesday. Is that not true?"

"I suppose it is," he said.

Dandre's eyes had never left the gentleman's face, and when Mr. Redding spoke of what awaited Mr. Chesterton in Manchester, the girl was convinced that she had been very wrong in her flippant dismissal of any other perspiration having been on that brow before. The expression that flitted across his face might have been tinged with disgust, revulsion, perhaps even pain—Dandre was unable to interpret the shadow precisely—but whatever else it was, it was first and foremost, definitely, unmistakably, an expression of bone-weary fatigue.

It was gone. He bowed stiffly and then raised his perfectly veiled eyes to hers.

"Miss Collin, I have been reminded of a duty I should more correctly consider a privilege. May my brother and myself call on you tomorrow morning to assure ourselves of your well-being?"

"Of course, Mr. Chesterton."

"Then we will leave you in the care of Mr. Woodley to see you home."

"I look forward eagerly to speaking with you again, Mr. Chesterton," she said. "At length."

Chesterton was about to mount his own horse, but he stopped midway and lowered himself to the ground again.

"I do not know that that will be possible, Miss Collin," he said, facing her once again, a hairline crack in his perfect composure.

"Oh, but I hope it will be." She urged her horse forward, past Mr. Chesterton, who stood without moving, watching her uncertainly.

"You stay on that side, Dandre," Mr. Woodley called across to her. "There is a shallow crossing back along this way."

Dandre raised her hand, assuring her uncle she would do as he bid. Mr. Chesterton, following her retreating figure for another moment, looked as if he desperately wished the girl would give him the same assurance. Finally he grasped the pommel of the saddle and pulled himself onto his horse.

"She fell into the stream," Mr. Woodley announced, opening the kitchen door and clomping noisily across the floor in his heavy riding boots.

Mr. Woodley and his niece had agreed it would be best to enter the house by the back door, considering Dandre's wet dress, which by now was caked with mud and had chilled her thoroughly.

"Dandre?" Mrs. Woodley asked, as if there were any doubt.

"Actually, the horse threw me off," Dandre said, defending herself as well as she could.

"Of course it did, dear. *Mildred!*"

Mrs. Woodley put her arm around her niece's shoulder, Mrs. Biggins answered her mistress's summons, and Henry was instructed to fetch water. The water was heated, the bath prepared, and thirty minutes after their arrival, Dandre sank back against the cool porcelain of the tub and closed her eyes.

As taken as she had been with her little puzzle of Mr. Chesterton passing as a workman in Manchester, she realized she had always assumed it was nothing more than a harmless prank in which the unexpected gentleman had been indulging himself. His alarmed, and alarming, reaction to his recognition of her had put an entirely different light on his masquerade. Whatever it was he was involved with, it was certainly *not* a harmless prank.

What could it be?

Surely he had no business dealings for which he would find it necessary to disguise himself. And it was equally as unlikely that he had a set of rough friends of the meaner class from whom he did not wish to distance himself. Just from the way her Aunt Beatrice had spoken when she said, "Mr. Chesterton is very rich, my dear," Dandre knew that Mr. Chesterton himself was very rich, as was his family, as had been his family, for generations. Life on Mr. Chesterton's stratum would never call for or even allow the possibility of that gentleman making friends of the meaner sort.

If it was not a prank, if it was not some legitimate business or social dealing, that only left something . . .

Dandre's eyes popped open. The soothing scent of bath oil was mixed with the steam in the air of the small, closed bathing room. The girl drew in her breath sharply and then had to cough the wet air out from her lungs again.

Good heavens!

If Mr. Chesterton was not involved with something harmlessly legal, he was obviously doing something *illegal.*

Dandre rubbed the washcloth slowly back and forth across the soap until suds dripped from around her fingers into the bathwater. She pushed the soapy cloth up and down her wet arms, across her neck and shoulders. She raised one leg and scrubbed diligently at a knee that had not encountered grime since she was thirteen and played with her brother in the meadow behind the house.

What had started out as an amusing little puzzle had suddenly taken on a much more sinister tone.

From Chesterton's reaction to his recognition of her and the troubling expression she had seen cross his face, *and* what she realized was irrepressible relief that he was forced to delay his return to Manchester for even a day when Mr. Redding insisted they come to pay their respects tomorrow, Dandre was led to only one conclusion: Mr. Chesterton had enmeshed himself in some difficulty, something that was disagreeable, taxing and, very likely, illegal.

It was not his fault, unquestionably. Dandre was a proven authority on the scrapes one could get into that might in no way be blamed upon one's own actions or intentions.

Now Dandre rose and stepped from the bath. The tiny rivulets of water that streamed down her creamy skin, skin smoothed and waterproofed by the bath oil, gleamed in the glow of the lamp Mrs. Biggins had left in the dark little room. Dandre blotted her damp hair between the folds of the thick towel, which Mrs. Biggins had also left, and then shook her head so that the light sparkled in the long strands, highlighting the red in them. There was a full-length mirror in the room. With her reflection framed in the glass, she might have been a painting by Botticelli, *Maiden Rising from Her Bath,* though her figure was more slender and less voluptuous than many of Botticelli's subjects. Nevertheless, the picture was lovely and even the most un-tutored of art lovers could have appreciated the beauty of the scene.

With no thought to the picture she presented, Dandre flung her towel aside and began to pull on her underthings and then the soft, loose frock Mrs. Woodley had sent up with her.

Her one thought, her only thought, was that Mr. Chesterton, *her* Mr. Chesterton, was in trouble, and she was determined to help him.

Mr. Braid's cotton mill on Withing Grove Street, near the Manchester Exchange, was very much like the other mills that girdled the central business section of the city. Taking advantage of the revolutionary mechanical devises introduced in the last half century and the seemingly endless supply of cheap labor available to Mr. Braid's mill, and every other mill in Lancashire, the Braid mill was helping to supply the world with textiles. Silk, wool, cotton. Cotton thread and cotton fabric.

Like Dandre's Uncle Peter, Mr. Braid and the rest of the mill owners and factory investors were able to hook their thumbs in the straining waistbands of their trousers, beam and nod their heads and assure their fellow businessmen that "business was booming."

It was a flush time at the mills.

The key grated in the lock of the dormitory at four-thirty Monday morning. Fourteen little boys and twelve girls, the eldest thirteen years old, struggled from their beds before Mr. Juggs could get to them with his strap. Poor Ned and Ben did not beat the lash and were beaten instead, until Mr. Juggs was quite certain they were up and awake and had thrown off their five hours of sleep.

Mary was up and pulling on the tattered sleeves of her jacket, but Mr. Juggs, the overlooker of these quarters and the children lodged therein, casually flung his strap in the girl's direction and was gratified to see her wince when the leather licked across the thin material that covered her back.

"Let's go! Let's go! Let's go!" he roared. "The spindles will be whirling by the time you amble down there." He cracked the strap he held, regretful that the sound was produced only by the belt striking itself and not flesh. But he smiled his smile of ice to see the shudders and starts the sound produced in the room.

The children, small, pale and thin, all of them, some appearing to be no more than toddlers, jogged from the stone hut situated to one side of the building they called Braid's, only because they were too young and had never received enough religious instruction to know about hell.

The smallest of them were pieceners, with little fingers that pieced together broken threads. There were also bobbin winders, warpers and reelers, and Mary, the oldest, had recently been moved to doffing. Doffing was a pitiless, exhausting labor that kept the girl running back and forth along the frames all day, removing flyers, replacing full bobbins with empty ones and then setting the frames in motion again. The girl hardly had energy to speak at the end of her day, and yet she was very thankful to be doffing. She had come there from the carding room.

Danny was seven. Like the other children brought here from an orphanage in London town, he had no recollection of parents. He was called Danny Fry. He assumed Fry was his last name, but in reality one of the sisters at Saint Augustine's orphanage left him out in the sun one summer day when he was a baby, while she and one of the other sisters indulged in a sinful discussion of the manly attributes of the coachman who made deliveries to the orphanage. The baby, when finally recalled and retrieved, was sunburned and Sister Francesca cried for two days because she had fried the poor little mite. Hence, Danny Fry.

Like the other children, he was frightfully thin and pale, and his bones, attempting to grow yet fettered by the unnatural position and unreasonable length of time the boy was required to spend on his feet every day, often stationary for hours, were beginning to ache, the joints to swell. Because he was tall for his age, at least when they brought him to Braid's, he was forced to bend over his frame all day, as well. He had seen other boys, fourteen or sixteen, who had been employed as he was, deformed and crooked now, unable to stand straight, their knees bent unnaturally. At night as he lay in his bed, massaging his aching knees, he thought of those boys and what was awaiting him, and tears would start to his eyes as much from the pain of the thought as the pain in his leg joints.

He had been here in the mill, let us think . . . almost five months now. Five months.

Back in the beginning, and it seemed so long ago, he had made that attempt to run away. The lads in the dormitory at night had whispered that it was possible, that a fellow could get clean away if he was fast and careful. But Danny had not been fast enough or careful enough. That horseman had knocked him down and old Juggs had caught up with him.

The beating had been terrible. Juggs had laid on with his strap and booted Danny's bony frame around the floor when he fell. Danny was left black and blue and so hurt he could not work for two days, but eventually his young body repaired itself and once on the line again he acknowledged that Mr. Juggs would probably have caught him anyway. He had long ago forgiven the stranger, who had suffered a knockdown and a sore jaw himself.

Like the bent knees and the thin frames, work in the mill seemed to sap spiritual strength, as well. Danny had not tried to run away again and in recent weeks had even stopped dreaming about it.

But perhaps that was because Vince had come to work at Braid's shortly after Danny's unsuccessful attempt to escape. Vince helped as much as he could, and he kept Juggs's strap off the children when he was there.

If it were not for Vince, Danny knew things would have been worse. He might have lost the will to live as well as the will to escape. He had certainly lost the will to get up and get to work.

Mr. Juggs pushed him along so that he nearly stumbled and fell. But he saved himself and hurried into the mill. At four-thirty in the morning it was seventy degrees. It would be dreadful cruel by five o'clock tonight. But perhaps by seven-thirty it would be cooling off again.

As he took his place in front of the frame, which had indeed been started up by the time he got there, he looked around hopefully, but his spirits sank. Vince was not there. He might come later; he had a devilish disregard of the three pennies that were docked from his pay for being fifteen minutes late, of the six pennies for a half hour, which took a sizable chunk out of even a man's wages. But Vince sometimes missed a day or two, even a week. He did not look like a sot, he did not have the flabby muscle tone or the red eyes of the habitual drunk and appeared to be healthier than any of the other grown workmen here in the mill, so Danny was at a loss to account for his absences.

But the man was unusually strong and knew the job, so he would be set to work whenever he presented himself to the mill foreman. The loss of employment was not a threat. That was not what troubled Master Danny Fry.

Vince was his hero and his savior. The man was kind and helpful, seeing to his own herculean tasks and managing to help a lad who ran out of space for the full bobbins or could not keep the ends straight that he held in his hand. He winked and smiled at the children and brought them bits of candy that were not covered with the suffocating cotton fibers that filled the air and the lungs. And if he did nothing else, he was there. Mr. Juggs did not employ the strap when Vince was around. True, the children who could not help but doze at their machines toward the end of the day were beaten awake, just as the few unfortunates were in the morning, but only when Vince was away, carrying some heavy load to another part of the building.

Mr. Juggs was a cowardly bully in the truest sense. Vince and he had never even exchanged words, but the look in the workman's eye had fully and immediately convinced the overlooker that he would tolerate no strapping of the brats while he was there.

Mr. Juggs still remembered the one day he had raised his fist to the lazy Bunting boy. Vince jerked his head up and fixed Juggs with an eye that froze the blood in his veins.

The one enjoyment this job offered Juggs could now only be indulged infrequently, cautiously, surreptitiously, when the tall, rugged stretcher was at least out of sight. With his strap and his foot, Juggs could always ensure silence.

Mr. Juggs noticed that Vince was not at his station this morning, too, and knew, as did Danny, that his strap would whistle today along the row of bony backs bent over the frames. And like Danny, Mr. Juggs shivered in anticipation.

Mr. Redding and his brother-in-law did stop at the Woodley home the next day. Quite early in the day as a matter of fact.

"Mr. Chesterton, Mr. Redding, you catch us still at breakfast," Mrs. Woodley said when Mrs. Biggins showed the two gentlemen into the dining room and the surprised family group gathered round the board.

Mr. Woodley stood to shake hands with the callers, knocking the table and causing coffee to slop over into the saucers. In confusion he dropped his napkin into his porridge.

"Oh!" he exclaimed. "Oh dear."

"Will you not sit, gentlemen?" Mrs. Woodley asked, saved the trouble of standing to greet the guests and so much smoother with her amenities. "Mrs. Biggins, bring the gentlemen some coffee, and get another napkin for Mr. Woodley. Would you care for a boiled egg? A dish of oatmeal? I am afraid we can offer you nothing more than plain country fare."

"We have just come from the breakfast table ourselves and our own plain country fare, Mrs. Woodley," said Mr. Chesterton. "But I would like a cup of coffee."

"He pulled us away before I could wipe my chin," Mr. Redding said, rubbing his face with the back of his hand. "I can only hope I am not coated with muffin crumbs and strawberry preserves." He laughed.

He was not, though their hasty ride so early in the day had not allowed him time for his careful hair sculpting. The long hair at the sides of his head hung down loosely almost below his ears, leaving his high white forehead exposed when he removed his hat, which he did when Mildred brought in the two cups of coffee for the callers and the clean napkin for Mr. Woodley.

Dandre, having convinced herself just last night while in her tub and then later as she lay staring at the ceiling in her darkened bedroom that Mr. Chesterton was involved with some felonious activity, studied that gentleman carefully to detect a telltale sign of crime about his person. There was none. There was a trifling muss to his hair when he removed his hat and a scent about him that was fresh and natural, as if he had gathered the morning into his arms as he and Mr. Redding rode across the short distance between the two houses, and now emptied it out before them, a gift he had brought to his hostesses. He also had a rosebud pinned to the lapel of his waistcoat. It was obviously freshly cut and was secured in the buttonhole. Mr. Chesterton had done all that this morning before poor Mr. Redding could get his hair molded or make sure he did not have any breakfast on his chin.

Mr. Chesterton looked into her eyes, surprising her in her careful inventory of his person.

"Miss Collin, are you as unharmed as you believed yourself yesterday?" he asked. There was real concern in the man's voice that touched Dandre. Mr. Chesterton was an extremely reserved gentleman who kept his emotions and responses in tight control, yet the sympathetic regard in his voice was unmistakable.

In response to his inquiry, Dandre put one hand gently over a bruise on her other arm and smiled ruefully.

"I will admit that I am a little stiff this morning," she said. "Mr. Redding was correct. Aches and pains sometimes wait to make themselves evident."

Mr. Chesterton shook his head gravely in commiseration and then, surprisingly, raised his own shoulder carefully, as if loosening a painfully stiff muscle.

"I understand completely, Miss Collin," he said.

"I had no idea our pleasant little ride of yesterday would be so hard on us all." She laughed softly.

"Oh, it is not that," Chesterton began, but stopped abruptly. The dining room grew very quiet as the whole party waited for his elaboration. After fifteen or twenty seconds it became uncomfortably clear to everyone that he was not going to elaborate, nor was he to be pressed for details.

Mr. Woodley finally spoke. "Yes, well, the flesh is subject to all manner of ills, I suppose. Will you hand me that marmalade, Mrs. Woodley?"

Mr. Chesterton finished his beverage and leaned forward in his chair.

"We must be going, I am afraid," he said.

"You will not stay?" Dandre asked, surprised. She had been planning a few quiet, private moments with Chesterton, expecting her questions to be answered.

"I could not convince my brother to spend the day at Timbrey, but only to delay his departure," Mr. Redding said, finishing his own coffee and reaching for his hat.

"I hoped, that is, I thought we might talk a little. Some. Perhaps take a stroll. The Woodley property is not large, but it does contain a very nice garden," the young woman said, grasping frantically to keep this opportunity from slipping away.

"Not today, I am afraid," Mr. Chesterton said, a puff of smoke seeping away through her fingers.

"A short walk?"

"Miss Collin, I should not have delayed my departure even this long."

Like everything else about Mr. Chesterton, that reply, and the urgency in his voice, was enigmatic. Mr. Chesterton, it seemed, who did not *do* anything because he was so very rich, did not feel as if he could neglect his "business," for want of a more illuminating term, in Manchester for more than half a day.

"When will we have the pleasure of seeing you again, Mr. Chesterton?" Mrs. Woodley asked.

Chesterton had been avoiding Miss Collin's careful scrutiny of him and now turned with relief to the girl's aunt.

"If I may be so forward, Mrs. Woodley, I shall be back on Sunday and would regard it a signal honor if I might join you for tea."

"Oh, Mr. Chesterton." Her aunt was a self-possessed, gracious woman of clear head and keen eye, but if taken completely by surprise, she was able to manage a girlish flutter now and then. "Why, we would be delighted. Would we not be delighted, Dandre? Mr. Woodley?"

"Delighted." Mr. Woodley beamed. This was quite a feather in the old Woodley cap to have the grand Mr. Chesterton engaged for tea in their home.

Mr. Woodley stood with the other gentlemen and accompanied them to the door.

Dandre went to stand by the sitting room window to gravely watch them ride away. Mrs. Woodley smiled indulgently at the girl, sure she must be envisioning the departing gentleman in some romantic setting, wondering when she would see him again.

Mrs. Woodley was not altogether wrong; Dandre *was* picturing the departing gentleman in another setting, in the dress and dirt of a common laborer, and wondering what direful intrigue was pulling him to Manchester.

Shwack!

The lash fell across Danny's shoulders, adding another red stripe to the ones already stinging on his back, but startling him into wakefulness again.

"Wake up there, boy! Watch what yer doin'," Mr. Juggs snarled as he prowled past the boy and down along the line of shuddering youths and children bent over their work.

It was hardest at the end of the day—the long day—when they grew fatigued. Danny had seen arms broken, fingers taken off, hands mangled in the machinery, all at the end of the day.

They were beaten in the morning as well, "to get ye in yer fettle," as Mr. Juggs laughingly told them, cuffing them so they all had bruises on their cheeks and necks. But the morning was never so bad as the latter part of the day. Though it was the beginning of the week, eyelids had been drooping since noon, drooping over eyes that had not been bright or alert that morning, and certainly not innocently wonder-filled, as the eyes of children should be. Not this morning, not this week, not, in most cases, in several years of the brief lives of these children.

Danny's head bobbed and he jerked himself awake, glancing furtively out of the corner of his eye to locate the overlooker. Mr. Juggs was at the end of the line, leering over poor little Penny, who was nervously smoothing a filling bobbin. But, the boy told himself, he needn't feel sorry for Penny. He knew other girls who had "made it up" to Mr. Juggs and fared very well. They were given the least taxing jobs, allowed the greatest leeway and never touched with that hateful strap. Mr. Juggs sometimes would pull a girl off the line altogether and take her with him into one of the offices upstairs or even outside for a while.

It must be very fine to be a girl, Danny thought, and sighed at the idea.

With Mr. Juggs so far distant and occupied as he was, Danny allowed his eyes to rise above his frame, to look at the stretching station where Vince usually worked.

The three men manning the station today, the stretcher that Vince usually handled alone or with one assistant, were markedly different from the boy's absent hero. These men had the thin frames, the pallid skin, the sunken eyes of the seasoned mill worker. Vince was tall and strong and tanned, as if he saw the sun and breathed fresh air sometimes. As if he got meat with his meals more often than once a week, and more than the few bits of bacon sprinkled in with the potatoes on Sunday.

Danny sighed again but cut it short and hurriedly dropped his weary eyes to the threads in front of him when he caught the motion of Mr. Juggs turning around at the end of the line to begin another pass.

He sucked his breath in sharply when he heard the snap of leather and saw the blur of motion. Dexter, a year younger than Danny, a boy at the end of the line, squealed with pain and Danny could hear the sound of gloating in Mr. Juggs's voice when he told the boy to "shut yer yap and get busy." It was a sound that made Danny's emaciated stomach turn over.

When Vince was here, Mr. Juggs never sounded like that.

Chapter Five

For the entire rest of the day, Mrs. Woodley treated Dandre as if she were a cracked hen's egg. She must sit in the softest chair, have the downiest comforter about her, put her feet up, her head back, rest and recover. Uncle Peter was instructed to speak softly and Aunt Bea was careful not to click her knitting needles together too loudly.

Owing to her aunt's careful ministrations, or perhaps in spite of them, Dandre quickly recovered from the fall from her horse. The bruise on her arm was fading by that afternoon, and on Tuesday there was not the slightest vestige of stiffness in her joints.

But Dandre felt a listlessness, nevertheless. Her aunt believed she knew the reason for that.

"How unfortunate that Mr. Chesterton is away from Timbrey this week," she said Tuesday morning at the breakfast table. "I am sure you would have found another excursion to the Hall enjoyable."

"But did not Mrs. Redding say she and her husband would be staying all week?" Mr. Woodley inquired.

His wife gave him an amused, exasperated look.

"Your niece's enjoyment of her stay will not be enhanced by Mr. and Mrs. Redding's presence, my dear."

"Oh, hmm, I see." Uncle Peter cleared his throat and then beamed at Dandre, who blushed faintly.

"I think we can manage without him," she murmured uncomfortably. Her aunt smiled.

For the rest of the day, if Dandre was looking out the window or allowed her attention to wander from whatever she was doing, Mrs. Woodley would smile again and attribute her niece's vacancy to a preoccupation with the gentleman from Timbrey. As usual, Mrs. Woodley was not entirely mistaken. But Dandre's thoughts were not of their impeccable host in formal evening wear, the candlelight gleaming in his dark hair, reflected in sparks off his white teeth when he smiled, lost in the depths of his eyes. She was remembering those eyes, true enough, but she always pictured their direct, intelligent gaze from a dirt-streaked, tousle-haired head. As interested as she was in the young man, she was actually more interested in him because he had returned to Manchester than she would have been had he stayed.

When she first arrived, Mrs. Woodley had warned that Dandre would find her stay with her aunt and uncle uninteresting this year. Dandre refuted the claim, but by Wednesday morning, after only four short days, it appeared that Mrs. Woodley's prediction had been correct after all.

Dandre rose late, ate a few bites of breakfast and wandered eventually into her aunt's little morning room.

"Good day, dear," Mrs. Woodley greeted her.

" 'Morning," the girl mumbled.

Mrs. Woodley put down her pen for a moment and studied her niece carefully. The girl's hair had not been smoothed entirely this morning and loose strands floated around her face. There were no dark circles under her eyes, but she looked as if there should have been. That is, her eyes had a dull veil to them; they were not at all the bright, flashing green they should have been first thing in the morning.

"Did you sleep well?"

"Mmm," Dandre said.

Mrs. Woodley had no idea what that reply meant, except that Dandre was bored and uninterested in both the question and her answer.

"It looks as if we are going to have a warm day today."

"Does it?"

Dandre glanced up at the window, and after following her gaze, Mrs. Woodley returned to the letter she was writing to a friend over in Yorkshire.

Dandre's inspection of the weather outside the window was brief. Instead of determining to go outside for herself to see if it was a warm day, as Mrs. Woodley had expected and hoped, the girl wandered from table to desk to mantel. Finally she pulled a book of uplifting tales down from the bookshelf, but after two minutes she closed the book with a snap and rose again. She prowled around the close confines of the library like a caged jungle cat, pausing in her circuit to gaze out the window again for a few moments before resuming her pacing.

"My word, child! Why do you not go for a walk?" her aunt finally exclaimed.

Dandre looked around innocently, surprised by the impatience in her aunt's voice.

"I do not..." she hesitated, listlessly picking up a porcelain figurine from the mantel and then carelessly replacing it as her aunt held her breath. "I suppose..."

The sound of the farm cart filtered into the room. Henry had been hauling broken tree limbs and winter debris from the Woodley lawn all morning, stretching a job that should have taken thirty minutes into three hours and four different excursions up the road with his cart.

"Perhaps I will go for a short walk. If you are certain you will not need me, Aunt?"

"Certainly not," Mrs. Woodley said firmly, leaving no room for any doubt that she would sincerely welcome

Dandre's quitting the house for as long as the girl would stay away.

Dandre tied a bonnet around her curls but did not stop to bother with a shawl. As her aunt had warned, it was warm enough without one, and the thought of the worsted yarn clamped about her shoulders was repugnant to the young woman, who was already feeling claustrophobic.

"Good morning, Henry," she called as she opened the front door.

The man looked around, surprised, before emptying his small armload into the cart.

"Gettin' to be almost to afternoon, Miss Dandre," he corrected her.

Dandre acknowledged the truth of his more exact greeting and then smiled. It was the first time she had smiled that morning.

She squinted against the sunlight until her eyes grew accustomed to the brighter natural light. The air was fresh, the countryside wide open. As Dandre gulped in the air, she, like her aunt, could not imagine what had been keeping her in the house on a day like today. Lengthening her stride boyishly, she walked along briskly, coming to the edge of the Woodley property in only moments.

She paused briefly at the roadway, glancing up and down its length, her feet impatient at even so slight a pause.

She turned west, inland, toward Huddersfield and, coincidentally, toward Timbrey Hall. The choice seemed entirely random to her, but Mrs. Woodley, glancing through the morning room window, noted with a smile the direction her niece turned.

The empty road stretched before her, sloping up and down like a lazy carousel, following the contour of the land. It ran more or less straight for as far as the girl could see, but Dandre was not put off by the prospect. She was a good walker and enjoyed the exercise immensely. In Coventry she was used to walking several miles every day, where the deserted country was even more extensive than here in Lancashire. Here one came upon a little village with a stream and a textile mill every mile or two. And Manchester itself was only ten miles away.

But for two or three miles around Timbrey Hall there was no clanking machinery behind stone walls and Dandre forgot their very existence in the fresh, quiet countryside that surrounded her.

She was on the broad lane that accommodated what public traffic there was, but which saw primarily the various travelers to and from Timbrey Hall. It was a lovely lane. The roadway was cleared regularly, but the meadows and woodland through which it had been cut were allowed to grow wild. In the early weeks of summer the shoulders of the lane were a mass of wildflowers. Tansy, chamomile, wild orchids, all in bloom, pushed one another aside vying for her attention. The air was not heavy, thick with the odor of decaying greenery, as it would be later in the season. The faint breeze was cool and wafted only a delicate hint of perfume to her nostrils.

Dandre was aware in a dim, subconscious way that she was headed toward Timbrey, and in that same level of awareness was the recollection of mystery that had not yet been solved concerning the very handsome master of Timbrey. When she had first come downstairs that morning to drive her poor Aunt Bea to distraction with her restlessness, that had been the question nagging at her mind, as it had since Saturday last, buzzing and annoying like a fat housefly trapped against a windowpane.

Here, though, in the air and the space, where one did not even notice the flies and gnats in the wide expanse of sky, she was willing to acknowledge it a silly question after all, one not really worth her obsessive attention. Rather than a felonious scheme, Mr. Chesterton had doubtless been involved with some harmless project, possibly connected with his properties but more likely a *private* matter. That was the key word. Private to Mr. Chesterton.

Out here, the sun pouring down on her shoulders, the warm rustle of breeze stirring the hair on her neck, she acknowledged the point and allowed the question to slip away.

Her steps had slowed and her stride had shortened. Now, besides the birds and the rustle of leaves, she could hear the hum of busy insects. The air that had seemed so still when she started on this walk was actually vibrating with a soothing buzz. Through the trees Dandre could glimpse a sun-filled meadow of tall grasses and pink and yellow flowers.

She began to drift in that direction, and when her feet left the smooth roadway she did not call them back but followed them instead to the field of waving greenery. The sun was very warm. The air stilled. Her eyelids felt heavy and suddenly her legs would no longer support her. She sank down to sit in the middle of the soft grasses, and in only a moment she lay prone, nearly hidden in the tall fronds, cut off from the lane by the spring growth and the tree trunks.

She pulled a handful of the long grass and lay twisting it lazily, braiding it with no particular skill but not bothered by that fact. Her fingers moved slower and slower, clumsy and inexact in their weaving. Her lids covered the green of her eyes and were too heavy to lift again. Her hands fell lightly to rest on her bosom as it rose slowly in the measured breathing of sleep.

She could not have slept more than a half hour, the sun overhead hardly having changed its position when she was roused by a clatter of hooves coming along the lane from the main thoroughfare. It was the first horse that had come this way since Dandre started her walk, and it came rapidly. Merely from the sound of the hooves on the hard dirt she could tell it was a big horse. Probably with a large man astride. The gradation of sound was subtle, but Dandre was fairly certain in her deduction.

To confirm her judgement she raised her head, just high enough to see over the tall grass to the portion of lane visible through the trees. Approaching she saw a gentleman, a large gentleman, on a large brown horse. The rapid approach of the horse slowed, and then, very considerately, the man drew his horse to a standstill directly across from her half-recumbent position in the meadow and she was able to study him at length.

He was a stranger. And yet . . .

Dandre was very sure she had never seen him before, but his features seemed, in a strange way, imperfectly and fleetingly familiar to her.

Even seated as he was on horseback, the girl could tell that he was tall. He had a broad face, heavy in the cheek, with curling brown hair beginning, like Mr. Reddings's, to recede from his high forehead.

His horse pawed at the ground, but the man pulled back on the reins and put his hand soothingly against the creature's neck. Leaning forward as he was, Dandre was able to see his face very clearly, and saw a determination in his jawline, a will unconsciously revealed that she could well imagine to be tenacious. He rather reminded her of a bull terrier, which, once its jaw is locked onto something, will perish before it will release its hold.

The man glanced up the road and then back the way he had come. He sat up straight and took a watch from his pocket. He glanced up and down the road again as he snapped it shut and replaced it in its pocket at the front of his vest.

Very obviously the man was waiting for someone, keeping an arranged meeting. He had ridden from the main road that led into Manchester and north to Leeds. His appointment could be with anyone, anyone at all, coming from the city as he had. Yet he had stopped here on the wooded lane that led to Timbrey Hall, so, a few moments later when he raised his crop in greeting, Dandre could not be surprised to hear a horse approaching from the direction of the Hall. She also was not surprised, although she should have been, to see that the rider was Mr. Chesterton, who was ostensibly in Manchester. Until the weekend, she believed her aunt had said.

Nevertheless, there was Mr. Chesterton greeting the stranger and reining his own horse to a stop in front of him. Dandre, suddenly very anxious to keep her presence unknown, sank down lower in the grasses. From that position she was able to see little else besides a bright and busy ladybug hurrying up one blade of the tall grass and down the next, and she was able to clearly hear even less.

She was extremely frustrated and strained her eyes and ears to understand as much as she could. She was witnessing some sort of clandestine meeting between the mysterious owner of Timbrey Hall and a notorious character.

The men, though not whispering, were talking softly, but occasionally one or the other of them would turn in the right direction so that the words were carried to her on the air.

"Chesterton!" she heard the stranger acknowledge the newcomer's arrival. His voice was raised a little, but as the younger man drew close the stranger's speech grew softer. She heard, "How is it..." But by then the men were face-to-face and she could not hear what "it" was or how it was doing.

Between the leaves of grass and the trunks of trees she saw Chesterton nod, but she did not hear any of his reply. The older man was facing her direction and she heard more snippets from his side of the conversation.

"...difficult?" he asked.

Chesterton shrugged, but it was a dismissive shrug, not a negating one. Whatever "it" was, it was difficult, but Chesterton had accepted that fact.

"...finished?" the stranger said. And then, in response to Chesterton's reply, he asked, "Much longer?"

The younger gentleman nodded, the stranger shook his head and said something in reply. Their discussion was lengthy and evidently still concerning time.

She heard Chesterton say "longer," and then heard the other man's partial reply, "running out of time." Dandre could see one of them and then the other shake his head or raise a hand in explanation, so she knew that there was some—perhaps not disagreement, but *convincing* going on regarding the time in question.

But at one point Mr. Chesterton turned his head slightly and spoke with added intensity.

"I will not leave them until then," she heard very plainly.

The stranger shook his head and put his hand on the younger man's shoulder, a gesture very like the one he had used to calm his impatient steed. The gesture drew him forward in his saddle again, closing the gap between the two men.

"I know," he said. Then he added something else Dandre could not hear. She did hear him say, "You cannot...alone...make a real difference...all of them."

Chesterton nodded.

"What...you found," the man said. It sounded like a request for a report of some kind. Chesterton motioned with his hands, waving them expansively.

"I have seen..." she heard him say, but did not hear anything of what he had seen or where he had seen it or when. The other man nodded, not surprised by what Chesterton was telling him.

"...means of punishment?"

Chesterton nodded again, wiping a hand across his eyes as he did so, as if he would wipe away what he saw there, what the man's words had summoned before him.

"...hours...ages..."

Again Chesterton spoke, and again Dandre could not hear any of what he said.

The stranger shook his head woefully at the young man's remarks.

"This is not an isolated case," he said. "I wish it were. There are hundreds . . . exactly . . . But they . . . only one objective . . . profit."

Chesterton nodded again. His horse pranced sideways and he took a moment to steady it. When the horse had quieted, the older man spoke again.

"We must give this information . . ."

"I know," Chesterton replied.

". . . weeks?" the stranger asked.

Chesterton hesitated and then seemed to agree, but perversely Dandre did not hear how many weeks more the man was willing to allow the younger gentleman.

The larger horse stood quietly underneath his rider, but Chesterton's horse was more skittish. Once again it pranced nervously, and the young man pulled on the reins, at last turning his horse so that the two men were sitting parallel, both facing Dandre. She was able to hear almost everything they said now and could easily fill in the words that did not quite reach her. To her utter chagrin, though, she still was unable to make sense of what she was hearing and seeing.

"What will you do now?" Chesterton asked.

"I must return," the man replied.

"Not today," the young man argued, but the stranger seemed immovable on that point. "Come," Chesterton invited. "Return with me."

"To the Hall?" the man asked. Even from where she was, Dandre could hear the surprise in his voice that almost might have been interpreted as alarm.

Chesterton shook his head.

"I am staying in Manfred's cottage," he said.

Even with that assurance, whatever that assurance meant, the stranger shook his head.

"I had better not," he said. "We should not be seen together."

"Even by my groundsman?" Chesterton asked with a half smile.

The man shook his head solemnly.

"Not by anyone. Servants, family or friends. I have real enemies, Vincent. Enemies everywhere."

"Not here," Chesterton repeated.

"Here, too. Anywhere there is money at stake. They call me a thief. They suggest that we are robbing the country blind." The man smiled ironically.

"They would not believe that if they had seen what I have seen," Chesterton said. His voice had deepened with emotion and Dandre could barely make out his words.

"Then we will show them," the man said.

Chesterton nodded and may have spoken, but Dandre could not hear him.

The stranger gathered the reins of his horse briskly.

"I will wait to hear from you, then," he said.

"I will contact you as soon as I am finished."

"Do not wait too long," the man warned.

"I have told you . . ." Chesterton began.

"I know what you have told me, but this is only the first step. You know what Michael wants."

Chesterton nodded, and then the other man raised his crop to the brim of his hat, then turned his horse and headed back in the direction from which he had come. He was out of Dandre's range of vision almost immediately, and in only a few moments more she could no longer even hear his departing horse.

The younger man did not leave right away but sat still for several minutes, looking through the trees. Dandre held her breath, certain that he was staring directly at her. In a moment, though, she could tell that his eyes were directed to the more distant countryside and not really focused on that.

Lost in thought, he took several deep breaths. Dandre could see the rise and fall of his shoulders with each inhalation and exhalation.

Slowly, reluctantly it seemed, with a last deep sigh, he turned his horse and headed toward Timbrey. Dandre raised herself slightly in the grass and strained her eyes to watch his departing figure. He sat tall and erect in the saddle, but from the crease of fatigue between his brows and the way he occasionally pulled up his slumping shoulders, she knew it was an effort for him. Somehow that effort touched the young woman's heart. She did not know what the weight was that he carried on his shoulders, but she fancied she could almost see the massive, dark bundle there, bearing down upon him, requiring all of his strength to support it.

If the conversation she had overheard had answered none of her questions, at least it had proven one thing: the disguise he had been wearing when he saved her life in Manchester was not the harmless masquerade she had at first assumed it to be. From his words, from this secret meeting, from his heartrending struggle to remain straight in his saddle, Dandre knew there was something more serious. Something more serious, more dangerous and much more demanding.

Mr. Chesterton had long since disappeared down the lane that led to Timbrey Hall, and more specifically to his groundsman's cottage, by the time Dandre rose to her knees and then stood. The sun was uncomfortably warm by now and the girl felt a trickle of perspiration inch down her back between her shoulder blades.

She shook out her skirts and brushed the leaves and grass from the back of her dress and off her shoulders.

She was a long time at the single task, finding one more bit of crushed, dried foliage, one more flower petal, one more beetle wing, painstakingly plucking off minute particles her aunt and uncle would never have seen, let alone found remarkable. But she was lost in thought, lost in consideration of a strange, handsome man with a mysterious mission.

"Is there any news of Mr. Chesterton?"

"News? I do not believe so. As far as I know, tea is still planned for Sunday."

Dandre asked her question casually. Testing the water.

The Woodleys and their niece sat at supper. By the time the girl had returned from her walk it was afternoon, and Aunt Bea and Uncle Peter had already eaten lunch, as had Mildred and Henry, who ate after the Woodleys. Still, Mrs. Woodley did not scold her niece. She had told Mr. Woodley that it was good for the girl to get out and to stay out as long as she pleased, that she supposed their home could be a bit confining at times.

A goldfish would have found the tiny Woodley home confining at times.

Mrs. Woodley was pleased to see the glow of healthy exercise on Dandre's cheek and a brighter light in her eyes than had been there when she left. Her aunt also noticed that the girl had calmed down and no longer fretted and paced. True, she seemed quiet and withdrawn for the remainder of the day, but Mrs. Woodley, who was not as young as she used to be and did not feel herself up to entertaining a bored young woman, was secretly relieved by that fact.

When Mrs. Biggins announced that supper was ready, Dandre and her aunt and uncle sat down together at the table. Dandre poked absently at Mrs. Biggins's very good sole and creamed potatoes, watching her relatives from under her lowered brow.

What did she dare tell them? How much did she want them to know? How much did they already know? Perhaps, after all, she was the only person in all of Oldham who did know *anything.*

"He is not returned to Timbrey, then?" she asked, pursuing the matter.

"Mr. Chesterton? Of course not. You heard his plans to be away this week, Dandre," Mrs. Woodley said, able at last, if she had not been before, to attribute her niece's unrest to a desire to see the Chesterton gentleman again.

"I thought he might have returned unexpectedly," Dandre said.

"We would have heard of that momentous event, you may be certain." Mr. Woodley smiled. "Our tiny little community allows no bit of news to go unreported, and surely Mr. Chesterton's unexpected return would be detailed in a special issue of the *Gossip Gazette,* delivered by more than one mouth, doubtless, to our very doorstep." Her uncle chuckled at his witticism, and Mrs. Woodley smiled good-naturedly, though she was a faithful and regular contributor to the neighborhood's verbal tabloid.

"Well then, I suppose he is still away," Dandre said.

"I am afraid so, my dear. But just be patient. He will be back on the weekend, and sitting at this table after service on Sunday." Mrs. Woodley patted her niece's hand comfortingly, and Dandre allowed herself to be comforted. She would force herself to abandon her pursuit of the question for the moment, but when next Mr. Chesterton sat at this table she intended to get some answers from him. Of course, that had been her intention almost every time she had met him, and so far she had failed miserably to live up to it, but Dandre did not allow herself to be daunted by such trifling consideration.

You have until Sunday, Mr. Chesterton, she thought to herself as Mrs. Biggins brought in the lemon pudding. *And then I want to know what you have gotten yourself into.*

Chapter Six

The remainder of the week passed with no further incident of note. Now Dandre took regular, daily walks that invariably led her in the direction of Timbrey, occasionally almost to the Timbrey door, but she saw no other sign of Mr. Chesterton. She did see Mrs. Redding daily, and Mr. Redding once. Mrs. Redding always waved to her, but Mr. Redding motioned her to the clipped grass of the front lawn to ask after her aunt and uncle. Dandre could find no place to casually work in an inquiry after Redding's brother-in-law, and she did not want to see on Mr. or Mrs. Redding's face the knowing look her aunt always assumed whenever she mentioned his name, so she excused herself in a few minutes without learning anything from the couple.

And then, for all of her planning and anxiety, when Sunday finally arrived, the girl slept in late. Too late to accompany the Woodleys to their church service. So late, in fact, that Mr. and Mrs. Woodley had returned home and it became uncertain who would arrive first at the groaning board and tea table, Dandre or the party from Timbrey.

When Mr. Chesterton and the Reddings did arrive—just after Dandre took her place in the sitting room in a charming yellow chiffon gown that suggested she had been up and dressed in it to greet the sun as it rose that morning—Mrs. Woodley, with the calm assurance of age and wisdom, who believed she could see directly into her niece's every thought, would have been shocked by the first thought that crossed Dandre's mind when she saw the man.

Good heavens, he looks terrible! she gasped to herself.

Mr. Chesterton did not really look terrible, of course. His clothes were as fine and fashionable as ever, his hair as clean, his cheek as shaven, his bearing at least as stately as when she first met him at Timbrey Hall. But Mrs. Woodley, who was not as fascinated by Chesterton and whatever was his difficulty in Manchester, did not see the weary dullness in his eyes, the crease across his brow, the chalky hue of his cheek under his tan. Yet even Mrs. Woodley had the nagging impression that Mr. Chesterton did not appear to be as robustly vibrant as she remembered him to be last Saturday.

The thought was foolish. Mrs. Woodley reminded herself she had seen him for the first time in years and years a week ago. Had met him in the evening, under artificial light. He might look very different in another setting, in the harsh light of day. He *did* look somewhat different. He might even be ill.

Mrs. Woodley could only hope.

She beamed at them all. "Come in, come in. Mrs. Redding, how good of you to come. You remember my husband, Mr. Woodley, and Miss Collin. Mr. Redding."

Mrs. Redding was passed along the greeting line that had somehow formed itself at the door of the modest Woodley sitting room and now came to stand next to Dandre.

For a moment longer Dandre turned to watch Mr. Chesterton bend stiffly over her aunt's hand and greet her uncle. Mr. Woodley clasped the younger man's hand and Dandre distinctly saw the shimmer of a wince at the corner of his mouth.

"This is a very small house," Mrs. Redding said.

Dandre's attention was claimed by the other young woman and she smiled at her words and then at the blush of embarrassment on her cheek.

"It is quite all right, Mrs. Redding. Some homes are distinguished by fine carpets, impressive art or silver collections, even past scandal behind their walls. I completely agree with you that the most remarkable thing about the Woodley home is how small it is. It reminds me of a dollhouse over which I used to quarrel with my sisters."

"It is lovely. Quaint. But warm. Very comfortable, I would imagine." Mrs. Redding fumbled for a flattering phrase that would soften her initial startled reaction.

Dandre only smiled again and faintly shook her head.

"Let us sit down," she offered.

The two young women left the gathering at the doorway and sat on the high-backed divan.

Mrs. Redding, recovered by now, asked after the well-being of everyone in the Woodley home. Her aunt and uncle still well, she assumed.

They were all doing famously. And the Reddings?

Fine, thank you.

It seemed there had been a flurry over a missing pocket watch of her husband's during the week. Mr. Redding had been certain it was lost or stolen, but his wife had endeavored to calm him and convince him it was only temporarily misplaced. To the joy and felicity of everyone in the household, the watch *was* eventually recovered.

Mrs. Redding was evidently telling the most thrilling thing that had occurred at Timbrey Hall in the past week. She did not even hint that she had seen her brother during the week, and Dandre surmised that was because she had not. When the stranger refused to accompany Chesterton to his groundsman's cottage, Dandre thought perhaps the young man would have returned to the Hall proper, but evidently he had kept his return from his family even then.

Like Mr. Chesterton's skittish horse, Dandre squirmed under the grueling details of Mrs. Redding's domestic tale of the pocket watch and wondered how the other young woman could endure, and evidently enjoy, the unremitting grind of such a tame country life.

But she was forced to smile at herself. It was the same country and the same life she had been enjoying for twenty years herself. And if Mr. Chesterton had not saved her from certain damage and possible death in Manchester, and then brought his disturbing mystery here with him, she might be perfectly contented still.

There he was, though, with his intrigue, looking heart-breakingly spent and worn this evening. She let her eyes wander beyond Mrs. Jacqueline Redding and her report on the health of her Persian cat to her brother, still standing at the doorway, an audience for whatever pleasantries were passing between Mr. Redding and her Uncle Peter. No doubt they were something along the same lines as what Mrs. Redding was sharing with her. Mr. Chesterton looked even less interested than Dandre felt.

He turned his head, ever so slightly, and looked into her eyes. Dandre imagined she saw a warning there, though the afternoon light was uncertain and there were dark shadows under Mr. Chesterton's eyes and in the hollows of his cheeks.

"Your brother looks a trifle worn, Mrs. Redding. I hope his ride from Manchester was not too exhausting?" she asked, inserting her question, which she hoped sounded perfectly casual, into a break Mrs. Redding allowed in her pleasant recitation of the exciting week at Timbrey.

Mrs. Redding glanced over her shoulder to the gentlemen, who were leaving the doorway and following Mr. Woodley into the room.

"Does he?" she asked, surprised by Dandre's suggestion.

"I thought so," Dandre confirmed.

"Oh? Perhaps it is just the light." Mrs. Redding narrowed her eyes. "I see what you mean, though," she agreed. "Vincent!" She spoke loudly to attract her brother's attention.

Chesterton looked across to the two young women and then excused himself from the grouping now, of Redding and Aunt Beatrice, to answer the summons in his sister's eye.

"What is it, Jackie?" he asked.

"Sit down here so I can look at you." Mrs. Redding spoke with the command in her voice that an older sister uses with a younger brother, no matter what their ages.

Chesterton dutifully sat on the arm of the divan next to his sister and Mrs. Redding took his hand in hers.

"Miss Collin says you appear to be weary, and I must admit that I agree with her. What have you been up to in Manchester that leaves you looking as if you were supporting the weight of the world on your shoulders, or had been moving it about this week anyway?" Now she put her hand to his face and smoothed his cheek with the back of her hand.

Chesterton smiled and captured the fingers, giving them a brotherly little kiss before releasing her hand.

"Nothing more strenuous than meeting with a few brokerage firms and losing a bit of money at cards."

Mrs. Redding laughed.

"That explains it then." She turned her smile on Dandre. "As my brother, the wicked beast, has told me before, there is nothing more exhausting to a man than losing money—" She turned to her brother with raised eyebrows. "A great deal of money?" she asked. Chesterton shook his head and waved his hand in casual dismissal. Mrs. Redding faced Dandre again. "At the gaming table," she concluded with another smile.

In the polite setting of the Woodleys' formal tea, Dandre could do nothing else but raise her own eyebrows and return her own little smile.

"I am flattered, though," Chesterton said, "to be the object of Miss Collin's concern. But really, you must not waste such admirable charity on such an unworthy subject."

Chesterton stood and bowed slightly, then turned to join Mrs. Woodley in her inspection of the tea Mrs. Biggins had laid out for them. Mrs. Woodley would never have admitted it, certainly, but his scrutiny unnerved her and produced a high-pitched querulous note in her voice, which was usually so low and self-possessed.

Dandre had not meant to instigate a confrontation when she asked her question of Mrs. Redding. She was hoping for some morsel of information, though she was actually expecting Mrs. Redding to pooh-pooh her suggestion. Instead, Mrs. Redding had put the question directly to her brother, who had manufactured a pleasing little excuse that satisfied his sister completely and did not satisfy Dandre in the least.

The "confrontation" had achieved one thing, though. Mr. Chesterton had made it clear that he would not be confronted. He would answer no question; he would offer no explanation; he would not even admit the exhaustion that was weighing so heavily on his shoulders that they drooped pitifully under the navy broadcloth of his coat. He did not appreciate Dandre's solicitation, nor would he admit her to the labyrinth of his private life, a life he kept private even from his sister.

Mr. Redding came to ask his wife's opinion of a heavy old brooch Mrs. Woodley was showing him from a family collection, and Dandre readily relinquished her place on the divan.

"Miss Collin, I did not mean to drive you away," Mr. Redding hurriedly assured her when the girl stood.

"Not at all, Mr. Redding. Please sit next to your wife and I will inquire if my aunt needs any help," she said.

Mrs. Woodley turned to her with such a look of relief when the young lady appeared at her side that Dandre could only assume that her aunt did indeed need her assistance.

"Oh, my dear," Mrs. Woodley gasped brightly. "Mr. Chesterton says he has not been able to see any of the plays on the Manchester stage. I told him I was aghast. That a young gentleman ought not to neglect the arts."

From the desperate tone of her aunt's voice, Dandre suspected Mr. Chesterton had not been able to tell Mrs. Woodley anything about Manchester society, fashion or scandal, either, which was the news from Coventry her aunt always required of her. No doubt Mrs. Woodley was assuming the gentleman was too serious, scholarly, too involved with high finance and the masculine business world to share her more social interests. But Dandre suspected there was another, more sinister reason Mr. Chesterton did not keep abreast of the metropolitan gossip, something else that kept him from the theater and the concert hall.

"I am sure Mr. Chesterton patronizes the arts to the full extent of his leisure hours, Aunt Beatrice." the young woman gently chided Mrs. Woodley. "You must remember that he must attend to personal matters when he is in town." She was careful not to turn a knowing eye on Mr. Chesterton or to infuse her words with added meaning. The smile she directed to him was pleasant and open and perfectly bland. As was the smile he returned.

"Which is precisely what I was about to tell Mrs. Woodley myself, Miss Collin," he remarked.

"That all may be very true," Mrs. Woodley said, "but it left us with no common topic of interest after we had both admired Mildred's arrangement of the table."

"You might have asked if Mr. Chesterton would not like to sample one of Mrs. Biggins's tarts or a little of this pâté."

Chesterton shook his head and murmured, "Not at the moment."

But Dandre's suggestion reminded Mrs. Woodley of her duties as a hostess and she hurriedly excused herself to put the other occupants of the room in motion toward the table.

For the moment the two of them were alone. It was the first moment of even semiprivacy since his recognition of her the week before when the gentleman had assisted her from the stream after her horse threw her.

Dandre waited until her aunt was out of earshot before raising her eyes to Mr. Chesterton's face. His look was wary. He reminded Dandre of a sleek, purebred wolfhound, suspicious, on guard, his upper lip quivering on the threshold of a snarl.

She assumed her most guileless expression—and Dandre Collin was fresh from the English countryside, so she was able to assume an extremely guileless one.

"Mildred really does make excellent tarts, Mr. Chesterton," she said, indicating the plate of fruit-filled pastries on the tea table in front of them.

"I am sure she does," he said, the wariness still in his eyes.

Dandre reached for one of the small plates her aunt had stacked on the table and took one of the tarts herself.

"I understand from Mrs. Redding that you missed a bit of excitement at Timbrey this week," she said.

Chesterton seemed surprised and raised his eyebrows questioningly.

"Did I?"

"Your brother-in-law's pocket watch was missing for a day or two," Dandre explained.

"Was it? I had not heard," Chesterton said.

"I believe it has been found."

"Ah. Good." Chesterton followed the girl's example and took his own plate, piling on it several of Mildred's varied dainties. He did so with an unmistakable air of relief. Perhaps the young woman was not going to grill him after all.

He stretched his hand toward the middle of the table for one of the thin slices of cold roast beef, then winced at the shot of pain the effort signaled.

His halted motion and his quick grimace were not lost on Dandre, who was furtively watching his every movement.

"Is something wrong, Mr. Chesterton?" she asked innocently.

"My shoulder is a bit sore," he said.

"Is it?"

"A bit."

"If I remember correctly, your shoulder was occasioning you some pain last Monday. Is this the same injury?"

"Not the same injury, the same cause," Chesterton told her cryptically, then turned without offering further explanation. "Jacqueline, Miss Collin tells me Jeremy lost his watch this week?"

"Only misplaced it," Mrs. Redding corrected. "It was that lovely old watch of his grandfather's, so for a few days, until we found it, he was positively disconsolate."

Mrs. Redding and her brother both chuckled, and Dandre smiled. She had come up cold against the shield Mr. Chesterton put around himself and his secret life in Manchester, and she saw no way of penetrating it. Certainly not here, not at the correct tea table of her dear aunt and uncle. Not when Mr. and Mrs. Woodley were both so pleased to welcome the illustrious Chesterton party into their home. How could she disrupt the delicate bubble of their pleasure with the discord her pursuance of the question would surely cause?

The Woodleys and their guests took their seats around the small sitting room, exchanging quiet comments about the weather and their health. Mr. Woodley announced that the market looked good right now, and Mr. Redding recited a silly bit of poetry he had heard just the other day, which he found delightful.

"The cook has burned the roast again,
The apples all are rotten,
But we are from dear Lancashire,
And thank the Lord for cotton.

"I heard some of the lads down at the stable singing it the other day," Redding said after he completed his recitation. "There are several more verses, but that's the only one I can recall offhand."

"What a charming little ditty, dear," Mrs. Redding commended her husband. And then, to Mrs. Woodley, she said, "Lancashire *is* a lovely part of the country. I cannot blame you Lancashire folk for believing it the sweetest place on earth."

Mrs. Woodley beamed, but Mr. Chesterton interrupted the pleasant exchange, sounding very serious.

"You miss the point of the song, I am afraid," he said. "I have heard it before myself and I do not think it is about the grandeurs of Lancashire. Rather, it is about the cotton industry."

"And what is more grand in all of Lancashire than that?" Mr. Woodley asked, smiling broadly.

"From your vantage point perhaps nothing," Chesterton said. Dandre was puzzled by the note of sorrow in his voice. "But the rest of the song tells a different story."

"What is the rest of the song, brother?" Mrs. Redding asked.

Chesterton shook his head.

"It becomes rather grim, I am afraid."

"Come, come, man. You cannot leave us in suspense now," Mr. Woodley cried.

Chesterton looked around seriously at the expectant party and acquiesced reluctantly.

"The next verse is not so bad, I suppose.

What though Mother beats her child,
And Dad's a drunken sotten?
We are from dear Lancashire,
And thank the Lord for cotton."

"It is a bit rough, but not so very bad," Mrs. Redding said.

"I am sure it is only a song," Mrs. Woodley protested.

Chesterton shook his head but did not bother to contradict the lady.

"It does not change my opinion about the industry, though." Mr. Woodley grinned.

"Another!" Jeremy Redding demanded.

Dandre was closely following the mild confusion in the sitting room, but Mildred interrupted her scrutiny.

"Miss Dandre?" the housekeeper murmured softly at the girl's elbow.

"What is it?" she asked.

Mildred stepped back through the doorway and Dandre was forced to follow her.

"Miss, I am embarrassed for Mr. Biggins and told him he'd have to come himself. He refused and so the matter has taken another hour at least. Can't get him to do anything he has decided he won't. Says it wasn't his fault, what with his busy work yesterday and this party today. Well, you know how Mr. Biggins is."

"What is it, Mildred?" Dandre asked impatiently, bringing a stop to the housekeeper's meanderings. The girl did not want to listen to Mrs. Biggins's complaints against her husband, which she knew from previous experience could go on for a considerable length of time. She wanted to be in the sitting room with the guests and *their* pleasant bickering, which might, conceivably, throw some light onto the mystery of Mr. Chesterton.

"Yes, well, it's the mail," Mildred said.

"The mail?"

"Mr. Biggins collected it from the boy on Friday and forgot to give it to you."

"To me?"

"There's a letter for you from Coventry, along with one or two for Mr. Woodley from uptown. I told Mr. Biggins it might be important, but he says it's just word from home and you won't mind so very much. Still and all, *he* wouldn't bring it to you. Made me."

"It is quite all right," Dandre assured her.

With a grateful sigh Mrs. Biggins took the few envelopes from her apron pocket and put them into Dandre's hand.

But the Biggins's concern over the delayed mail had prevented the girl from hearing the denouement of the conflict in the sitting room. By the time she returned, the subject of the song had been abandoned, evidently without Mr. Redding having coerced his brother-in-law into giving them another verse.

There were once again separate conversations going on simultaneously: Mrs. Redding and Uncle Peter were discussing poultry raising, while Mrs. Woodley listened to Mr. Redding and Mr. Chesterton discuss the latter's plans for his departure early the following morning.

"If you want to drive it yourself, you are quite welcome to the cabriolet," Redding was saying. "Your sister and I can get along without it this week."

Mrs. Woodley looked up as her niece entered the room.

"What did Mildred want, my dear?" she asked.

"Henry had neglected to give us the Friday post," Dandre said. "I left Uncle's business letters on the secretary in the library, but I am afraid there was some unsettling news for me."

"What?" Mrs. Woodley sounded concerned but not alarmed, since Dandre herself did not sound alarmed.

The girl held up the opened letter in her hand.

"It is from Mother," she said. "She writes that Katherine has caught the influenza. She does not believe it is anything too serious, but she suggests that I come home."

"Oh!" Mrs. Woodley sounded very disappointed.

"Only for a week or two. She assures me I can return to finish the summer," Dandre consoled her.

Mrs. Woodley thought it strange that Mrs. Collin would have her daughter make the long, expensive trip on so slight a pretext as her younger daughter contracting a mild illness, but Mrs. Woodley had learned long ago that there was no accounting for Katey Collin. It was easiest just to enjoy her company and overlook her quirks. That is what Mrs. Woodley's brother, who had some interesting quirks himself, had learned to do.

"When do you need to leave?" she asked her niece.

"As soon as possible. This evening. Tomorrow morning. Of course, I only need to go into Manchester, where I can catch the train to Stoke-on-Trent," she said. She looked beseechingly around the room, passing quickly over Mr. Chesterton and settling her gaze instead upon Mr. Redding. "I do hate to bother my uncle or even Henry to make the trip to Manchester so early in the morning," she sighed.

"Nonsense," Mr. Woodley protested.

But Jeremy Redding, having received a sort of revelation, cut the older gentleman short.

"This is capital!" Redding cried. "Vincent, surely you would be willing to share your cabriolet with Miss Collin into town tomorrow morning?"

"I . . ." Chesterton hesitated.

"If you leave early enough, you can deliver the young woman to the station and still have plenty of time to get to the Exchange by the time it opens. You do not mind leaving early in the morning, do you, Miss Collin?" Redding asked.

"Not at all," Dandre said. "The earlier the better."

"Now, Dandre, there is no point in putting Mr. Chesterton out. Henry can get you into Manchester in plenty of time to catch the train," her uncle said.

Dandre was just barely able to keep from turning to him with a look of pique. As it was, she feared for a moment that Mr. Chesterton was going to agree with Mr. Woodley. Finally, though, he shook his head, replacing his teacup on its saucer.

"Certainly not," he said. "I am perfectly willing to take Miss Collin into Manchester with me. I am afraid my brother is correct, though. We must leave very early. Shall we say three o'clock, Miss Collin?"

The hour was very early, but if Mr. Chesterton was hoping to discourage the girl, he was doomed to disappointment.

"I can have no objection, whatever the hour, Mr. Chesterton," she said. "I will be ready to leave tomorrow at three o'clock."

"In the morning," Chesterton warned. He wanted to make it clear that he was not talking about tomorrow afternoon.

"Yes, in the morning." The girl understood.

"Well then, perhaps we had better get back to Timbrey," Chesterton said. He stood up and replaced his dishes on the sideboard. "It has been delightful, Mrs. Woodley, and we would stay longer if your niece and I did not have such a long day in front of us tomorrow."

"I understand completely, Mr. Chesterton. And thank you for your kindness."

"It is entirely my pleasure, Mrs. Woodley. Mr. Woodley. Miss Collin."

Mr. and Mrs. Redding also took their leave, and Mr. Woodley accompanied them all to the door.

"Well, that was a lucky thing," Mrs. Woodley said. "Oh, not that poor Katherine has the influenza or that you have to leave, of course. But that Henry should forget to

give us the letter until today, while the Reddings and Mr.
Chesterton were here. How fortunate that Mr. Chesterton
would be returning to Manchester so soon.''

''Very,'' Dandre agreed.

''Now, my dear, you will have to get packed. Mrs. Biggins and I can finish up down here. But you must be all
ready to go tonight, and then you will have to retire very
early if you are to leave with Mr. Chesterton in the morning.'' Mrs. Woodley turned to survey the disorder of the
room, shaking her head and murmuring, ''An ungodly
hour. Mr. Chesterton's business in Manchester must be very
pressing.''

''Perhaps I will go pack a few things,'' Dandre said. ''I
may only be going for a day or two, but I suppose I ought
to prepare for an extended leave.''

Before she went up to her room, though, she stopped at
the foot of the stairs to reread her mother's letter before she
slipped it back into its envelope.

Dearest Dandre,

Everything is very well here. I am convinced your
father is improving daily with his fiddle lessons and
will amaze you by the time you get home. Your sisters
are both well and happy, though they miss you terribly. Paul writes that his Latin is very difficult, but he
thinks he is getting better at it. He closed with *abeo*,
which is doubtless Latin for goodbye.

We hope you are enjoying yourself. Give your aunt
and uncle our best and enjoy your summer with them.
We will see you sometime in September. With love and
affection, your mother, K. Collin.

Chapter Seven

As early as three o'clock came, it did not catch Dandre unawares. She awakened several times during the short night, each time lighting the candle to read the face of the little locket watch she usually pinned to the bodice of her shirtwaist or carried in her reticule.

Midnight. One-thirty. Two-fifteen.

At two-thirty she rose and splashed a little water onto her face. She was already in her traveling ensemble by the time her aunt tapped at her door to alert her to the hour.

"Oh, you are up," Mrs. Woodley said, opening the door and peeking around the frame.

"And dressed," Dandre said. She stood before the mirror on the dresser, her image lighted by the candle that had already lighted the room several times this night. She was pulling her tortoiseshell brush through her hair, carefully working out the tangles before she gathered the whole mass into the curly bun atop her head.

"Everything is ready to go?" Mrs. Woodley asked.

Dandre pointed with her brush to the carpetbag on the chest at the foot of her bed.

"I am only taking that. It holds a change of clothing and some personal articles."

"Do you think that will be enough?" Mrs. Woodley eyed the bag uncertainly. To a woman who understood matters of feminine toiletries, the bag looked very small.

"That will get me home, and anything else I need I can find there."

Her aunt, with another uncertain glance at the carpetbag, went to summon Mrs. Biggins to get something for her niece's breakfast. Although Mrs. Woodley managed to rouse the housekeeper from a sound sleep, insisting she leave the warmth of Mr. Biggins's broad back, Miss Dandre did not have a chance to take even one bite of the hastily concocted cornmeal mush.

"He is here!" Mrs. Woodley called. She had stationed herself by the window at the front of the house. "Mr. Chesterton has come! Hurry along, Dandre. You must not keep him waiting."

Dandre dropped her spoon and started up from her chair. Mrs. Biggins looked on in disgust and determined within herself that if she was called to get a breakfast at three o'clock in the morning that nobody ate, then, by heavens, they would eat it cold and hard at seven o'clock.

Mr. Chesterton was better looking than he had any business being before the sun even rose.

"Good morning, Mrs. Woodley," he called from the little carriage. He met the older lady and Dandre at the door and took the bag from the young woman. He, too, seemed surprised by the modest volume of Miss Collin's luggage, but unlike Mrs. Woodley, he did not try to convince the girl to reconsider.

"I am afraid it is entirely likely that we will get to Manchester before a train is scheduled to leave for Coventry, Miss Collin."

"Stoke-on-Trent," Dandre corrected.

"I beg your pardon?"

"The train will only take me to Stoke-on-Trent," Dandre explained. "From there I must take the coach to Coventry."

"Well, I do not believe a train will be leaving for Stoke-on-Trent until later in the day, either," Chesterton said. "And I fear my business is rather pressing. I hope I will not seem too much of a cad if I leave you waiting at the train station?" He looked mildly apologetic, but only apologetic, and only mildly so, not as if he would change his plans on her account. Which suited Dandre very well.

Mrs. Woodley did not look nearly so well suited. She looked scandalized, but since she had not been consulted on the matter, and Dandre appeared to be satisfied with the arrangement, there was not a great deal she felt she could say.

A soft, "Oh, Dandre, do you think...?" was as much as she ventured, and that was ignored.

"Certainly not, Mr. Chesterton," Dandre said, settling onto the thinly padded seat of the cabriolet. "Rather than a cad, you are a knight in shining armor rescuing a hapless damsel. Now, Aunt, I shall be perfectly all right." Mrs. Woodley had known her niece since she was a child; she certainly knew her well enough to accept her assurance with a grain of salt. "I shall send word as soon as I arrive to let you know how Katherine is, but since it is very likely that I will be on my way back to you by the time a letter could get from Oldham to Coventry, I will convey your regard and I do not suppose you need to write." Especially since it would alarm her parents to read that one of their daughters was ill and the other one had come home to nurse her, when they had seen no evidence of either. Dandre really hoped her aunt would not take the trouble of sending a letter after her.

"Very well, my dear. I will wait to hear from you," Aunt Bea said in partial compliance.

Chesterton raised his crop to Mrs. Woodley and the carriage was on its way.

Travel in the chill, predawn hours was—invigorating. Dandre was determined to put as good a face as possible on this situation, since, after all, she had precipitated the whole thing.

Chesterton was maintaining a stony silence. Like the girl, he was aware that being alone, isolated as they were, presented the perfect and, until now, the only opportunity for questions and answers and lengthy explanations.

Chesterton was not willing to answer those questions, was not going to give her any explanations, short or long, and it especially irritated him to realize that he found this meddlesome child appealing. She had a country innocence about her that was refreshing to a man who had spent recent years in the teeming cities of England and Europe. With her open countenance, her gentle touch, even her charming tendency to mishaps, she was like a delightful breath of fresh air. As the carriage jogged along behind the trotting horse, the two of them for the moment silent, Chesterton was forced to admit to himself that he needed some fresh air in his life right now.

Dandre turned toward him. Chesterton clenched his jaw.

"This is a pleasant drive. Even so early in the morning. Do you not think so?"

Chesterton did not answer immediately, the girl's question not being the one he expected.

"I really had not considered it before," he said.

"No? You surprise me, sir. I thought a gentleman like yourself would appreciate the beauty around you."

"It is dark, Miss Collin."

"It is not always dark when you travel this road, surely. But even now, without the beauty of the scenery, there are the pleasing sounds of the sleepy songbirds just beginning to awaken, the serenity of the hour. And if nothing else, you must enjoy the fresh air."

"As a matter of fact, I do like fresh air, Miss Collin. I was just this moment past reminding myself that I like nothing better than a breath of fresh air."

After their innocent, innocuous exchange, the natural silence of the hour and the deserted countryside settled over them. Occasionally one or the other of them would make a comment on the road or the landscape that was slowly becoming distinguishable as the dawn approached. And once Dandre asked her companion if he had any brothers or sisters other than Mrs. Redding. He did not. That was the only personal disclosure she demanded of him, and Chesterton, who had been dreading the time they would be alone together, was surprised that the ride, which was usually so long, should be over so quickly that morning. By four-thirty they had reached the outskirts of Manchester, where the air was not so fresh, and ten minutes later Chesterton had them at the train station, which was, just as he warned, deserted of people and trains at that hour.

He looked around at the bare tracks and empty benches.

"Perhaps you have a relative here in Manchester? I do not like to leave a lady unprotected."

"I know you do not," she said, softly and sweetly. "You very gallantly proved that once before." When she finished speaking she was almost whispering. Yet it was still quiet enough, even in the city, for the gentleman to hear her.

Chesterton looked into her eyes and then quickly turned his own away. Her comment had taken him by surprise, though it really should not have. He should have known that she would not let it go, could not put the whole episode behind them—behind her.

"Will you not tell me what it is all about?" she coaxed.

Damn the woman, she coaxed very prettily.

"Miss Collin, I thought I had made it clear that I did not want to discuss the affair. I had hoped you were bright enough to grasp that fact. Evidently things must be made crystalline clear to you. What I do in Manchester is my concern."

"But I think—"

"And *not* yours," he said, cutting her request short.

"Mr. Chesterton, I am sorry to cause you distress, but I suspect, I am afraid, that you are in some sort of difficulty, and—" She hesitated, laying a soft hand against the back of his that held the reins. He could feel the warmth of her fingertips and the palm of her hand even through the material of her glove and his own. As lovely as the young woman's green eyes were, as delightful as he found the red highlights in her hair or the unmistakable pleasingness of her firm, provocatively rounded figure, this hand, its gentle touch, was the thing about her that he found most appealing. There was no hesitancy, no aloofness in the tender caress, no demand in the curve of her fingers around his, no coercion in the pressure of the palm. There was only compassion and the desire to assist. "And I would like to help you, if you will let me."

He shook his head, following the course of the lamplighter who was coming toward them along the street, extinguishing the feeble candlelight that had become unnecessary by now. A yawning newsboy had appeared on the corner, where he stooped to roll his newssheets, keeping careful watch out for his first customer of the morning. Keeping a careful, hopeful watch, in fact, on the gentleman and young lady in the little trap at the end of the lane.

"There is nothing you can do, Miss Collin," he said.

The girl laughed softly.

"I have been told that," she replied.

"That is not what I meant. You are a very capable young woman, I am sure," Chesterton mumbled uncomfortably, then added, "And I do appreciate your not saying anything to my family. Nor, I hope, yours."

"You are the only one to whom I have made any mention of the incident," she affirmed for him.

"Good," he said.

"My dear Mr. Chesterton, have you had a—a run-in with the law?" she asked softly, trying to minimize the scandal she was suggesting.

Chesterton's lips twisted in a wry smile, but he shook his head again. Dandre could not tell if he was replying to her question or indicating that he could not reply to her question.

A number of people had appeared in the concourse by now. The lamplighter had passed by them and a woman with a box of apples had joined the boy on the corner. They had already each sold one item of merchandise. The ticket seller had appeared in her cage, although neither Dandre nor Mr. Chesterton had seen her arrive.

It is curious that Mr. Chesterton was aware of all that. What he was immediately, and he believed exclusively, aware of was the tiniest increase in the pressure of Miss Collin's hand on his. He released the reins he held to fold his fingers around hers.

"Miss Collin," he began, with a plea in his voice he feared was useless, "I have asked you not to interfere. What I am doing I must do alone. I do not want or need any help from you, which you could not give me anyway. Just leave it alone." He spoke firmly, sounded, he was sure, intractable, and yet when he looked into her face her eyes were wide and dark, full of question and compassion. If Dandre's heart had been touched by his effort to keep his shoulders straight, his was pierced by the look in her eyes.

The gray light of morning was still dim, though it hardly cloaked them any longer. Chesterton raised his hand and hooked his index finger under her chin. With a slight motion of his shoulders and a tiny exertion of pressure he pulled her toward him as surely as if she were tethered at the end of a strong rope. He looked down into her eyes for just a moment, but without waiting for her permission or even her complete comprehension, he bent his head and pressed his lips against her own. In the cool morning air they felt very warm, their pressure both soothing and demanding.

Dandre, quite inexperienced in the arts of love, responded intuitively with her own warm desire. Caught off guard as she was, her defenses did not come into play immediately, and by the time it had occurred to her to protest his familiarity, it had also occurred to her that the kiss was very pleasant, and what, exactly, did she want to protest?

When they parted again, Dandre opened her eyes to study his face.

"Miss Collin...Dandre," he began hesitantly, aware that he ought to apologize for the liberty he had taken but not sorry for it at all. "I did not mean..."

"It is all right," she said softly, resting her fingertips at the corner of his mouth. "We will pretend that everything that has happened at this station has been a dream."

He nodded slightly.

"Yes, perhaps everything at this station *has* been a dream. Everything." He looked deeply and seriously into her eyes, requiring her agreement.

That was not what Dandre had meant, but the gentleman seemed determined to take her at her word. She could not resist making one last attempt, though.

"Mr. Chesterton, will you not allow me to help you?" she pleaded softly.

"You cannot," he said.

"Surely there is something..." she began. She was interrupted by the faint sound of a train whistle in the distance.

Chesterton jumped. Hastily he drew back and took his watch from its pocket.

"Good heavens!" he murmured. "I must go."

"Mr. Chesterton, let me..."

As if he had never kissed her, as if it all really had been a dream, Chesterton shook his head at her words, dismissing them, and her, with casual impatience.

"There is nothing you can do for me, Miss Collin. Go home."

"Can you not even tell me what it is all about?"

"Not now," he said. He spoke with such cold implacability she thought he would leave her there without another word, but he looked into her eyes and allowed a glimmer of his kindlier emotions to shine through once again. "You will return, Miss Collin?"

"That is my intention."

"Perhaps then." His promise was vague, but her expression immediately became eagerly hopeful. "But not until then," he warned sternly.

Without another word he jumped down from the carriage. He helped her down and retrieved the carpetbag from under her seat. He looked behind him at the train station that was continuing to fill, and now his concern was that it would be too crowded for the girl. But the train whistle sounded again, reminding him of the time, and he realized that he no longer had a choice.

"I must go," he repeated. "Are you sure you can make it to your train?"

"I shall manage very well."

"I trust you will have no difficulty," he said distractedly, half-turned by now to the carriage. No one who knew Dandre Collin had ever made that statement to her. Mr. Chesterton had only been with the girl on two or three occasions, and even he sensed something disquieting in his words.

"None at all, I am sure," she said.

He had taken his place in the carriage driver's seat again.

"Take care of yourself, Miss Collin. And return to... Oldham. Very soon."

He spoke with such a boyish shyness it almost made Dandre smile. But she did not smile. He did not seem *that* boyish, and his kiss certainly had not been.

Their eyes locked for a moment, then he flicked the reins, stirring the horse from its nap. The cabriolet clattered along the cobblestones and Dandre watched as Mr. Chesterton guided the horse out into the mainstream of traffic, which really had become a mainstream by now.

"Actually, I will not need to return, Mr. Chesterton," she said under her breath, "because I have no intention of leaving."

She raised her hand and immediately a hansom stopped for her. Without waiting for the driver's assistance she quickly climbed aboard and then looked up into the man's surprised face.

"Do you see that small carriage?" she asked, indicating the roadway in front of them and the several carriages of varied shapes and sizes.

"I see a bunch o' carriages, miss," the driver confessed.

"The one being driven by the young gentleman in the tall hat and the light-colored coat. See him there?" She pointed in a very unladylike manner, but following the line of her outstretched finger, the cab driver was able to identify the vehicle and the driver to which and to whom the girl was referring.

He nodded. "I see 'im, miss."

"You must follow him," she said.

"Where to, miss?" the driver asked.

"Wherever he goes," she said. At that moment Chesterton turned a corner. "Oh, hurry, or you shall lose him!" she gasped.

The driver snapped his crop against the horse's flank and Dandre was thrown back against the seat as the hansom started forward.

The cab turned the same corner and Dandre was relieved to see the little cabriolet ahead of them. They traveled several of the long city blocks, turning a number of corners, moving from the smart section of the city, which catered to the moneyed set, to the domestic section and then a very mean residential quarter. At last she saw the carriage stopping in front of a tawdry-looking tenement building. Dandre leaned forward to pull on the jacket of the driver.

"Stop here," she called softly.

"Thought you wanted to catch up with 'im," the man said.

"No, I am only—" She paused for a moment to consider what exactly it was she was doing. "I am plotting his route," she explained.

The driver nodded sagely and pulled the hansom cab to the side of the road. As original as her explanation had sounded to Dandre, evidently it was one with which a cab driver in the city was familiar.

Chesterton climbed from his carriage and looked down the lane in the opposite direction from Dandre's cab. A group of young rowdies was clustered a little way up the road, and the man hailed one of the boys. The lad held up a finger in acknowledgment and came in answer to the summons. The man and boy stood consulting in the doorway of the tenement for a minute and then Chesterton handed the youngster something.

Chesterton turned from the boy to the stairs that led to the narrow building. But before climbing them, he took his hat off and ran his fingers roughly through his hair, shaking his head as he did so, so that in only a few moments he had attained a very unkempt appearance. Then he mounted the stairs and entered the smoke-grimed building.

The ruffian waited at the doorway for a beat and then stepped to the curbside, where he grabbed the reins of the carriage and started leading the horse back up the street toward Dandre and the cab.

"He is stealing the carriage!" the young woman gasped.

"I don't think so, miss," the driver said.

But Dandre was not convinced. Indeed, the evidence of her eyes told her otherwise.

"Stop him! Stop him!" she demanded.

The driver sighed. He was well enough acquainted with the thievery of young hooligans in Manchester to know that this was not their usual *modus operandi*. Never before had he seen the victim beckon the thief, the two of them talk, the victim thoughtlessly leave his property on the street and the thief amble away with it.

But the girl was not to be denied. If he did not apprehend the "thief," she was very likely to.

"Ho, there! Boy!"

The scruffy lad looked up at the driver in surprise.

"Wha' you want?" he called back.

"Is that your carriage, boy?"

"Not 'ardly likely, is it?" He grinned, revealing a mouth full of crooked teeth.

"You stealing it, then?" the driver asked, half-smiling himself.

Now the lad laughed out loud, a hard, short laugh.

"Hoo! And where d'ya think I could sell such a fine and useful toy 'ereabouts?" he asked. "Nah. A gen'l'man wants me to take it to the stable for 'im. Said to leave word 'e'll pick it up on Saturday next. Give me two bob, 'e did." The boy held up the coins to verify his words. "A sight more'n I could get for sellin' this thing outright." The boy nodded briskly at the driver and passed on, pulling the horse behind him.

The driver turned. "The boy said he was paid to..." he began.

"I heard what he said," Dandre stopped him.

"What now?" the driver asked.

"I...I am not..." She faltered, but before she could come to any conclusion, the door to the tenement opened again and a rude mill worker came out, slamming the door behind him. He stopped to pull on a pair of fingerless gloves before starting down the road. He was bareheaded, his hair in disarray. He was dirty, or at least the rags he wore were dirty, and his shuffle along the boardwalk was easily accounted for by the huge, heavy shoes that flopped around his feet every time he took a step.

Dandre grabbed the cab driver's arm in a grip he found neither compassionate nor comforting.

"That is him!" she whispered fiercely.

"Oo? 'Im?" the driver asked. "No, miss, the fellow you were following was a very fine gentleman, not an old mill rat like that one."

"It is him, I tell you," she insisted. The driver shook his head again, but Dandre did not have time to let him try to talk her out of something she knew. She grabbed her carpetbag and jumped from the cab, landing on the ground with a long, jagged tear in the skirt of her gown. Her various ascents and descents in and out of vehicles that morning, plus the breezy ride from her uncle's home into Manchester and her cab ride through the city streets, had rumpled her clothing and dislodged her carefully arranged hair, loosing strands to fly about her face, a face that was still very pretty but now undeniably travel-stained.

"How much do I owe you?" she asked, fumbling through the little coin purse she had withdrawn from the bag.

"Miss, I'm tellin' you..." the driver protested.

"Come, come. I have no time. Here—" She pulled a bank note from the little leather bag. "Is that enough?" She held it up to him.

"It's enough, miss, but you're makin' a mistake."

She waved the note impatiently and at last the driver was forced to take it. The girl closed her bag smartly and started down the street toward the tenement dwelling. The cab driver watched the straight-backed little figure hopelessly, then sighed and jounced the reins again. He turned the cab on the deserted street and headed back toward the railway station.

It was a habit of his to share the events and diverse patronage he had served that day with his good wife every night at the supper table over a bowl of stew. But he did not believe he would tell his wife he had left a fine-looking young lady by herself in the mill dwellings. There were other women down here, certainly. Younger women, older women, women as old as his good wife, still trying to work the mills. But none of them, including his wife, would have paid him for an eight-block ride with a five-pound note.

Dandre hurried along the rough walkway toward the door out of which she had just seen the transformed Mr. Chesterton come. She shifted the carpetbag from one hand to the other, feeling for the first time since she had arisen that morning how very early it was she had arisen.

At the apartment entrance she pushed open the door and found herself in a dim entry hall. To one side was a cluttered desk with an empty doorway behind it. Dandre went to the desk and put her bag on the floor beside her.

She cleared her throat.

The doorway remained empty.

"Is anyone here?" she called softly.

There was a rustling beyond the opening and in a few moments a tired form appeared to lean against the frame. Dandre decided it was a woman, though the person did not possess any feature that suggested even a dim and distant feminine softness or beauty. She wore a gray sacklike gown of some kind with a faded housecoat over the top of it. Her hair was frowzy and she had dark circles under her eyes, though whether they were bruises or signs of exhaustion, Dandre could not tell in the uncertain light.

"Wha'?" the woman growled.

"Do you know where the gentleman was going who just left here?"

"Which gent is that? We got a whole building full of gen'l'men 'ere, from top floor to cellar." The woman coughed thickly.

"Well . . ." The girl hesitated, unwilling to disclose anything about Mr. Chesterton in this place, to this person. If he was keeping his Manchester identity secret from his Oldham acquaintances, might he not be hiding his elevated Oldham position from the people here in Manchester, as well? "When he came in he was wearing a light-colored coat and hat, though his hair was somewhat disheveled."

"Ah. You must mean Vince."

"Vince?" Dandre repeated carefully.

"Vinnie Chess. 'E might be mistaken for a gen'l'man in that getup of 'is, I suppose. One fine suit of clothes 'e 'as. Inherited 'em from a dead cousin, I think. Wears 'em on the weekends to impress the ladies." The woman leaned across the desk and squinted at Dandre. "Wha'? Did 'e impress you, then, lass?"

"Where did he go?" Dandre asked, ignoring the woman's leer and her assessment of the girl's own mussed hair and torn skirt.

"Where they all go. 'E's gone to the mill. Long gone, though not so long ago as most, I suppose. Ol' Vinnie's often late of a Monday morn, and seems to 'ave little care for the dock from 'is wages, though the loss would ruin another man. 'Course, Vinnie's got no family of six or eight brats to feed, no slattern of a wife to keep or girlfriend, neither, that I've seen. 'E can afford a fine room on the ground floor 'ere—" the woman glanced down the corridor to half a dozen thin, narrow doors that evidently led to the deluxe ground-floor apartments of the tenement "—and bacon with 'is potatoes two or three times a week. I guess that kind of money does take a girl's breath away, aye?"

The woman grinned knowingly at Dandre, and the young lady was embarrassed to feel the heat of a blush on her cheeks.

"Do you know to *which* mill he has gone?" she asked stubbornly.

"Oh, my girl, you can't see 'im at Braid's, not unless you want to cost 'im 'is job. They wouldn't let you in, anyway. Only way to get in there is with the workers. And a good-lookin' thing like yourself could earn better money outside the mill," the woman advised. Though she was referring to prostitution, it was not a lewd suggestion but a sound piece of business advice she was trying to pass along.

The young woman ignored the landlady's words with an unblinking air that indicated she had no idea what the other woman meant. The landlady shrugged. There were foremen and overlookers inside the mills who would demonstrate her meaning right enough.

"And where is Braid's mill?" the girl asked instead.

"Up on Withing Grove Street." The woman pointed her chin toward the door and Dandre assumed she could just turn in the direction Mr. Chesterton had taken. "Near the Exchange."

Dandre turned back toward the entrance.

"'Ere now," the woman barked, "where is it you think you're goin'?"

"To Braid's mill, I believe you said," Dandre replied.

The woman's hand flew across the desk to grip Dandre's arm tightly.

"Didn't you 'ear what I just said, girl?" she snarled. "Your goin' up there will cost the man 'is job."

Dandre was shocked by the woman's hold on her and intimidated by the tone of her voice. She looked through the doorway and back toward the lodging rooms uncertainly.

"I have to speak with him," she said.

"You can talk to 'im after work," the woman said, releasing the girl's arm.

Dandre rubbed her arm where the woman had gripped her.

"I . . . do not . . ." she began hesitantly.

"You need a room, then?" the woman asked. She smiled and dropped a heavy eyelid over one eye. "Or was it your plan to stay with Vince?" She shrugged. "It's another three shillings either way."

"I do not have . . ."

"No money, is that it? Well, you can get your own self a job at Braid's, right enough. Just don't go 'avin' Vince try and get you one, 'ear?"

Dandre backed toward the door, leery of the woman and the physical restraint she might use. The woman seemed willing to let the girl go now, but as Dandre opened the door she cautioned her one last time.

"You wait for a break to talk to Vince, and you tell 'im . . ." Dandre had the door open and the woman called loudly after her, "You tell Vince it'll be another three shillings if there's to be two in that bed of 'is!"

Dandre went down the stairs, then stopped to give her teeth the chance to stop rattling and her knees the chance to stop knocking. As smoke-filled as the air was out here, it was a hundred times better than the air inside the building, thick with the confined odors of sweat and cabbage and urine. How horrible that people actually lived in a place like that, the girl thought.

Dandre had no idea.

She went in the direction Mr. Chesterton had gone, turning at the corner where she had seen him turn. Every stranger she passed made her clutch the handle of her carpetbag tighter as she became more and more convinced that she was carrying in her little wallet more money than any of these people saw in a month, maybe a year.

Eventually she came to a street marked Withing Grove and saw that it was lined with six or eight textile mills. They were great stone buildings whose six-inch walls could not completely insulate the hum of the engines that had revolutionized more than Lancashire's cotton industry; engines that had altered the course of the world.

One of the buildings had a carved block of stone above the door that proclaimed it had been Founded By Joseph Braid, 1765. This, then, was Braid's mill. It looked no better or worse than the other businesses along Withing Grove Street, but nevertheless, as Dandre pushed open the door, she could not help but feel as if she had become mired in a thick muck that would not release her but was pulling her inexorably into some dangerous swamp.

The din of machinery was deafening inside, yet another set of doors was blocking the workroom, still shutting off some of the noise.

There was a small waiting room just inside the building. In one wall was a door with a glass panel in it and a metal nameplate identifying the office that was doubtless behind it as belonging to Mr. Braid. In the other wall was a heavier, solid door. It had no markings on it, but the steady throb of engines and the muffled buzz of activity left no doubt that it led to the workroom.

Sitting outside Mr. Braid's door was a small boy. A painfully thin boy, with dark hair and large eyes and a dark smudge smeared across one cheek. A cheek that was not so round and not nearly as ruddy as a little boy's cheek should be. He was evidently waiting for something. When the outside door opened he looked up curiously and smiled shyly at Dandre.

"Hello," she said, sweetly returning his smile.

"'Lo, miss," the child said.

"Are you waiting for your mother?" she asked as the door shut behind her and she tried to get her bearings and decide what, exactly, should be her next course of action in this, her first attempt at very amateur sleuthing.

"No, miss," the boy answered, smiling as if Dandre had made a fine joke. "I'm waitin' for a note."

"Mr. Braid's note?"

"I'm to take it down to the Exchange for him," the boy said proudly.

Taking Mr. Braid's note down to the Exchange was obviously a signal honor.

"You are a messenger boy?" Dandre asked.

"A messenger boy? La, miss, I'm just a piecener."

"A piecener?" Dandre asked blankly.

"Usually, but I get to take the note today."

"You! Boy!"

Their conversation was interrupted, and Dandre was not allowed to pursue a more illuminating explanation for the child's presence in this place as Mr. Braid's door opened and a man in shirtsleeves appeared in the entrance, holding a large white envelope. The boy jumped to his feet and stood at attention. The man put the envelope into the dirty little hand and the child clasped it convulsively.

"Now you know what you are to do?"

The boy nodded.

"You ask at the door and they will summon the gentleman for you. What are you to say if someone offers to deliver the note for you?"

"'This here note's for the gentleman named on the envelope and no other,'" the boy recited woodenly.

"Very good," the man said. He held the door open and the child ducked under his arm, but the man grabbed his collar before he was through the arch. "Now, Danny, you come straight back. You know that it is not usual for the pieceners to deliver these notes. You don't want to make any trouble for me or thee, now do you?"

The boy looked up at the man and shook his head solemnly.

"No, sir. I'll be right back. You have my word of true honor."

The gentleman smiled a small, tight smile at the boy's promise, but nevertheless he released his hold on the shirt and the boy ran down the steps.

The man shut the door and turned. Dandre assumed that now he would acknowledge her, but he looked down at the board he was holding in one hand and began to compare the information on the paper clipped there to a sheet of paper tacked up on the wall next to his office door.

"I beg your pardon?" Dandre finally asked softly.

The man wore a visor and looked from under it at the girl, watching her while keeping his own eyes shaded.

"Yes?" he inquired.

"Mr. Braid?" the girl asked timidly.

The man smiled another thin smile and shook his head. "Not quite," he said. "Mr. Howard Braid is either in his office at the Exchange or up in his house on Cheetham Hill."

"Oh . . . well, I . . . I am looking for . . ." Dandre faltered, the landlady's stern warning ringing in her ear.

"If you are looking for work, you do not want to speak to Mr. Braid anyway. You will have to speak to Mr. Donner. He does the hiring for the mill."

"Oh," Dandre exclaimed softly. Her thinking, already slowed by the brief three hours of interrupted sleep she had been able to snatch the night before, had been thrown into confusion by the young man's assumption of what it was she was looking for and his clipped, impatient explanation. "But where is . . ."

"*I* am Mr. Donner. What do you do? Fine spinning?" He sounded hopeful. The girl looked quick and clever, and Braid's could always used a trained fine spinner.

Dandre shook her head.

"Coarse spinner, then?"

She shook her head again.

"You do not sound as if you have spent much time in the carding room. Hand weaver, perhaps?"

"No, you see..." she began.

"Have you not worked in a mill before?" the man asked, frankly surprised.

"No. Never. I was wondering..."

"I am not certain..." He stopped to study her carefully, this time raising his head and the shade he wore to reveal pale eyes set close together in his sallow, narrow face. "We can start you down on the floor as a peicener, I suppose, and move you up to coarse spinning if you catch on quickly."

"I..."

Mr. Donner had returned to his study of what Dandre could now distinguish as close columns of figures. He waved his clipboard at her.

"You can start tomorrow. We have slowed down for a while, so work does not commence until six o'clock. You will need to come in by five-thirty, though, so we can get you started." He half turned from her and then glanced back up. "You will need to wear something cooler and less restricting. We would not want you carried away by the wheel the very first day because you fainted from the heat, now would we?"

Dandre had been dismissed and was forced to give up. Humiliated, she would have to wait for Mr. Chesterton now at that abominable place of his. She was not sure that she could find her way back to the train depot, and even if she did, she did not want to go to Coventry but would be forced, she supposed, to return directly to her aunt's home in Oldham. She would have to manufacture another tale to explain her quick return for her aunt and uncle. Neither her lies nor her quick return had been her intention when she started on this foolhardy adventure, but she was not foolhardy enough to want to return to this place. Just from the dark sound of the word when Mr. Donner mentioned it, she thought she agreed with him when he said she did not want to be carried away by "the wheel."

But even then, Dandre had no idea.

Chapter Eight

Dandre returned to the apartment building Mr. Chesterton had entered and Mr. Chess had exited that morning. She was reluctant to put herself within its reeking confines again, so she sat on the steps that led to the front door, pulling her thin little carpetbag close against her. She waited. The morning grew warmer, then hot. Dandre slept. The step grew very hard. The smell of cooking potatoes began to waft through several of the open windows along the street. The girl's stomach growled loudly.

"Would you sell me anything to eat? Or tell me where I can find something?"

She had abandoned her position and reentered the building. The woman came to the front when she heard the door open, and though Dandre had assumed the landlady had but lately risen from her bed when the young lady first came in that morning, the woman still wore the loose gray sack dress and housecoat, which Dandre had also assumed was her sleeping attire.

"You again?" the woman said.

"I have been waiting for Mr. Chester... Mr. Chess," Dandre said.

The woman neither replied nor looked surprised. Like the cab driver who had helped other girls plot the route of young fellows, the landlady had evidently seen other girls station themselves at a young man's rooms.

Dandre repeated her inquiry about the food and the woman glanced over her shoulder toward her living quarters.

"It's only potatoes and an onion," she said.

"Anything," Dandre breathed.

"Cost you fourpence," the woman warned. Dandre nodded carelessly and the landlady regretted she had not asked for more. The girl would just as readily have paid four bob. "Wait 'ere," she told the girl, and returned to her cooking operations. After a few minutes more, after the food began to smell scorched, she returned with a chipped plate holding a few slices of fried potato. If she missed the chance to ask a more inflated price for her fare, the landlady had determined to make her profit in another direction.

Dandre did not complain but rather took the dish and burned herself on the first hasty mouthful.

After a very few mouthfuls the plate was emptied and Dandre returned it to the woman.

"More?" the landlady asked. "That'll be another..."

But Dandre shook her head. "No. That is quite sufficient." The few oily potatoes had quieted her hunger and taken away any remaining appetite. She took the coin purse from her bag and four coppers from the purse. "I was wondering, though, if I might wait in here," she asked hopefully.

"'Ere?" The woman looked around the bare, close entryway.

"Perhaps..."

"Oh, in *'is* room. Well..." She looked Dandre up and down one more time, as if she had not noted before the tangled hair, the tired creases at the corners of the girl's eyes, the torn skirt, grimed by now after her trek to Braid's and back. But she also considered the fine complexion, which showed none of the discolored bags, puffs, creases or pockmarks of the other girls on the street. She noted the pretty face and the healthy figure, which was another physical aspect so unusual down here. "I guess your friend would be pleased enough to find you waitin' for 'im. After you two 'ave 'ad a chance to—greet each other—you be sure to tell 'im it'll be three pence more a week."

The woman came around her desk and led the way down the dark hallway to one of the doors. She opened it for the girl and closed it behind her, returning to her own room and the contemplation of three more pence a week in her coffer.

The final bell did not ring until seven-fifteen. The workers were paid to work until six o'clock, which was when they believed the bell rang. Chesterton had a small watch pinned to the inside of his shirt and knew that an extra half hour, even an hour and a half, was often wrung from the workers, many of them women and children, already teetering on the brink of utter exhaustion at six o'clock after twelve hours spent on their feet.

Juggs came along the line, pushing the children before him, as Chesterton stood wiping his hands and brow with a scrap of cotton material. But the overlooker did not use his thong on any of the backs with the other man looking on. He even stopped and impatiently pulled one of the brats to his feet when he stumbled.

Chesterton took a step forward.

"Danny?" he called.

The boy, the one who had stumbled, looked up and managed a weak smile.

Chesterton smiled back and motioned him to his side.

Danny started toward him, but he was stopped by Mr. Juggs, who laid the handle of his strap against the child's thin chest.

"Where is it you think you're going?"

Danny looked up with an expression of such piteous pleading it would have melted the heart of a stone statue.

"Vinnie wants to talk to me," the boy whispered.

"I think you've had all the special favors you need in one day. Off to the Exchange and away a good thirty minutes. I guess you boys don't think we know how long it takes to run down there." He pushed again at the boy with the handle of his strap.

Juggs had exaggerated the time to the boy. Danny had run as fast as his little legs would carry him to and from the Exchange, not daring even to breathe the clearer outside air deeply for fear of taking too long and abusing the special privilege he had been afforded.

"Vinnie..." he begged.

"You know the rules, and Mr. Chess knows the rules. Last bells ring and you brats are back in your quarters. Unless you don't want any supper? Unless you don't need any sleep?" He asked his questions loudly enough for Vinnie to hear, though they did not require an answer. Danny's painfully thin body and the lids that drooped across his sunken eyes answered the questions in volumes.

"Yes, sir," Danny mumbled, joining the moving line of boys and girls once more, casting a sorrowful look back at Vinnie as he did.

The workman cleaned up the frame and gathered his few belongings with a black expression, unable to do anything for the boy or any of the other children whose fragile bodies and souls were being consumed by the mill. Juggs was right. If the children were not returned directly to the gray stone buildings that were their prisons, they would not receive any supper, none of the thin gruel and few boiled potatoes they were allowed. They would be locked out for the night, and if they did not return to the workstations tomorrow they would be hunted and beaten and dragged back to their places. And when their bodies and spirits completely drained, when they had nothing left to give, they would be discarded, useless refuse that would quickly perish, making room for the next crop of defenseless humanity. The workhouses and orphanages contained an endless supply.

But endless and nameless as the mass of mill children were, little Danny Fry had captured Vinnie's heart in an extraordinary way. In fact, Vince had presented himself at Braid's mill as an employee with the express purpose of finding and helping the child. And now here, in daily contact with the boy, he found Danny Fry to be typical, yet unique, among the mill children. Typical in that he had arrived at the mill with unlimited potential and was daily having his vitality sapped from him. Unique in that his eyes had not lost their glow of life, even after months in this numbing place. The clear blue of them still sparkled, still shone from the dark shadows of exhaustion that circled them liked bruises.

Chesterton slammed his fist against the frame in frustration, setting it and the attached belts and wheels to quivering. If only he could do something. Something more. He looked around him at the workroom, where the lights had been dimmed and a door opened somewhere to finally let in some of the evening air.

What he was doing was valuable, was necessary, and would in time help numberless children. But would Danny Fry survive the time? He wanted to do something for that child.

Unexpectedly, the image suddenly sprang to his mind of Miss Collin and her soothing touch. She would not have hesitated, she would have taken the child and cared for him. But Vincent Chesterton was not Miss Collin, and in his present disguise he could not afford to do more than see that the children were not actually beaten by that troll Juggs.

Chesterton had left the mill by then and was on his weary way back to the Mill Street apartments where he stayed while he was in town. They were not luxurious, but they were the best he could get in this place, and he needed to be here. At least he wasn't in a cellar or in one of the covered alleyways. And it was not Little Ireland. In the warm summer evening, Chesterton shuddered at the thought.

When he reached the tenement building, he let himself in quietly and was relieved that Mrs. Bink was not at the desk. If she was there—"lying in wait" was the impression Chesterton always got—she would insist on talking, flirting. She would question him and regale him with sordid rumors at which she would laugh and wheeze and cough and then begin the whole distasteful process again.

Tonight he could hear her in her rooms, probably preparing supper in whatever kitchen she had, although Chesterton had never been behind the desk through that doorway, nor did he know of any tenant who had. Quietly he hurried past the desk and down the hall to his room.

He heard a clatter from the kitchen and hastily pushed his door open and slipped inside. With his eye suspiciously on his closed door—Mrs. Bink had been known to summon him from his room if she had a particularly juicy morsel of gossip to tell him—he removed his jacket and pushed off those great iron boxes that encased his feet all day at Braid's. The only luxury he absolutely insisted on bringing with him from Timbrey was a soft, comfortable pair of calfskin slippers. If he was ever summoned from this room after work, he merely slipped them off and answered the call in his bare feet.

With his poor, aching toes released at last, he backed to the edge of his bed and with a sigh dropped to the thin mattress to reach for the slippers he kept under the bed.

There was a motion on the bed behind him and a hoarse, unmistakably feminine "Mmm."

Chesterton started violently and sprang to his feet.

"Miss Collin!" he cried.

Dandre's eyes popped open in alarm.

"Oh—oh!" she stammered, trying to collect herself, make certain she was decent and rise, all at the same time.

The loose springs under the mattress did not support her efforts, and her generally flailing limbs carried her, eventually, off the bed and onto the floor on the opposite side from where Chesterton stood witnessing the exhibition, frankly agog.

"Miss Collin!" he finally repeated when the thud of her body on the floor jolted him to action.

Grasping the iron framework of the bed for support, Dandre pulled herself up to peer at the bareheaded, barearmed and barefooted gentleman across from her.

"Mr. Chesterton," she said. Although she had many questions for him, she did not feel as if she were in a position to ask any of them at that moment, so she waited for him to ask his.

His first question touched her.

"Are you all right?" he said, a look—of all the looks he might have worn—of genuine concern on his face.

"I am uninjured," she told him. Encouraged by his words and tone of voice, she pulled herself to her knees and then pushed herself to her feet.

By now her untidiness was bordering on tatters and she stood watching him with ducked head, still waiting for his cry of outrage. But her mussed hair and torn dress, and most especially her humble attitude, reminded Chesterton keenly of poor, defenseless Danny Fry, quivering under Juggs's strap.

"Miss Collin, what are you doing here?" he asked, managing to keep his voice calm and reasonable. Recognizing, though, that the girl's presence threatened serious consequences.

"I was waiting for you," she said.

"Waiting for me?"

"I hoped we might..."

"Might what?"

"Talk?" she suggested timidly.

"Miss Collin, you and I have nothing to talk about."

"I thought that after the train station and your... well, when we... surely you remember?"

"Of course I remember the train station and I take full responsibility for my advances. But that does not explain what you are doing here," he said impatiently, hoping that his regrettable lack of self-control was not being interpreted as anything more than that by the girl.

"I told you. I thought we might talk."

"Our 'talking' aside for the moment, how did you know I would be here?" he pressed.

"I... well, actually, I suppose you could say I followed you," was her weak explanation.

"You *followed* me?" he asked, his reason and calm slipping.

"I was worried about you."

"Worried about me? You tracked me down because you were worried about me? Really, Miss Collin, is a man not to be allowed any deliverance from your compassion?" Chesterton shook his head in condescending wonder, which, understandably, raised Dandre's ire.

"No. I mean, yes. Yes, I was worried about you. Both weekends when I had the opportunity to see you in Oldham—" she was sorry she had to make that sound like such a privilege "—you looked more and more worn and spent. I knew something, something very serious, more serious than a pleasant game of cards, was preying on your mind and strength here."

"In Manchester, you mean."

"Yes, in Manchester."

"Then are you telling me that you did not miss your train at the depot, that you followed me to this rooming house *intentionally?*"

"Now, you see..." she began.

Chesterton narrowed his eyelids suspiciously. "I thought you were returning to Coventry. To nurse your sister," he said.

"No," Dandre said softly. And then, even more softly, "She does not require nursing."

"She does not?"

"My sister is perfectly healthy, Mr. Chesterton. There was no summons from my mother."

"No?"

"I came to help you."

He exhaled his breath loudly in a sound of absolute exasperation.

"Miss Collin!"

"Mr. Chesterton, all is not well with you. The life you are leading here suggests some great difficulty."

"I thought I had made it clear to you that I am in no difficulty," he said.

Dandre raised her eyebrows, glanced about the very small room and then dropped her doubtful gaze from his head to his arms and finally to his naked feet.

"I find that difficult to believe," she said.

"You may believe it. You may also go away and leave me alone with an absolutely spotless conscience."

"I want to help," the young woman offered.

"You want to pry," Chesterton accused coldly.

Their little moment of mutual gratification had been very pleasing that morning, he was sure. But it had been a long day at the mill, of backbreaking labor mixed with nerve-racking espionage, and he was simply not in the mood for this infuriating young woman and her meddlesome curiosity.

"That was not my intention," she said softly.

Chesterton was prepared to sidestep any inquiry, to quash any interest, to prevent any intrusion in his affairs. What he was not prepared for was the catch of emotion in the young lady's voice.

"You are not going to take no for an answer, are you, Miss Collin?" the gentleman asked, a weary tone to his voice.

"I do not know how I can..." she began again, but Chesterton sighed and held up his hand to stop her.

It had been a very long day.

He pulled the room's single stool away from the wall and *plunked* down upon it. He motioned to the bed facing him, and uncertainly Dandre sat, or rather sank, there.

"Miss Collin, you have defeated me. I have managed to maintain my anonymity here in Manchester and lead my double life unsuspected at Timbrey Hall for two months. I have been scrupulously careful so that no hint of my doings would leak back to my sister, her husband or my friends. I have spent hours and hours circumventing their scrutiny. Lying, living two lives, shouldering both workload and social obligations in an effort to be undetected. And in one day an ignorant child from the country has found me out."

Once again Chesterton struck a belittling, insulting chord. He may not have been the least tactful man in the kingdom, but he seemed quite willing to vie for the title in his present humor. Ignoring the furrowing of Dandre's brow at his latest condescension, he sighed and waved his hand.

"You are obviously a determined girl who will not be dissuaded and who will also—" he shook his head dismally "—go to any lengths to satisfy your curiosity. You have proven yourself discreet, so with that proviso, ask your questions."

Dandre took a surprised breath.

"What are you doing here?" she began. "Why are you dressed like that? Why do you live here during the week?" Her questions began to pick up speed. "Is your sister aware of what you do? What *do* you do? Who is that Mr. Donner and why in the *world* do you go to that horrible mill?"

She stopped to take another breath, but before she could start again, Chesterton had a surprise question of his own.

"You went to the Mill? You spoke with Mr. Donner?"

"That is where the lady at the front desk said you went to work. Do you work there?"

"What did you say to Mr. Donner? About me?" Chesterton's spine had stiffened and he leaned toward the girl.

"I did not have a chance to even mention your name. I said, 'I am looking for...' and the man said, 'A job. But you will have to see Mr. Donner.' I asked, 'Where is...' and he said, '*I* am Mr. Donner.' Then he asked if I had ever done fine spinning, or coarse spinning or even hand weaving. And finally he said I would have to start as a piecener and could advance from there. That, in its entirety, was my conversation with Mr. Donner and the full complement of what I said to him of you."

Chesterton relaxed again.

"Mr. Donner is the head clerk and paymaster of the Braid Cotton Mill. And yes, I do work there."

"Oh!" Dandre gasped. In a moment her eyes were brimming with sympathy and despair and Chesterton feared in another moment they would be brimming with tears, as well. She extended her gentle hand, but the distance between them was too great, and Chesterton regretted that. "What is it? A gambling debt? An investment that proved worthless? A former—*indiscretion*—that haunts you? But surely there are more profitable avenues to pursue to regain your fortune?"

"I act as a jack-of-all-trades at the Braid mill in an effort to assist Mr. Michael Sadler in his fight to improve working conditions in the textile mills," Chesterton said.

Dandre drew in her breath sharply. There was hardly a soul in all of this island kingdom, and certainly not in Lancashire, who did not know of Mr. Michael Thomas Sadler, member of the House of Commons and sponsor of the highly publicized Irish Poor Law Act.

"Mr. Sadler of the Parliament?" she whispered.

Chesterton smiled and nodded his head.

"The same. Though my contact with the movement has not been primarily through him. Tell me, Miss Collin, have you ever heard of Richard Oastler?"

Dandre's eyes grew wide. Richard Oastler! Of course! That was the man who had met with Chesterton on the lane that day, not some notorious outlaw. Not a hunted criminal but rather a man famous for his attempted social reform. She had read of him and even seen a sketch of him before, which explained why his features were imperfectly familiar to her.

"Mr. Richard Oastler? The man who has done so much charitable work among the poor?" Dandre asked.

Chesterton nodded.

"He has," Chesterton affirmed, a solemn, almost reverential note in his voice. "I had heard of him before, of course. Like you. I knew of his activities, I knew he was distrusted by some and disliked by others, though I did not stop to give his notoriety much thought. But my attitude toward Mr. Oastler and Mr. Sadler and their cause was altered dramatically one night several months ago." He stopped and gazed past Dandre, gazed past the room and the evening, as well, seeing another place and another time.

"What?" she asked, prompting him, calling him gently back to her.

"I came upon a child trying to escape from the mill one night. It was the middle of winter and the lad was dressed in tissue-thin rags. He might have frozen to death. He was recovered by the mill overlooker." His voice faded again and Dandre got the distinct impression that the child freezing to death was not the worst thing that could have happened to him. "I determined then to offer my assistance to Mr. Sadler in his attempt to better the lot of the children who are forced to work in the textile mills."

"Children?" Dandre asked uncertainly. "Do you mean children work inside that mill?" Her mind flashed the picture of the very small boy outside Mr. Donner's office who seemed so pleased to be delivering a note. "Mr. Chesterton, I talked with a little boy outside Mr. Donner's office this morning. At first I assumed he was the child of one of the mill workers, waiting for his mother perhaps. But he said he was a piecener."

Chesterton nodded.

"That child *works* in the mill? He could not have been more than seven, if that old," she protested, trying to convince the man before her that he must be wrong. A sweet little boy like the one she had seen that morning surely could not be set to work at the machinery she had heard clanking heavily behind the workroom door.

"If he was seven, he is not even the youngest child working in the mills, not by a year or more. Little children work behind those stone walls, Miss Collin. Very little children. I have heard Mr. Oastler speak of them myself and call them 'infants.'" He paused, and Dandre, watching him with horrified fascination, saw a shadow of pain darken his eyes. "And I have *seen* them myself, Dandre," he murmured. "Infants."

"And when you made your resolution to help Mr. Sadler and Mr. Oastler help these children, what did you decide to do?" she asked.

"I decided to speak to Mr. Oastler and offer my services."

"Your services as what?"

"As a mill worker."

"A mill worker?" Dandre repeated slowly, struggling to be very clear about what Mr. Chesterton was saying.

"Mr. Oastler introduced me to Mr. Sadler, who accepted my proposal that I go to work in one of the textile mills here in Manchester. In Mr. Braid's mill, to be specific."

"What is it Mr. Sadler wanted you to do in the mill?" Dandre asked. Her questions had become slow and thoughtful.

"Observe," Chesterton said simply. "He asked me to observe conditions inside the mill. Government inspectors see only what the mill owner wants them to see. The rest is either hidden or obliterated by money. The inspectors fill their pockets and sell human lives."

"And *why* does Mr. Sadler want you to observe?"

"It is his intent to propose a law that will prevent the employment of children under nine years of age and limit the working time of those children nine to thirteen to no more than eight hours a day. He wants a universal law of a ten-hour workday for every man, woman and youth forced to toil in the mills. But before such a bill can be passed, those industrialists who cry that such a reduction of labor would mean the ruin of the British Empire must be silenced by public outrage. And the country will be outraged, Miss Collin, if we can show them the truth."

"And that is what you are to do?" Dandre was awed by the stature of the man before her and the importance of his mission.

But Chesterton shook his head in dismissal of the girl's admiration.

"I am a very small cog in this wheel of reform," he said. "I could testify myself, but my word, the word of a wealthy landowner against the industrial mill owner, would not hold much sway before the House of Commons. But Mr. Oastler can take the information I give him, then go to the workers themselves and get the testimony of the men and women, the abused children. Only..." He stopped without finishing his thought.

"Only what?" Dandre prodded gently.

"Only I do not know what I can tell them. Juggs, the overlooker—"

Dandre looked puzzled by the term.

"The man who sees that the children work, he is intimidated by me. He has not actually mistreated any of the children or women since I stopped him the first day I was there. But I will not witness such villainy without putting a stop to it, regardless of what testimony Mr. Sadler requires."

Chesterton clenched his fists. Fire had replaced the shadow in his eyes.

Dandre spoke softly, diverting his train of thought.

"And your sister and brother-in-law, they do not know what you have been commissioned to do?"

Chesterton shook his head.

"It was a confidential assignment. I was to work during the flush summer season and make my report to Mr. Sadler to allow him to prepare his bill before the end of the year. But I do not know how much more information I can gather. And honestly, I do not know how much longer I can work there without taking some kind of action."

"You must fulfill your duty," Dandre said.

Rather than becoming perturbed by the girl's insistence, Chesterton nodded wearily.

"Yes. I must. I could not desert the child—the children—now. Not just when the work is picking up." Then, very softly, to himself rather than Miss Collin, he murmured, "He would not survive it."

"What you need," Dandre said, her voice even and eminently reasonable, "is another observer. One who is not a threat to this Mr. Juggs, who will see what is hidden from you."

"I am already known to Juggs. And it would be the same at any mill in which I worked. I am, regrettably, healthy and able-bodied." He smiled ruefully, but the young woman's expression remained serious.

"Not you, Mr. Chesterton. Did I not just say it must be someone Mr. Juggs would not find threatening?"

"Mr Juggs is a great bully and hence a great coward. Who would he not find threatening?"

"Me."

"You?"

"Me, Mr. Chesterton. I have already been offered employment at the mill. Mr. Donner said he could start me on the floor, which must not be so very difficult if he believed I could do it with absolutely no experience at all. I could be where you cannot and see the things that are hidden from you. I could be your eyes and ears."

"What are you saying?" Chesterton sputtered.

"I am saying that I could become an observer, too."

"An observer? Absolutely not!" the man roared. "That is ridiculous! Impossible! Ludicrous!"

"You just said you are unable to get any more information. Therefore, someone else must help you. Must get the information needed by Mr. Sadler and Mr. Oastler."

"*They* do not need another observer to help me. And *I* certainly would not send *you* inside that mill."

"You would not be sending me, Mr.Chesterton. I would go of my own accord."

Chesterton had managed to calm himself enough to see that the girl was not to be convinced by wild outbursts of emotion. He assumed his most reasonable tone of voice, which was certain, instead, to absolutely infuriate her.

"You do not know what goes on in those mills, Miss Collin," he said.

"No, it is you who does not know. I came to Manchester to help, Mr. Chesterton. I would still like to help."

"You cannot. I could not allow it. It is not a place for a lady..."

"Is it a place for a gentleman?" she countered.

"For a gentleman who can take care of himself, yes. I beg of you, Miss Collin, be reasonable. The conditions in those mills are unspeakable. And I do not mean only the working conditions. Things go on..." He paused, unwilling to describe to the girl before him the absence of morals, the utter bestiality of the men and women trapped behind those walls. He extended his arm and caught her hand in his, pressing her fingers urgently. He knew from experience that the girl was determined and headstrong. And he knew as admirable as those traits sometimes were, in this instance they could be very dangerous for her. "Tell me," he said, "that you will not even think such foolish thoughts. I will take you to a respectable hotel tonight and put you on a coach back to Oldham, if that is your preference, in the morning. I promise to see you when I return at the week's end and tell you what has happened. Will you do that?" He tried to search her eyes, but she lowered them before his gaze.

"It seems I have no choice," she said.

"You have no choice," he agreed.

"And you, must you not be to the mill at six o'clock in the morning?" she asked, raising her eyes again, eyes filled with guileless innocence.

"At five forty-five," he corrected.

"How can you hope to be there if you are taking me uptown to a 'respectable' hotel and then putting me into a coach?" She paused but the gentleman had no answer to her question. "You cannot," she answered for him. "I will stay here tonight," she said, "and hire a cab to take me to the station. I saw a number of coaches for hire on my way to this place, and I am perfectly capable of making my own arrangements for the return to Oldham."

Chesterton faltered in his resolve. The girl was right. He could not hope to do all of that and still be in the mill before the doors were closed and locked against latecomers. Mr. Donner was a harmless enough fellow and had nothing against Chess, who was surprisingly intelligent yet still and all a good worker. But Overlooker Juggs had Donner's ear, and if Chesterton gave him the excuse the overlooker would demand his dismissal.

"Your landlady indicated that the rooms on this floor are perfectly acceptable—" Chesterton humphed derisively, "—so if you will arrange accommodations for me, I will retire and leave you to do the same."

Chesterton still hesitated, but the young woman had answered all of his objections, and in the end he agreed to get a room for her among these apartments and to allow her to make her own way back to Oldham.

"We are not talking about the voyage of Marco Polo, Mr. Chesterton. It is ten miles from here to Oldham, and if all else failed I could *walk* back."

With a shrug, Mrs. Bink, the landlady, took Chesterton's money for the rent of the room down the hall from his.

"The money is the same," she said, "no matter what bed the girl sleeps in. Your money would go twice as far if it paid for her bed *and* her company, but that is your choice."

A half hour later, after showing Dandre to her room and personally checking the accommodations, which were very mean but relatively clean for all of that, Chesterton stood once more outside her door. His expression was doubtful and troubled.

"If you are unable to secure transportation, come back here and I will invent some sort of excuse that will free me from the mill for a day or two." He spoke vaguely because he really did not know what excuse he could possibly manufacture that would release him from his job and allow him to return to it two days later. If a man was injured or sick he was simply released and expected to find another job once he was on his feet again. Chesterton would easily have been able to find more work in the mills, and that prospect may not have daunted him except that Danny Fry had found a place beneath his protective wing and Chesterton could not abandon him. But just as difficult for him, as a gentleman, was to abandon Miss Dandre Collin without escort or protection in this city. He was a man in a quandary.

Dandre looked up at him and smiled at his whimsical expression of confused distress.

"To ease your mind, I will leave a short note for the coachman to post to you the moment he delivers me to the Woodley home."

Still the gentleman had misgivings.

"You must not worry about me," she said. "I shall be perfectly all right."

She put her hand against his chest and could feel the strong beating of his heart against her palm. She raised herself up onto tiptoe and leaned against his chest. Still he watched her warily, too worried about her to enjoy her playful advances. She smiled and touched his rough cheek with her own cheek of velvet.

"I will be all right," she whispered.

She turned her head slightly and kissed his cheek, then, with her palm still against his chest, she pushed him away from her and began to close her bedroom door.

Doubtfully, Chesterton backed away and turned toward the door of his own room.

Dandre did not close her door immediately but shut it slowly, watching the man as he walked away and stopped at his door. He raised his eyes, but the girl swiftly finished closing the gap so he did not see her watching him. He also did not know she stood silently behind her door after it was closed, with her ear against the wood, trying to interpret the sounds of his door opening, him entering his room and then the closing of the door behind him.

When she was certain that all was quiet and the hallway was deserted, she opened her door a crack and then slipped out of her room. She tiptoed down the hall, being careful to make as little noise as possible, though she doubted that Mr. Chesterton was poised listening behind the door of his room.

"Pardon me?" she called softly across the desk when she reached the front of the apartment building.

The landlady's unlovely form, wrapped in her unbecoming garments, which had not been changed this day, and Dandre wondered if it had not been several days since they were changed, appeared at her doorway.

"What do you want?"

"I need to post a letter. Where can that be done?" the girl asked.

The woman looked at her for a moment without speaking, then raised her chin toward the door. It was a gesture almost identical to the one she had employed to indicate what direction Mr. Chess—Chesterton—had taken when he left the tenement. This morning Dandre had been glad she had seen Chesterton leave and had some clue beforehand of what his heading had been. Now she was without any idea of where the landlady's motion was directing her and she was momentarily distressed. Fortunately the woman offered a single sentence of explanation.

"Across the way there," she said.

Dandre went to the door and opened it to look across the street in the general direction Mrs. Bink's chin had pointed.

"The livery there?" Dandre asked uncertainly.

"Man makes a pickup there. Comes early in the morning, though. You'll 'ave to get your letter across to 'im in good time," Mrs. Bink warned.

"I believe I shall be able to get it in before the post goes out," Dandre said, then nodded to the woman and returned to her room.

She sat on the bed, using her carpetbag as a desk, and wrote by the faint glow of the single candle that had been provided her.

Dear Aunt Bea,
Katherine is well enough, but I shall stay another week at least. Mother and Father send their best and ask

that I include their salutations, since Father is busy with his violin and Mother does not think she will write.

She mentioned a few other details of home, things she was relatively certain had not changed since she left Coventry. She hoped the letter would assuage her aunt's concern, and, again, she hoped it would discourage Mrs. Woodley from writing to Coventry herself.

She held her little timepiece close to the candle flame. It was only nine o'clock, but it might have been midnight, judging from the silence in the building and of the street outside. And Dandre was exhausted. She had been up before three this morning and would have to be up very early again tomorrow morning. She decided not to write any more letters or even to try to decipher by the light of the candle the words in the book of nature lectures she had packed among her things. Instead she would go to bed immediately and no doubt fall directly asleep. The girl did not know when she had ever been this tired before.

But, once again, Dandre had no idea of what real exhaustion was.

Chesterton woke at five o'clock and rolled from his sagging mattress. The notice had been tacked to the wall yesterday that work would begin at five forty-five the next morning. The starting time would be moved earlier and earlier from now until the end of the summer, as the cotton was harvested and received at the Liverpool docks.

He wet his face and haphazardly scraped his straight razor back and forth across his cheek, under his jaw, in and out of the crevices of his chin.

He pulled on his trousers and then his undershirt, his work shirt, his woolen vest and the oversize jacket. The walk to Braid's would be cool in the morning air, but the articles of clothing he donned would be shed quickly during the morning hours until, by noon, he would very likely be clad in only the trousers again.

When he left his room he glanced toward Miss Collin's door, feeling the qualm of his conscience but unable to indulge his misgivings right then. The girl said she would send word to him when she had arrived at her uncle's home, so if he did not receive a letter by tomorrow he would have to go looking for her. But tomorrow would be soon enough to contemplate that necessity.

He let himself out the front door and once on the sidewalk noted several other informally clad figures trudging toward the ring of mills that girdled the Manchester Exchange.

He arrived at Braid's only moments before the door was shut. Leaving his coat and the woolen vest at the front, he took his position at the stretching frame just as the machinery growled to life.

It took more than a quarter of an hour for him to get squared away, before he could even look around him. Danny Fry and the other little pieceners, who tied together the broken strands as they spun onto the bobbins, were down on the main floor. Chesterton checked his machine one more time before he went to the ladder that led from the scaffolding to the ground floor and the site of his labors. At the railing he stopped to look over the row of sleepy children to make sure all was well with them this morning. Or as well as it could be for children, ages six to twelve, closed in a stuffy room, breathing lint-filled air, stationed in front of dangerous, sometimes deadly machinery, threads of cotton whirling past them faster than their eyes could follow.

He located Danny, saw that he seemed alert and felt distinct relief to note that Juggs was nowhere near the boy. Before descending the steps of the ladder he took another moment to locate the overlooker.

Juggs was at the other end of the line, leaning against the far wall, watching one of the girls work. Chesterton was aware that he did that occasionally, and the thought made his flesh crawl. The girls who worked on the line were compelled to keep their attention strictly on what they were doing, had to be quick and precise in their movements. Because of the demands of their labor and the heat of the room, Chesterton knew they were encouraged to wear as little as possible to cover themselves yet maintain some semblance of modesty. And Mr. Juggs, fully aware of their distraction, took every opportunity to ogle their thinly clad bodies.

Chesterton glanced at the poor girl with whom Juggs seemed to be fascinated today and his foot halted suddenly in midair as if frozen there by a blast of Arctic air.

The girl was Dandre Collin.

Chapter Nine

Vincent Chesterton said he had to be at work by five forty-five. He would be rising at five. Dandre was up, dressed and out of the building by four.

It was still perfectly dark outside, but the streets were not entirely deserted. An old man shuffled along the board-walk toward her, and a huge woman was headed in the same direction she was on the opposite walkway. The distance between them made it impossible for Dandre to tell if the great bulk of the woman was really mounds of flesh or if bundles or layers of clothing accounted for some of her immense size.

She left her letter at the stable with a livery hand more asleep than awake, praying as she did so that her letter would be posted and she would not become the subject of a massive search within the next few days.

Then she turned from the stable in the direction of the Manchester Exchange and the mills. A light or two gleamed in a few windows along the way, and as she neared the mills she was joined by half a dozen workers on their way to their jobs. Four of them were young children. Dandre, studying them in frank amazement, calculated the eldest to be ten, if that old. It was so hard to tell with these children. The pinched, pale faces that gazed out at her from under caps and scarves were all aged by world-weariness, but they sat atop emaciated, sometimes crooked little bodies that were underdeveloped for whatever age they were.

The other two workers were young women like herself, without her fresh color or bright eyes or healthy figure.

"On yer way to the mills?" one of them asked. The questioner was the last to have joined the heavy-footed procession. She was a blond girl, or at least her hair was not brown or black. But to call the dust-colored, greasy lanks of her hair "blond" was an insult to lemons and gold and pale daffodils. The thin material of her dress revealed a protruding, drooping belly, and the loose flesh that swung on her upper arms suggested her figure had once been much fuller than it was now.

"Mr. Braid's mill, yes," Dandre replied.

The young woman eyed Dandre's person appraisingly and raised her upper lip in a cold sneer.

"I guess you're hoping not to have to work too hard," she said.

Dandre looked down and realized the plain shirtwaist and skirt she had chosen that morning were really quite grand compared with the skimpy, worn dress this girl was wearing and the other girl up ahead of them, too.

"It is my first day," Dandre explained defensively. "I wanted to make a good impression."

"I'll bet," the girl said. Then she called, "Fay! Hold up!" to the other young woman ahead of them, bringing the conversation to an abrupt end.

Dandre was sorry to see her hurry to catch up with her friend. She had been hoping to steer the discussion to the mills and the work they would be expected to do there.

But she arrived at the forbidding door of Braid's mill fifteen minutes later, as ignorant of what was involved in spinning thread and weaving cloth as she had been when she left Oldham, or Coventry, for that matter.

She did have a definite plan of action, though.

With a great show of confidence she entered the building and stepped to the office door inside, the door by which the visored Mr. Donner had catechized her yesterday on her experience in weaving. The door had been then open so that Dandre could see the cheap little desk and the wooden chair that were evidently as generous as Mr. Braid cared to be with his business manager, who ran the mill while Braid sold the product and reaped the profit at the Manchester Exchange.

Now the door was closed and Dandre knocked lightly at the thin panel of wood, dropping her hand to the latch. There was no answer to her knock, and the latch would not give. She had fully expected to open the door and see Mr. Donner seated behind his desk, and for the first time it occurred to her that the business manager probably would not come in until later in the day; not until he had washed and dressed and breakfasted. Not until the sun had risen.

"What are you doing there, girl?"

With a start, almost guiltily, Dandre dropped her hand from the door and turned to face her questioner.

Dandre Collin had grown up in a sheltered home and neighborhood surrounded by good people, regardless of their eccentricities, who loved her and cared for her. When she turned she took a surprised and frightened step backward, which put her shoulder blades against the unyielding office door. She had never been in close quarters with a truly bad man before. She had never *seen* as truly bad a man as was Mr. Eldridge Juggs.

His close-cropped hair greasily clasped his skull, which was not round but looked as if it had been pushed forward when it was not yet hard and set, so that the back of his head was flat and the front, his brow, hung heavily over deep-set eyes. Bushy, dark eyebrows further shadowed his eyes, until all one saw of them was a hard reflection of light now and then.

His nose was crooked and his teeth were crooked. There was a discolored mark on one cheekbone, but Dandre could not tell if it was a temporary irritation, a scar or a birthmark. She did not care to study his face carefully enough to determine which it was. It was too near the glitter of his eye.

Mr. Juggs was not tall, and he was not flabby. Rather, his frame was packed solidly, so that even with his moderate height he gave the impression of a great and powerful mass.

His was not a handsome countenance, but more than any one feature, it was their entire combination that suggested his evil character. That, and something more. Something almost like a shadow, a dark aura, that emanated from him. Men automatically did not like Mr. Juggs, but it was only innocent women and children who sensed the blackness of his soul.

"I . . . I was looking for Mr. Donner," Dandre stammered in answer to his question.

"Donner's not here," the man said, stating the obvious.

"Yes. I see that. Well then, I suppose I had better . . ." The girl's voice faded away uncertainly and she took a small, hesitant step toward the entrance and the blessed freedom she realized she had left on the other side of those walls. Juggs did not move aside and Dandre did not take a second step toward him.

"Lookin' for work?" he asked her. His eyes glittered and their darkness moved over her body.

"Yes . . . perhaps . . . Mr. Donner said something yesterday about being able to start me on the floor. I am not very skilled. I believe he was hoping for someone with more experience. But I thought I might appeal to him today . . . when he comes in. Later, perhaps."

There was a clatter of machinery behind the workroom door as the big engines roared to life, and Dandre was forced to leave off her nervous explanations.

"You'll have to try your appeal with me," Mr. Juggs said. Again, it was not merely the raspy quality of his voice or the stress he put on the words "appeal" and "me." It was the thick heaviness of his tone, the permanent half sneer of his lips, his offensive familiarity that made his speech sound like the way raw liver feels.

"Later, I think," Dandre repeated, fussing with her hair and the collar of her blouse, giving the impression that she was about to leave, watching Mr. Juggs from beneath her brow to see if he would take the hint and move. He did not.

"Now is when the day begins, girl. If you want to work here you start with the others. I'll square it with Donner when he comes in."

"I am not . . ." Dandre began.

"Do you want a job or not?" Mr. Juggs asked impatiently, and Mr. Juggs's impatience seemed dangerous.

Dandre understood now, after only a brief five minutes with this man, why Vincent Chesterton was so adamant about her not coming down to the mill. It was that thought which summoned the young man to her mind, and she recalled his expression last night as they stood together outside her room, his desire to arrange her safe journey at odds with his commitment to his duty here.

And the thought of his duty summoned another picture, the picture of a little boy, a thin, pale, beautiful little boy, so happy to be able to go outside to run an errand.

What Chesterton was doing here was very important, was necessary to ensure that the little boy she had seen at Donner's office—and all the other children she had seen shuffling through the dark toward this and the other stone buildings that enclosed the mills and kept out the slightest breath of fresh air—would get to go outside more often. And play. As children were supposed to do. And she had convinced herself that Chesterton's complete success depended on her.

Dandre pulled herself to her full five feet four inches of height.

"Yes, sir," she said. "I do want to work here."

Mr. Juggs's sneer deepened until Dandre realized it was his smile. Her noble intentions and heroic resolve seemed to shrivel and harden in the pit of her stomach under that smile.

"Very well, girl. Come with me."

At last he stood aside, but Dandre's opportunity to dart from this place into safety again was gone. Juggs pushed open the heavy door that led into the workroom and Dandre followed him into what sounded like the chaos of hell.

It was a big, echoing room with a ceiling open to two or three stories overhead. In that first room were several uniform lines of tall wooden tables. From each table rose belts and bars attached to spinning gears and more steel bars, steel bars that ran the length of the long room, cranking the bobbins that spun below and the reels of thread that spun on top of each worktable. The air hummed with life; the engines growled a dangerous warning.

A few women were stationing themselves in front of their worktables as the cranking rods overhead churned to life, driving the shafts that turned the wheels that spun the thread that filled the bobbins.

But the majority of the workers who had taken their places, wiping the film from their sleepy eyes and across their dirty faces, were children. Little children. Tiny little children.

Dandre caught her breath in surprise and then had to stop and cough violently for a few moments to clear her throat of the cotton fibers she had inhaled. As the spindles whirled to life, clouds of lint rose into the air. Other, more ragged coughs were heard around the room, coughs from the women and children whose lungs could not be cleared of the thick dusting of fibers they had been inhaling for months, perhaps years.

"We'll start you out down here," Mr. Juggs shouted up to her, over the sound of the machinery, as he descended the short ladder into the room.

Dandre was forced to turn and climb down the ladder herself, with Mr. Juggs leering up at her.

On ground level she turned and followed the man as he led her past the children intently watching the thread winding onto the bobbins in front of them. As Dandre walked down the aisle one little girl lunged forward toward the machine, throwing herself into the very middle of the shafts and gear wheels. Dandre gasped, certain she was about to witness some frightful accident. But the child reached between the wheels to grab the end of a thread with her left hand. She ducked her head under the machinery to find the other end of the broken thread, which she retrieved from the close confines of the spinning apparatus with the tiny fingers of her right hand.

She tied the two ends together and then released the thread to continue winding onto her bobbin.

In this close proximity, Dandre could see that each of the little pieceners was watching two or three threads. The blur of the machinery and the damp heat of the room made Dandre feel nauseated, and she could not imagine how these people, how these *children,* could stay alert enough to do their jobs.

Mr. Juggs had come to a stop in front of one of the wooden frames, the last frame on the line.

"You'll be set to work here," he said.

"Doing what?" Dandre asked.

"You'll be a reeler," Juggs told her.

"A reeler?"

The glitter of the overlooker's eyes sparked across her face and body for an uncomfortable moment.

"A reeler," he repeated. "Don't you know what you're to do?"

"I...I am afraid not," Dandre said.

Mr. Juggs turned impatiently, pointing and demonstrating as he spoke.

"Your job is simplicity itself. You stand here and wind the thread onto the reels. When your reels are full you take them down and replace them with empty reels. Understand?"

"Where am I to put the full reels?" Dandre asked, glancing around her to make sure the answer would not be embarrassingly obvious. She saw no full reels of thread piled on the floor or on any of the worktables.

"There," Juggs said, motioning vaguely to the end of the room. "Keep your lines tight and the winding smooth," he warned, already half-turned to make his pass along the line. Dandre was too relieved to see him leave to detain him, not stopping to consider that she was not at all certain yet what her job was or how she was to accomplish it.

The empty reel was spinning dizzily before her eyes. She looked from side to side at other girls younger than she was, smaller, their faces white, with sunken cheeks and dull eyes. But their reels were all filling, and though she saw one of them reach forward to smooth the thread once, she did not see from whence the thread was coming or how it had been attached to the reel.

"Grab it there."

Dandre jumped and looked down. Standing at her side, having appeared from nowhere, was the same little boy she had seen in the waiting room of the mill yesterday. She bent toward him and smiled.

"Well, hello again..." she began cheerfully, but the boy shook his head and looked after Mr. Juggs with an alarmed expression.

Dandre followed his fearful glance, the boy's alarm infecting her. She straightened hastily and only looked at the child out of the corner of her eye, without turning her head. He pointed under the lip of her table, and Dandre, bending down to get to the child's eye level, saw the end of a thread slapping against the post that supported the frame. Dandre pinched the end and pulled it up to her. She found the notch on the lip of the table and passed the thread through it and then the large eye in the thin steel rod in front of her empty reel.

So far so good. Glancing around her, she could see that was the general setup in front of all the other girls. Still, though, she could not see how she was to attach the thread to the spinning reel.

"How do I start it?" she asked softly.

"Hold it against the reel while it turns. There. Like that. Wait until it's wrapped in."

The two of them were so intent on watching the revolutions of the reel and the end being captured under the succeeding rounds of the thread that they did not see Mr. Juggs turn, take notice of them and approach down the aisle between the workstations. Other of the young women and children fearfully watched him pass and cringed to one side, but Juggs was too intent on the two at the end of the room to enjoy the effects of his passage. The first intimation Dandre and the boy had that they had been observed was the whistle of the strap through the air just before the thick leather thongs struck the child's bony back.

Both of them jumped violently, but though tears started to the boy's eyes, he did not cry out.

"What's going on here?" Juggs growled.

"How dare you!" was Dandre's outraged protest. "He was only showing me how to begin."

"Oh, he was, was he? To your post, boy."

Danny Fry scurried back to the two threads he was supposed to be watching at the next station but one from Dandre's post, Nan's station. One of the threads had broken in his absence and he quickly pieced the two ends together and set the small bobbin winding again; when it was full, Nan would wind the bobbin's thread onto her much larger reel, just as Dandre was doing at her table. He was actually very relieved that he had gotten by with a single blow of the strap, and he knew that if Mr. Juggs were not so interested in the pretty new girl he would have fared much worse for his disregard of the rules.

"You don't talk to each other, girl," Juggs was saying to Dandre. "And you don't *ever* talk to me that way. Do you understand?"

The man was standing so close to the girl that she could distinguish the large pores in the purplish skin that covered his nose, and close enough for her to smell his sour body odor and the foul stench of his breath.

"He was helping me start..."

The man actually growled at her and raised the thongs threateningly.

"Understand?" he repeated.

Dandre nodded silently, her eyes wide with fright. Mr. Juggs continued to hold the strap before her face and Dandre hoped that she could be as brave as the little boy had been and not cry out when she was struck.

But Juggs did not flip his hand to bring the strap to life. Instead, he bounced it gently so the fringe of thongs was a constant threat.

"We have rules here in the mill, and penalties for breaking those rules, but nothin' that says the two of us can't be friends." His sneer deepened again as the glitter of his eyes roved over her body. He held his strap steady, putting the end of it under her chin to raise her eyes to meet the dark indentions of his. "And I treat my friends very well," he said, dropping the level of his voice to an intimate whisper.

Dandre raised her head imperiously to clear it from the handle of Mr. Juggs's strap.

"I am not asking for special favor," she said.

Mr. Juggs dropped the strap to his side, where he once again began to flick it restlessly. Dandre could not help but watch it, mesmerized by the pain and violence it represented.

"Maybe not yet. But when you do want a favor, keep in mind that they don't come free," he said. He nodded his head slowly, certain the girl understood exactly what he meant.

Mrs. Katey Collin had always been perfectly frank with her young children and their innocent inquiries into the mysteries of reproduction, unlike most women of her day, but as frank as Mrs. Collin was, Dandre could not have even imagined, *exactly,* what the man meant.

Mr. Juggs snapped the thongs sharply and pointed with it to her worktable.

"We'll talk of this again," he said. "Now you best get back to work." Like his strap, his voice held the suggestion of pain and violence, too.

"And keep your mind on what you're doing. Keep your mouth shut and your eyes open. I'll be watching you."

Dandre turned to her workstation again. In the time it had taken Juggs to strike the boy and make his unsavory offer of friendship to her, the thread from the smaller bobbin had almost completely been transferred to the large reel.

True to his word, Mr. Juggs remained behind her, watching her nervous, unsure actions as the last few revolutions unwound the thread from the bobbin under her table.

"Tie the ends together," the overlooker said.

Dandre glanced over her shoulder at him and then leaned down to find the beginning of her next bobbin. Still Mr. Juggs did not walk away. He backed up to lean against one of the support beams and continued to gaze at her unnervingly as she fumbled to join the two ends. Once the threads were tied she released the taut line in her right hand so it could continue winding onto the reel, and watched for snags as the loose thread that had piled onto the floor from the smaller bobbin was taken up.

"Watch yer spool. Make sure it's smooth there," Mr. Juggs cautioned behind her.

She ran her hand along the reel, like a potter smoothing out the bumps and dents from the clay urn on his wheel. When the wrapping of white cotton thread was even against the spool, Dandre stood back to admire her handiwork, modest though the labor had been.

"Enough, enough," Juggs said. "Get your next one started."

For the first time Dandre noticed that there were two more empty reels on the apparatus, and glancing down the length of the room, she saw that all of the women were watching at least two or three—and sometimes as many as six—reels filling at once.

Checking below her workstation again she found other piecener's bobbins filled and waiting to be rewound. Clumsily she started her second reel, fumbling with the notch and the eye and then unable to get the filament to stay against the smooth metal of the turning reel long enough for the wraps to secure it. Finally that thread was in place and with more skill she started her third reel.

"Keep the line taut," Mr. Juggs warned.

Dandre found the limp thread to which he was referring and pulled on it until the slack was gone. Then, without his warning, she smoothed the surface of her second reel of thread, which had begun to bunch.

By now her first reel was almost filled and the girl realized with dismay that she did not know what to do once one of the big wheels of thread was filled: how to detach it; where to put it; where to find another empty one.

Her little friend was too busy now with his own work to help her, even if Mr. Juggs would allow it, which he would not. And she did not want the boy's help again, if to give it cost a lash across his pale skin.

She also would not ask Mr. Juggs. Not even if her ineptitude cost her a lash across her own back. Better by far her back than the little boy's. The material of the light shirtwaist she was wearing looked thicker and more substantial than the poor child's skin.

Now the thread was threatening to spill from the filled bobbin. So she would not have another reel filling before she had disposed of this one, she broke the thread and heaved the thing off its spool. It was heavier even than it looked, and Dandre staggered back beneath its weight. She searched the length of the hall. Surely she had not been the first to fill a reel of thread this morning? But if others had been filled and removed before hers, they had been well and cleverly hidden.

The weight of the reel of thread was making her arms and back ache, and the second reel was nearly full now. She tried to turn and search the gray wall Mr. Juggs had loosely indicated when she originally asked what to do with the filled reels, but unfamiliar with the machinery of the mill, she ran her hip into a projecting wooden handle and staggered back in surprised pain. The floor was uneven and her skirts, the lightest she owned and had worn that morning, were heavy and clinging with dampness by now. Yet she held on to the reel, and even as she felt her knees giving way beneath her, two strong arms caught her, one supporting her elbow, the other encircling her waist.

Mr. Juggs pushed himself away from the pillar where he had been leaning and enjoying the spectacle the girl was presenting, waiting in pleasant anticipation for her fall, expecting to view exposed limbs, hoping for her tears of pain.

"Here now!" he cried, shaking his strap but not actually raising it in threat. "What are you doing away from your place?"

"The young lady needed some help," the quiet voice said above her head. "I was the only one available to supply it."

Everything had happened so quickly that Dandre was still not sure on her feet before she recognized the voice and glanced behind her.

"Aren't you the fine gentleman, though?" Juggs sneered. "But you'll have your hands full if you intend on doing your job and the job of every clumsy girl in here, Mr. Chess."

There were two or three snickers the length of the line as most of the workers looked up to watch the unusual drama unfolding at the end of the room. The usual drama of Mr. Juggs lashing one of the children and their shrieks and moans hardly elicited notice, but someone defying Mr. Juggs was worthy of attention.

"If she can't do the work alone, she'll be let go," Mr. Juggs continued.

"The girl has to know what her work is before she can do it," Vince said. He turned in disregard from the fuming overlooker and took the heavy reel from the girl's arms.

"Mr. Chester..." Dandre began.

"It's just Mr. Chess, miss, or, better still, 'Vince' here in the mill," he corrected, a casual note in his voice but a bright glow in his eyes that was part warning and part surprise and a great part anger, and back behind the other emotions was a light that might almost be called admiration. "You put the filled reels over here," he said, leading her to a tall gray bin against the wall that she had not noticed before.

The rim of the receptacle came almost to her eye level and she could just barely look over into it to see the few filled reels already in the bottom.

"And the empty reels are here, in this other side." Vince indicated the other half of the bin but opened a cunning door at the bottom to release another of the large reels. There was another latched door, not as wide, which Vince indicated. "That holds the smaller bobbins for the piece-ners."

Together they turned from the bin and saw that Mr. Juggs was no place to be seen.

"What the *hell* are you doing here?" Chesterton whispered to her furiously. Mr. Chesterton was not a cursing man and Dandre might have considered it some sort of special achievement that she had been the spark to ignite the gentleman, who had never sworn in front of a lady before in his life, to swear *twice* in her presence.

"I came to help," the girl said.

Chesterton gave her a look of profound exasperation. "And I suppose you call this helping? Juggs was correct, I will have a formidable task before me to do my own job and yours, too."

Dandre grabbed the empty reel from him and placed it on its wheel at her workstation.

"I can learn my job, *Vince*, and I can be an invaluable asset, if you do not close that prejudiced mind of yours."

"Miss Collin . . ."

"I suppose if we are working here under assumed names, you had better call me Danny," she said.

Chesterton did not reply for a moment but looked down along the line and then back at the girl before he spoke.

"I already know one Danny," he said. "But as I consider you both, I think 'Danny' would be entirely appropriate for you, too."

"You! Girl! And, Chess! Mr. Donner wants to see you both. *Now!*"

Their attention was claimed by Mr. Juggs's bellow. He stood at the other end of the long room, yet his loud summons filled the echoing space, nearly drowning the rumble of the machinery.

The two gave each other a warning glance and then together walked the length of the room. As they passed the third station, little Danny Fry was watching them fearfully, afraid for them and what was about to transpire in Mr. Donner's office, and afraid for himself, too. But Vince looked down and winked broadly as he passed. The girl saw the boy's wide blue eyes and smiled at him sweetly. Danny returned his own brave smile, but it was a great effort for him.

"Mr. Juggs has informed me of some irregularity on the line this morning, Mr. Chess. You know the rules." Mr. Donner, his green visor shading his eyes, spoke with head bent over papers on his desk.

"Yes, sir, I do know the rules. But the girl does not, nor did she know anything about her work, the reels or the machines."

"Then perhaps the girl has come to the wrong place to work," Mr. Donner said.

"Oh no, sir," Dandre coaxed. "I catch on very quickly. I believe I am perfectly capable of doing the job."

Mr. Donner looked up at her and studied her through the green haze of his eye shield. He paused for a moment before answering her, and then only nodded.

"Perhaps," he said.

The girl and her plea were dismissed. Mr. Donner turned his attention instead to Vincent.

"Nevertheless, Mr. Chess, we must maintain discipline here in the mill if we are to avoid chaos. Still..."

Dandre held her breath, Chesterton drew in his breath, and Mr. Juggs breathed heavily through his nostrils.

"Braid's mill does not like to lose an able-bodied laborer."

Dandre had seen one or two of the other men who worked here in the mill, and by comparison, calling Mr. Chesterton "able-bodied" was like calling the Egyptian pyramids "mounds of clay."

"Mr. Chess will be fined twelvepence, Mr. Juggs. Note that, please. You two gentlemen may return to the floor. I don't want to hear of any further disturbance. The girl and I will review the mill rules and then Miss..."

"O'Brien," Dandre supplied, choosing her mother's maiden name. Her mother was a great joiner and champion of lost causes and would have wholly approved of her daughter assuming her name in this undertaking, which undertaking she would *not,* of course, have approved in the first place.

"And then Miss O'Brien will return to her workstation. Where she will labor *without* assistance," Mr. Donner warned.

The two workmen left the office, both giving every appearance of being reluctant to do so, and Mr. Donner began opening drawers in his desk and riffling through the papers. As the door closed behind Mr. Chess and Mr. Juggs, he seemed to find what he was looking for and pulled a stained and torn sheet of paper from the second drawer.

"Can you read, Miss O'Brien?"

"Yes, sir," she said.

Mr. Donner glanced up in surprise, raising his visor so far as to be able to look directly into the girl's eyes.

"Very well then, these are the mill rules," he said, handing her the paper. "Read them over carefully. Consult with me if you have any questions. You must adhere strictly to the rules of this establishment if you want to work here, and you must understand those rules to be able to abide by them."

"I am sure I will understand your rules, Mr. Donner," Dandre said coolly, looking down at the paper.

1. Door closes ten minutes after work begins. Fine: 3d. per minute late.

2. Every power-loom weaver must be present at loom while machine is in motion. Fine: 3d. per hour absent per loom.

3. Weavers are to supply their own scissors. Fine: 1d.

per day without scissors.

4. All shuttles, brushes, oilcans, wheels, window-panes, etc. must be paid for by employees responsible for them.

5. One week's notice required if a worker wishes to end his or her employment.

6. Every operator caught speaking to another, singing or whistling will be fined. Fine: 6d.

Fines also issued on inferior work. Work to be inspected often, with deductions reflected in the worker's wages.

"And what is my wage that is subject to so much reduction?" Dandre asked, looking up from the paper when she reached the bottom and handing it back to Mr. Donner.

Mr. Donner took the rules and replaced them in his drawer.

"Your wages will be one shilling tenpence per day, Miss O'Brien. Payment will be made at the end of the half day on Saturday, with all fines subtracted from the total. That ensures that all workers will be present on Saturday. If you still wish to work for Mr. Braid, you may return to your station. Do you understand your job now, Miss O'Brien, or shall I instruct Mr. Juggs to assist you?"

Dandre was barely able to suppress a shudder at the thought.

"I believe I understand my job," she said.

"Very well. We will disregard the irregularity of this morning, since, as Mr. Chess pointed out, that while he knew the procedure here, you did not. Now you do, Miss O'Brien. Mr. Juggs is a careful overlooker, and I allow him the leeway he requires to maintain order on the floor. Do you understand me?"

"Perfectly, Mr. Donner."

"Good," Mr. Donner said. "You are dismissed then."

Dandre left Mr. Donner's close office and returned to the heavy air of the work floor. She walked directly to her station, but she did not hurry. She was not anxious to put herself under the scrutiny of the frightening Mr. Juggs and the leeway of discipline he was allowed.

The memory of his strap whistling through the air raised gooseflesh on her arm, but even still, she had seen Mr. Juggs' authority defied. By Mr. Chesterton.

And by little Danny Fry.

Chapter Ten

For twelve hours Dandre stood at her station. The work was not demanding. By the time she had filled one more reel after her return from Mr. Donner's office she was thoroughly familiar with all of its intricacies. She worked three reels, each holding four and a half of the smaller bobbins filled by the pieceners. True, the filled reels were heavy, the back one on her machine especially hard for her to lift off its rod. But she was able to do even that, and watching the thread spin through the notch and eye of the rod and onto the turning reel was not difficult. It was dizzying and hypnotic. Whenever she looked away her stomach rolled just a bit and she felt as if she were swaying, which, in fact, she sometimes was. But really, she could not understand Vincent Chesterton's near horror when she suggested doing this work, his avowal that she would not be able to do it.

That is, she could not understand it at seven o'clock in the morning. It was then, though, that her stomach had begun to roll from hunger instead of vertigo and she wondered when they would call a break so she could eat her few slices of bread and plum preserves. Vincent had procured the supplies for her breakfast from the bakery down from Mrs. Bink's rooming house the night before, when he believed she would be breakfasting in her room before her departure for Oldham. Last night they had appeared to be substantial enough, but by seven-thirty in the morning they seemed pitifully inadequate.

She glanced down the aisle and saw that Mr. Juggs was at the other end of the line, and she also saw the girl running the station next to her with an earthen bowl on her table from which she hurriedly snatched a spoonful of what looked like bread and milk. Some of the children, she saw, were nibbling slices of bread, one even a gray potato she hoped was cooked. Evidently they did not call a break for breakfast.

She had left the box that held her bread and jam and the little meat pie that had also been purchased for her lunch under her work bench, for which foresight she issued a sigh of relief. She had debated whether she should bring it down onto the work floor with her or leave it out by Mr. Donner's office.

She was forced to open the box and snatch the slice of bread while she watched her line, untangling a snag, putting a little tension on one lax thread. She considered the plum preserves but realized that in raising the bread from the box to her mouth the sticky spread would collect a thick coating of the lint that filled the air. She snapped the lid of her box down on the untasted preserves, but before she could take a bite of the dry bread she had to take off a full reel, replace it and start the thread around it.

By ten o'clock, having been on her feet since four o'clock that morning, carrying the heavy reels to the bin and the empty ones, which were also heavy, back to her station, and forced as she was to stay alert and intent on the three separate strands of thread, she was beginning to feel a weariness that was totally unknown to her.

At noon a loud whistle sounded, startling her out of a trancelike state in front of her station. She had not been asleep, but neither had she been entirely conscious of her whereabouts or the labor in front of her.

She looked around her, trying to find Chesterton, hoping they could talk, the recollection of his strong arms around her, supporting her, vivid in her mind. He was nowhere to be seen, though, and Mr. Juggs stood surveying the room from atop the short stepladder, so she did not want to draw attention to herself or "Vince" by wandering around looking for him. Besides, she was starved.

She claimed the box under her table and searched for someplace to sit. The little boy who had helped her that morning at such serious consequence to himself was sitting against the wall. He put his hand in his shirt and withdrew a piece of dark bread. Though it never had been a traditionally shaped slice, it had probably been more uniform and less compact that morning.

The boy glanced up to find the young lady's eyes on him. He smiled and raised the hand that held his luncheon in invitation. Dandre smiled back and went to join him. She was forced to admit that, considering Mr. Chesterton's present mood, the delightful little boy was going to be much pleasanter company anyway.

As she approached she saw that the smashed piece of bread was not going to be his only lunch. He unrolled a dark kerchief to reveal two small boiled potatoes, one of which he bit into and had almost devoured by the time she lowered herself to sit next to him.

"How'd it go for you?" he asked, serious concern in his young voice.

"Not so well to begin with," she said. Then leaning closer, she confided softly, "Mr. Juggs was unhappy with me, but he did not lash me. I am so sorry he struck you."

"Oh, it's just Juggs. A fellow has to get used to that," the boy said, shifting uncomfortably where his back rested against the block wall.

"But Mr. Donner explained the rules, and I learned how to change the reels, and after Mr. Chess helped me . . ."

"Ain't Chess a swell, though?" The boy sparked to life. He spoke with a surge of warmth and pride and a small boy's hero worship. "He's helped me some, too. Betcha ol' Juggs didn't like that much, did he?" There was a soft little purr in his voice that Dandre realized was the boy's laugh. It seemed unfamiliar to him, and Dandre wondered if he used it once a week or even once a month.

She readily joined in his laughter to encourage him. The boy finished his first cold potato with a smile on his lips.

"Now," Dandre said, opening the box that held her lunch and eyeing the boy's mashed bread. "My name is Dandre O'Brien, but you may call me Danny. And if I remember correctly from seeing you in Mr. Donner's office, Danny is your name, too, is it not?"

The little boy purred and smiled again.

"Danny Fry. I'm afraid that's the only name I have that you can call me."

"Well, Danny Fry, it seems to me that the two Dannys working at the same job ought to be best friends. What do you think?"

The boy grinned for a moment, but then his expression faltered.

"*Best* friends?" he asked.

Dandre nodded.

"I . . . I already have a *best* friend," the boy said.

Dandre could see the dilemma was real to him, so she refrained from smiling. Instead, she assumed a thoughtful look and appeared to be giving the matter grave consideration.

"And I suppose one can only have one best friend, is that not so?"

The boy nodded, his eyes big and soulful. His world was sparsely populated with friends and he hoped he had not alienated this pretty new one. But Vince—well, there would never be a better fellow than Vince.

"Hmm," Dandre continued. "I still want *you* to be *my* best friend."

Suddenly Danny's face brightened.

"I know!" he cried. "You can be my best friend, and Vince can be my *very* best friend."

"Oh, it is Mr. Chess who is your friend?"

Danny nodded again. Dandre extended her hand.

"I am honored to be your best friend, Danny Fry, as I am certain Mr. Chess is to be your very best friend."

Now the boy smiled and put his small hand in hers to seal their agreement with a handshake.

"Now if I remember correctly, best friends do nice things for each other," the young woman continued, still very serious. "You did a very nice thing for me this morning when you showed me how to run my machine, for which kindness you received unwarranted punishment."

Danny shrugged. "Juggs straps everybody. Most everybody. Some girls he don't."

He looked up at her under his brows and Dandre got the distinct impression that it would be better by far to be strapped by Mr. Juggs than to accept the alternative that he offered some girls.

"Nevertheless," she said, "you helped me and you were very brave. And friends do that for each other just because they are friends, not because they expect a reward. However—" she reached into her box and pulled out the little jar of plum preserves "—friends also share. I believe this will make your bit of bread there taste a little better."

Danny looked uncertainly at the jar of preserves and the spoon Dandre had also produced from the box.

"What is it?" he asked.

"Spread for your bread. It is very good," she answered him, her heart beating painfully at the realization that this beautiful little boy did not know what fruit preserves were, had evidently never seen them before.

Danny scooped a little spoonful from the jar and put it on one corner of his pulp of bread. He just wanted to be polite and take a nibble of the purple stuff, but when the sweet-tart flavor touched his tongue he hungrily bit off that corner and then slathered a great mound of the preserves on the rest of his bread and ravenously gulped it all down.

In seconds he smiled a purplish, happy smile at Dandre, the happy part of which she returned.

She had by now taken the meat pie from her lunch receptacle and her stomach contracted painfully when the aroma filled her nostrils and saliva flowed into her mouth. Nothing had ever smelled so delicious to her and it would not be an exaggeration to say that she had never been this hungry before and no one in her family had ever been this hungry, excepting perhaps her brother, Paul, who had spent an adolescent year or two feeling perfectly hollow.

It was a very small pie, and infected by Danny's enthusiasm, she felt as if she could put the whole thing into her mouth in one bite, but before she could give the idea serious consideration, her attention was caught by the small boy at her side.

He was looking at her pie with a wide-eyed fascination that bordered on awe. His look was not covetous, for surely a pie with actual meat in it was too grand for such as he; he just wanted to watch her eat it, wanted to see the way such a marvelous thing was done.

Dandre inhaled the delicious odor one more time before taking the pie in her two hands and breaking it. The larger half she handed to the little boy.

"For me?" he gasped.

"I really could not eat the whole thing by myself," Dandre said, unable to keep the faint note of regret out of her voice, even in the face of such stunned gratitude as little Danny Fry showed when he held the delicate crust in his grimy fingers and took a bite. He was a growing boy with an appetite that had never been wholly satisfied in all seven years of his life. Yet the bite he took was moderate and he managed to chew it slowly and actually taste the delicious flavors that were so unfamiliar to him.

The young woman and the little boy ate their halves of the meat pie together in silence, exchanging glances and smiles, Danny occasionally making an appreciative noise.

The pie, when whole only six or eight bites big, was gone in very short order. Dandre brushed at her lips and shook the crumbs from her skirt. In a moment she looked around her.

"Is there someplace where we can get a drink of water here?" she asked.

"The pump's up by the front office," Danny said, springing to his feet. "I can go fetch you a drink if you'd like."

She smiled. "I would like that very much."

The boy was gone in a flash. Dandre tightened the lid on the plum preserves and secured the top to her lunch box. She sighed wearily and rested her head against the stone wall. It was very noisy in the mill. The machines were not clanking as much during this, the dinner break, but there was talking, and now and then a coarse cackle or guffaw. And there was the cacophony of much "doings," although the noise could not be specifically attributed to any one source but rather was the result of human beings and metal machinery enclosed in a large, open room.

In only six hours Dandre had become accustomed to the noise, had ceased to give it conscious consideration. Now, as her head found support against the hard wall, her only conscious thought was that the pump was either a great distance away or little Danny was having difficulty drawing the water. That second idea occasioned a twinge of concern, but Miss Collin was too exhausted to hang on to the thought, and her concern, along with all other thoughts, floated away on a stream of unconsciousness.

She thought she had barely closed her eyes—and certainly she could have dozed no more than five minutes—when suddenly an intuitive alarm jolted her awake.

"Not a lot of time for shut-eye here, I think. But I could arrange somethin' for you. Just say the word, girl. A soft bed, a private room. And somethin' extra besides..."

It was Mr. Juggs. He leered down upon her, an evil ogre in this mill world of half reality.

Dandre scrambled to her feet, confused and embarrassed and instinctively frightened, as most women are by snakes.

"I...I was resting. Did I miss the bell? Is it time to get back to work already?"

In her flutter of motion she brushed the man's arm. He stepped back heavily and Dandre was surprised to feel water splash into her face and onto her arm.

"It's almost time to start up the machinery again, but I thought you wanted a drink of water first."

Now Dandre could see that he held a dented tin cup in one hand, which he offered to her, but with a bent elbow so she was forced to step nearer to him if she wanted it. Unfortunately, she was very thirsty by now, after her lunch and the long morning. The little water girl had passed by her station only once with the bucket and dipper.

Reluctantly, she took a half step forward and then extended her arm and bent toward him to grasp the dented cup rather than voluntarily coming any closer to the man.

She gulped the water like a desert castaway, and only when the cup was drained did she stop to consider that Mr. Juggs had brought her the drink little Danny Fry had gone after.

"Where's the boy?" she asked, wiping droplets of the tepid water from her lips with the back of her hand.

"I thought he was stealin' the cup, the hellion."

It was a relatively innocuous remark, but the gruff timbre of the man's voice, and the man who said it, sent a hiver through the girl's slender frame. This man was very dangerous.

"What have you done to him?"

"Stealin' warrants a strappin'. Company rules."

"He was not stealing the cup," Dandre cried.

"So 'e said." Juggs smiled coldly. "But you can't trust any of these little toads."

Dandre, despite a fear that was deepening with every word Juggs spoke, opened her lips in further protest, but before she could say anything else, a loud bell clanged.

"Back to work, girl. And I don't fetch water for line workers. You'll get your own drink next time."

"Where is Danny Fry?" she asked stubbornly.

"By the time I get this cup back to the pump, he'd better be at his post. And you, too." He snapped the thongs of his trap. "Else you'll both have a meetin' with my friend here."

With one more flick of his wrist, he turned from her. Dandre could only watch him leave. She might have remained mesmerized by her horror of him, but the view of his departing figure was often blocked by other women and children returning to their stations, reminding her to get to hers. There was no doubt that he would strap her if she did not return to work. There was no doubt that he would enjoy it and was beginning to look for the opportunity with relish.

She did not know what he had done to little Danny Fry, but she realized there was nothing she could do for him right now. Nor would she be able to help him later if she allowed herself to be beaten senseless now.

Numbly she returned to her worktable. She got one of the reels threaded and spinning, and looking up she saw that Danny had returned to his bobbins, as well. There was a red welt across his cheek and his eye was beginning to swell shut. Dandre's heart missed a beat and tears sprang to her eyes, but she saw Mr. Juggs make his turn at the end of the line, and like everyone else along the line, she bent her head over her work and, like everyone else along the line, silently and fervently prayed that Mr. Juggs would pass her by this time.

The machines were in full production by six o'clock in the morning. That is to say, the workers were at their posts to bring the factory to life beginning, some of them, at five o'clock or even four-thirty. The bell for lunch rang at noon and they were told they were allowed twenty-five minutes for lunch. But Dandre suspected the break had been no longer than fifteen minutes. She knew it could not have been more than twenty minutes, even taking into account the two or three minutes she had dozed off.

After the bell rang everyone got back to work and remained standing at their worktables until seven o'clock— Dandre also suspected it was nearer to seven-thirty than seven o'clock.

In the afternoon, probably at about four o'clock, they were allowed to stand back from their machines and two little water girls hurried through the building.

Dandre had no idea how she managed to stay upright and even semiconscious during the long day. She really did not have any idea what she was doing or what she had done as the afternoon lengthened and began to turn to evening. Her knees were weak and her legs did not seem strong enough to support her. Yet she stayed upright at her table, feeling like a powerless marionette, her stiff arms and legs held and maneuvered by an outside force. An evil force.

Mr. Juggs.

He was omnipresent and merciless. When her eyelids began to droop she was usually startled to wakefulness again by the chilling crack of the strap and some pained outcry. Even above the machinery the warning snarl of his voice could be heard, blackened by a note of glee.

Usually she was roused by the sound of his passage, but not every time. Once, an hour or more after the ten-minute water break and years since lunch, decades since her rising that morning, her eyelids, as heavy as stones, slid down to cover her eyes. Her head nodded. Her shoulders sagged. Without warning, no whisper of sound alerting her, the hateful strap snapped across her back. As her eyes sprang open, they filled with tears. Her little cry of surprise was barely audible above the clanking of her machine as it whirled the reel.

"Wake up there, girl! Watch your lines. And you can watch your back as well if I catch you sleepin' again."

Juggs stood behind her, bouncing his strap in his hand. He did not resume his patrol of the room immediately but stood watching her. Dandre imagined she could feel his hot breath on her neck.

At last he turned, coolly flicking the strap toward her as he did so. The thongs lashed across her derriere in a painful caress. Dandre jumped but did not cry out again. This time she was not imagining that she heard the ominous rumble of his laugh.

There were no actual marionette strings holding her up, though, and Dandre's half of the little meat pie had been burned up hours ago. Her personal reserves had been called upon and burned away, as well, but she found inspiration in that impossibly long day in Danny Fry as he worked gallantly at his post, nodding sometimes, even, like her, strapped once, but struggling to stay alert. Then, when Juggs was in another part of the room, the child would look at her and smile bravely, as concerned for her as she was for him. She also felt a strange jolt, like an electrical shot of energy, every time she was afforded the occasional glance of Vincent Chesterton as he carried his heavy loads of filled reels, five and six at a time, from the spinning room to the weaving room, or as he attended to the frames and the machines that became fouled. His job, as he had told her, was that of a handyman and jack-of-all-trades. Besides a porter and a mechanic, he was also a carpenter, an engineer for the steam engine and a cleaner and sharpener of the carding frame.

His various jobs kept him busy and moving all of the day and evening. He saw Dandre and the boy several times during the day, but his diverse duties called him away most of the time. Whenever he passed through the room he saw that the two of them appeared to be alert and unharmed, or at least awake, and Mr. Juggs was always in another part of the room.

But after the lunch break, when he had been called to the throstle room to tinker with the drive shaft of the main engine for a while, he passed through the spinning room again and noticed that Danny's cheek was red and his eye appeared to be swollen some, evincing the fact that Mr. Juggs was not *always* in another part of the room.

As he walked back along the line, carrying a number of reels that had been filled, he carefully studied Dandre's face. It was drawn and pale, in one day the cheeks sunken with a fatigue that clenched his heart in a way he was reluctant to acknowledge, even to himself. But she did not appear to have the mark of Juggs's strap on her.

He would kill the man if he ever harmed her.

As the murderous thought passed through his mind, his eyes narrowed, he gritted his teeth and tightened his grip spasmodically around the reels he was carrying. At that moment the young woman looked up and saw him. She smiled a smile of such sweetness it seemed to bathe the whole dark room in a wash of soft light. His teeth unlocked, his grasp loosened, but his resolve became an iron vow.

Finally, long after the bell in the Manchester town hall had struck seven o'clock, the bell in Braid's mill sounded and the machines ground to a halt. As the reels on her machine whirled slower and slower and finally stood still, Dandre experienced a giddy sensation, like a sailor used to weeks of adjusting to the constant motion of a ship deck suddenly finding himself on stationary land.

Dandre rested her hands against the front board of her work frame and was surprised to find herself sinking to her knees. It was over. She could stop. She could sleep.

She pushed herself up, a groan escaping her as she did so. She reached under her table for the little lunch box she had packed so optimistically that morning and turned to find her way first to Danny Fry, then to Vincent, then to the door.

Her way was blocked by a grim, dark form.

"And where do you think you're goin', girl?" Juggs asked.

"Home?" Dandre whispered.

It was too cruel. Work was finished, the day was over at last. Surely the horrid monster would fade away with the rest of the nightmare.

It did not. He did not. With his strap he pointed to the machine behind her.

"Not until your machine is cleaned. The reels have to come down, the metal oiled, the wood dusted, the floor swept. And when you've finished with your machine, do that one." He jerked his wrist and the thongs of the strap cracked against the workstation next to hers. Dandre jumped nervously.

She would have thought her will had been quashed in this place, but a spark of it flared again.

"*That* machine?" she cried. "What about her?" With her chin she pointed to the young woman who had worked coolly beside her all day. They were not allowed to speak, but the girl had refused to return Dandre's smile or even a friendly nod.

The girl was short, dumpy and decidedly homely. Mr. Juggs put his arm familiarly around her waist.

"Doll's gonna be busy herself for a while. You just do what I tell you, girl. And as you're workin', you just remember that Doll could be cleanin' *your* machine, if you say the word."

"Wha'!" the other girl cried, tugging petulantly on Mr. Juggs's arm. The hand she pulled around her was the one that held his leather strap, and impatiently Juggs snapped the thongs against her broad hip and legs.

"You'll get what's comin' to you," he promised, though it sounded more like a threat.

The girl quailed and tried to draw away, but Juggs held her in a steel grip. Dandre's indignation turned to pity. Hers was the happier lot by far, to be required only to clean two machines.

"Very well," she said, turning back to her post.

Mr. Juggs left, pulling the other girl beside him.

Dandre looked over and under and all around the two stations for cleaning utensils. She found a small oilcan on Doll's frame, but there was no cloth for dusting and no broom for sweeping. She glanced around the room and saw other girls industriously employed with rags. She discovered where they had acquired their cleaning cloths when one young woman, the girl who had spoken to her on the way to the mill that morning, pulled up the hem of her skirt and tore off a piece of the ragged petticoat underneath.

The idea seemed perfectly practical to Dandre, and without a moment's hesitation she exposed her own petticoat, now soiled and limp. She pulled on it and was pleased to hear the tearing of threads and to see a long piece of the white linen come away in her hands. In fact, it was really too long to work with, so she tore it in two and tucked the second scrap under the waistband of her skirt.

"I'll help you," a small voice at her side offered.

Dandre looked down to see Danny next to her. A faint mark was still on his cheek, and his eye was still puffy, though neither irritation appeared to be causing him any real pain now.

"Oh, Danny, I am so sorry," she cried, dropping to sit on her heels so they would be at the same level. "Did he hurt you?" She brushed the back of her hand tenderly against the red mark on his cheek.

The boy shook his head bravely.

"Not much," he said. "He thought I was stealin' the cup, I guess."

"I guess so," she said softly, her eyes glistening.

"But here, I can help you now. Especially if you have to clean Doll's machine, too. Lucky Doll."

Dandre turned in the direction Mr. Juggs had been pulling the other girl and shook her head.

"I do not believe Doll is very lucky at all," she said quietly.

Danny looked behind him in the same direction and nodded faintly.

"No," he said. "I don't really think she is, either."

"Well, here, if you can help me and would be willing to, perhaps you could just show me what it is I am supposed to do," Dandre said, quickly dismissing the painful subject, fearful of the explanation she might be asked to give, more fearful still of the adult explanation she might hear from the child's lips.

Danny did not seem anxious to pursue the topic, either. Instead, he held out his hand and Dandre gave him the other bit of torn slip tucked under her waistband.

"You have to wipe here, and here, and under here. And don't forget the spindles. Mr. Juggs always checks the spindles before the machines start up in the morning. If there's any dust there you either get docked or strapped. Sometimes both." The boy spoke offhandedly of corporal punishment and fines against their meager wages as he showed Dandre where to dust and how to reach the nooks and crannies that had to be wiped clean and then oiled. Dandre cleaned her own station, following the little boy's example on the other machine.

The process did not take long, actually, and being at last allowed to talk, she and Danny carried on a lively conversation that warded off their fatigue.

When the workstations were cleaned, Dandre looked about her at the littered floor.

"Mr. Juggs said I was to sweep up the floor, too, but I do not see any broom or brush."

Danny knelt down and put the now grimy rag against the floor, pushing the debris in front of him.

"This is my broom," he said, "and that's yours." He nodded toward the rag she held, and like a seasoned charwoman, Dandre knelt on the floor beside him, pushing her own pile of threads and lint and cotton scraps and oily dirt away from her machine.

"Where does it go?" Dandre asked him.

"Right about here," Danny said, grinning as he stood and shook out the rag onto the collection of trash he had pushed directly into the walkway between the machines and the wall, where it would be certain to be scattered through the mill within minutes tomorrow morning.

"Well now, what is going on here?" a voice asked behind the two of them. Both recognized this voice, too, and both turned a delighted look on the speaker.

"Mr. Chess…" Dandre began, with more pleasure in her voice than she would have believed was retrievable five minutes ago.

Danny cut her off with his cry of "Vinnie!"

Softly Dandre revised her greeting.

"Vincent."

The little boy ran to the man and hugged his hips, which was as far as his short arms could reach.

Chesterton laid a strong, fond hand against the little boy's shoulder.

"I think you have done enough work for one day, Master Fry," he said. Then his eyes dropped to the girl, the lovely woman, her cheeks streaked with dirt, her beautiful eyes glazed with weariness, who still knelt on the hard stone floor, her hand holding a filthy rag. "And I think you have, too, Miss—"

"Danny's her name, Vince—same as me—Danny O'Brien," Danny supplied with shy delight. He suddenly realized he needed to be the matchmaker for these two perfectly suited people, but he was a little unsure of his responsibility.

"Miss O'Brien," Chesterton finished gently. Then he shook the boy's shoulder. "Here now, I think the children have left for their rooms. I came to find you so you wouldn't get locked out. I don't want you to miss your supper, but just in case..." He put his other hand in his pocket and withdrew a small square of dried beef.

"For me?" Danny gasped.

"All for you," Vince said. "Now slip that into your pocket and hurry along. Look, there goes Ben now. You catch up with him and all will be well."

Danny turned, but before he had taken three steps he stopped and turned back to look at Dandre with a worried expression.

"Miss Danny's havin' a time of it, Vince. You'll take care of her, won't you?" he asked.

"Yes, I will," Chesterton said, "very good care."

Danny was satisfied. If the girl was to be protected by Vince, no harm could ever come to her. He hurried away, drawing even with Ben just as the other boy was closing the door behind him.

Chesterton held down his hand and Dandre grasped it. Effortlessly, like pulling his shadow behind him, he helped the girl to her feet and drew her to his side, where he supported her with his good, strong arm.

If he could, if she would let him, he was forced to admit to himself at least, he would very much like to care for this contrary, willful, infuriating woman for the rest of his life.

Chapter Eleven

"I do not know how they can do it. How can they do it, Vincent, day after day for those inhuman hours? I would not have thought human beings capable of performing such awkward, wearisome labor for so long for even one day, let alone weeks. Or years. How can they do it? Ow!"

Chesterton and Dandre had returned to Mrs. Bink's rooming house, Chesterton sustaining most of both their weights on the trek. When they stumbled up the steps and into the front door, Mrs. Bink came to her desk and was not surprised to see the two of them go into the young woman's room. The landlady shook her head and clicked her tongue.

"Could have saved themselves the bother of traveling back and forth," she murmured. Who did they think they were deceiving, anyway?

Inside Dandre's room, Chesterton had the young woman sit on the chair. He pulled the box in front of her and sat on it. She had not been able to decide whether the box was meant to be a stool or a table and had almost decided it must be the latter, when the gentleman demonstrated how handily it could fill the other role.

Ignoring Dandre's weak protests, he took one of her feet into his lap, removed the heavy walking shoe and began to massage her aching sole.

At her cry of surprised pain as his broad thumb struck a particularly sore muscle, he eased his pressure but did not cease his operations. Firmly he pressed the heel of his hand into the arch of her foot, then he encompassed her whole foot with the fingers of his hand and squeezed it like a sponge. In just a moment he released the pressure and then very lightly ran his fingers along the top of her foot and underneath. She smiled faintly.

At last he spoke thoughtfully, sorrowfully, in answer to her question, while he continued to rub her foot.

"They can do it so their families can eat, so they are not separated and sent to workhouses. Have you ever seen a workhouse?"

Dandre shook her head. "I have not. But surely they cannot be any worse than that place?"

"They are like grim prisons, gray walls and iron locks and not even the comfort of family members."

"But little children . . ." Dandre began in protest.

"The mills will hire little children when men can find no work at any wage. True, a child only earns two shillings and sixpence a week, which is not a great deal. Not when bread is sevenpence a loaf and sugar sixpence. Not when a week's rent in one of the rat holes in the workers' quarter is three shillings and sixpence. But families are large, and if a man can set his children to earning two shillings a week as soon as they can walk, then the family can survive."

"And Danny? Little Danny Fry? Is he helping to keep his family together?"

Chesterton did not speak for a moment. Instead, he gave Dandre's right foot a final pat and put it on the floor, exchanging the right foot for the left. As he was removing that shoe he spoke.

"Danny has no family," he said.

Dandre's eyes opened wide in surprise.

"Then why is he . . . ?"

"When the mill owners discovered that children could work in their mills, that tiny fingers could more easily seize the threads and tiny bodies required less food and less clothing, and that tiny mouths could not make their protests or cries of agony heard, they started bringing children from other parts of the country, shipping them in by the hundreds and enslaving them. Children in orphanages and workhouses in the south are rented out to manufacturers for a certain number of years. They are lodged, fed and clothed in common and worked sixteen hours a day until they are used up. The supply is endless." There was an ache in his voice that matched the one in her heart.

"So Danny..."

"Is an orphan. Purchased for Braid's mill. He and some of the other children are boarded in one of the stone huts outside the mill. Eight children arrived from London's Saint Augustine's orphanage last February. Six of them still labor at Braid's."

"What of the other two?" Dandre whispered.

"Some children get used up faster than others. The boy's head was crushed by the wheel and lockjaw followed the injury."

"He died?"

Chesterton nodded. "The girl, I understand, was beaten so severely by an overlooker one day that she could not return to the hut. She managed to drag herself into the drying room, where her lifeless body was discovered the next morning."

The man's voice was choked with emotion and abruptly he stopped speaking.

He seemed to be concentrating all his mental powers on Dandre's foot. He rubbed it and smoothed it and closed his fingers around it, but the girl could tell that his thoughts were elsewhere.

Dandre lifted her foot from his knee and rose from her chair to kneel on the floor at his side. She took his hands in hers, hands of a wealthy landowner, which ordinarily would be smooth and well kept but were, instead, dark with ingrained dirt and rough with calluses earned in Braid's mill. She looked into his face. His brow was furrowed and lines of sorrow cut deeply into his temples from the corners of his eyes because he was unable to prevent all of the cruelty and injustices in the world. As she had done with Danny, she laid the back of her hand against his cheek. He looked down at her and she smiled.

"You are a good man, Vincent Chesterton. You care, and you try, but you are not a god."

"No," he said, sounding apologetic, as if it were his fault that he could not do everything.

"Of course, I will never tell Danny you are not a god. He would not believe me, anyway," she said, laughing softly.

"Do you not see, though?" he said, not returning her laughter. "You were right. They cannot survive the conditions. *He* cannot survive much longer. Something must be done, and soon. Very soon. But nothing happens quickly in the Houses of Parliament. Old men will not believe that all is not well, that merry old England can, in fact, do something wrong.

"But I do not know why I blame Parliament only. The workers themselves are so hesitant, so slow about making changes. They do not know that any changes made would not worsen their condition. But how could their condition worsen?"

Dandre patted his hand and shook her head and finally began to talk.

"When you guided me from the mill tonight, I knew that I could never go back there."

"Well, at least you realize that," he said, relief and approval in his voice.

"Now I know I cannot stay away," Dandre continued, ignoring him.

"What?" the man cried in dismay. Was this woman *never* going to see reason?

"I have enough food, good clothing—" she turned with a rueful smile to look across the room "—and a comfortable bed to sleep in. If children with none of those things can go back to the mill tomorrow, I suppose I can, too."

"You foolish child," he said, cupping her cheek and chin in the palm of his hand. "You know what it is like. You *saw* what it is like. I cannot allow you to return."

"If I remember correctly, I have not required your leave heretofore."

He frowned. "No. You have not. With no thought, without even an idea of what you were getting yourself into, you ignored my warning and any levelheaded thought that may have wandered into that head of yours unexpectedly and flung yourself into the lions' den. You saw the workplace, you stood at that terrible post for fourteen hours, and you still suggest that you would return. How can I make you understand? I cannot protect you when you are in that mill."

Dandre inhaled sharply, but Chesterton continued, as if unaware of the responsibility he was assuming and what that seemed to mean.

"As you so justly brought to my attention, I am not a god. I cannot be omnipresent. It angers me beyond words to know that Juggs mistreats Danny and the other children. I would prevent that if I could. But I cannot always be there. It sickens me to imagine what Juggs is capable of if left on his own. And if he were to harm you I do not know what I would do." There was a grim, implacable tone in those words.

Much as Dandre hated and feared Mr. Juggs, she did not mention the lash she had taken from him. Her back would heal, but the overlooker would not if she told Chesterton of his ill-usage.

Instead, she turned her head and kissed the palm of his hand.

"It is you who do not understand," she whispered. "If you cannot be there to protect Danny, perhaps I can. If you're going to return, I want to go with you."

His eyes filled with bemused hopelessness. What was he to do? What was he to do about Danny Fry? What was he to do with her? He was only one man.

His desire to do good, to do the right thing, was so touching Dandre's eyes filled with tears. Vincent lowered himself from the box to sit beside the young woman on the floor. He put his arms around her and drew her to him, holding her so closely that now he could feel the beating of her heart. His forearm crossed the tender stripes that still burned on her back, but she did not pull away from the embrace. Rather, she put one arm over the muscled bulk of his shoulder and clung to him desperately. She raised her chin, he lowered his head, their lips met and parted. Mr. Tuggs and his strap and the spinning reels that had filled her world all day, even little Danny Fry, were all forgotten in a new world. A world filled with fire.

He lifted his lips from the soft contour of her mouth. He kissed her cheek, then the pink folds of her ear, the white satin of her neck. He put his fingers in her hair, tangling them in the strands. Extricating himself, he pushed back the hair that had fallen around her face and began his trail of kisses again.

In a moment he drew back from her and placed his hands against her face, studying its lines, delving into the depths of her green eyes, wondering at her beauty. He fingered a few of the long hairs near her face, looking for the red the sun highlighted. He touched her cheek and would have compared it to porcelain if he had been in a poetic mood. Her perfect lips, the delicate jut of her chin—everything about her was charming to him.

Even in his arms like this, Dandre would have been sur
prised by his admiration. She considered herself only pass
ably pretty and would not have understood his adoration
might even, in a moment of mad foolishness, have contra
dicted him.

Vincent was another story altogether. When they drew
apart, Dandre ran her slim fingers through the waves of his
hair, could admire his strong jaw, his noble profile, his eyes
dark with determination and commitment. He was most
decidedly the handsomest man she had ever seen.

And at that appraisal Chesterton would have laughed out
loud.

But their thoughts were silent, their mutual admiration
unspoken, and in only a moment the space between them
was closed again as they found a more tactile way to ex
press their pleasure in each other.

The tender skin of her neck was scratched by the rough
stubble on his unshaven chin. It burned with a pleasant
pain she would delight in for days to come. Just as she had
when he massaged her poor, tired feet, Dandre relaxed at
his touch, reveling in the sensations he aroused.

Though his hands roved over her body, down her side
and the length of her thigh, though he pushed impatiently
at the material of her clothing between them, he did not
make any demands of her or take advantage of the fatigue
that may have weakened her resolve. Instead, when she
murmured a protest, weak and greatly lacking in sincerity
though it was, he ceased the exploration of his lips and
hands and simply held her close to him in his arms.

"I am starved," she mumbled.

They were still half panting with their passion, seated on
the floor of her bedroom, resting their backs on the stool
or table or whatever the box was supposed to be. Her words
surprised a loud laugh from Vincent.

"Yes, I suppose you are. What did you take with you for
lunch this morning?" he asked.

"A meat pie," she told him.

"Ah."

"A very small meat pie."

"Being the delicate creature that you are," he said.

"And I gave half of that to Danny."

Chesterton smiled and nodded. "With your meat pie and my bit of salted beef, little Danny Fry will have eaten very well today. Now let us attend to ourselves."

He stood and pulled the girl up to stand in front of him, very close to him, so that he could feel the rustle of her skirts when she moved, feel the warmth on his face when he exhaled.

"I do not know that I am properly attired for an evening in one of Manchester's restaurants," she said, glancing down at the simple shirtwaist and skirt that had been clean that morning. She did not need the evidence of her mirror to know that she must now look wretched. To learn that Chesterton thought she was beautiful seeing her like this would have amused and amazed her even more.

"That was not my plan," he said.

"Oh?"

"That is *never* my plan when I return from the mill. Primarily because I am too exhausted, but also because I am posing as a workman of limited means. Dining in an elegant restaurant hardly conforms to that image. But Mrs. Boyle, just around the corner, serves a very passable meal designed to fill up hungry mill workers. And one need only wash one's face to sit at one of Mrs. Boyle's tables. Come along now. You wash your face." He stopped to rub at a smear on her cheek.

"And you comb your hair," she said, running her fingers through his hair again, which was the primary reason it was in such a disarray now.

"And I will meet you by Mrs. Bink's desk in five minutes," he said.

"Three minutes," she corrected. "I am *very* hungry."

The little eatery that Mrs. Boyle oversaw was, as Chesterton said, just around the corner from the apartment building. It was a small establishment, obviously meant to cater to mill workers who could only just afford to buy their meals out. Still and all, considering its location and her clientele, Mrs. Boyle seemed determined to keep her kitchen and the dining area clean and pleasant.

When Vincent and Dandre entered, there was no raucous talking or drunken laughter going on. Rather, the well-behaved patrons sat at their tables, eating with correct utensils, using the worn napkins Mrs. Boyle provided, as they quietly discussed the day's events with their tablemates. True enough, more than one of the women across from her companion had obviously been hired for this particular evening for dinner and "dessert," as it were, but at Mrs. Boyle's everyone conducted themselves like ladies and gentlemen.

Mrs. Boyle worked with another middle-aged woman at the cookstove behind a short counter. When Dandre and Chesterton entered, the owner looked up and Chesterton raised his hand in greeting. Mrs. Boyle smiled and bobbed her head, then raised it again to study, with surprise, the young woman beside Vince. To her recollection, Vince Chess had never come in here with a doxy before. Hers was the distinct impression he did not employ their services. In fact, she had always admitted to herself that Vince would hardly have to pay for what every girl who worked at the mills would have given him for free.

But as she studied the young woman who took the chair across from him, she could see that this one was not a professional. Mrs. Boyle wiped her greasy hands on her apron and went to ask what the two young people would have tonight. As she neared their table and got a better look at the girl, she decided that not only was this one not selling it, she wasn't even giving it away.

"I see you brought a friend with you tonight, Vince. Evenin', miss. What can I get for you?"

"Mrs. Boyle makes the best stew in Manchester, Miss Collin," Chesterton said.

"Miss O'Brien," Dandre corrected him under her breath.

He appeared confused for a moment and then flustered as he quickly corrected himself.

"Miss O'Brien. Of course. Well...yes. As I was saying, the best stew in Manchester, in all of England, I would wager, is to be found in Mrs. Boyle's stew pot."

"Then by all means I must have some," Dandre said, smiling her pretty, innocent smile up at the older woman, a smile not one of the other girls sitting in here could have duplicated.

"Make that two bowls," Chesterton said.

"Two *large bowls,*" Dandre added.

Mrs. Boyle chuckled and turned to procure the order.

The stew did taste better to Dandre than any she had eaten in her life, but that was not proof positive it was the best in England. Dandre would have found a fried cat palatable at the moment.

When the bowl, a very large bowl, in compliance with Dandre's specification, was half-emptied, the young woman finally slowed the rapid movement of her dented spoon and looked around her.

Several of the tables were occupied, some by couples, some by men alone. One woman sat at a table in the corner, keeping to herself and unmolested. Dandre's impression of these people was the same as the one she had had in the mill. The men were all thin and pallid, with stringy, skinny arms, sunken cheeks and sunken eyes. The young women, even those with paints and powders generously applied to their faces, could not hide the fact that they, too, were pale, wan, undersized and misshapen. The most common irregularity of form seemed to be a curvature of the spine and legs bent and twisted inward. Many squinted at their companions, trying to bring their faces into focus after a day spent gazing at long parallel rows of fine thread Occasionally she heard a dry, raspy cough.

The people sitting in Mrs. Boyle's eatery were no healthy. They were not the strength of the nation. And yet despite their haggard, listless appearance, she suspected that none of them were out of their twenties. And these were the healthy ones. These had been the strong children and youths who had entered the factories. The others, the weak ones, even the ones not so determinedly robust, had been destroyed, killed outright or their bodies worn away to uselessness by the mills, then discarded onto the rubbish heap that was weakening this nation. Her uncle spoke with pride of the wealth and recognition England's factory out-pourings were creating in the world, but her uncle had no seen this, had not witnessed what they were losing—no what they were throwing away—for a few dollars. For their thirty pieces of silver.

Suddenly she did not feel as if she could finish her stew. She pushed the bowl away from her.

"Something?" Chesterton asked.

"I do not feel hungry anymore," Dandre said, looking around her mournfully.

Chesterton followed her gaze.

"It was days before I could eat at all," he said in under-standing. "But you will need your strength, Dandre. Try to finish the stew."

She pulled the bowl back in front of her but did not take up her spoon again.

"At least finish the meat," he advised. "It will provide more sustenance than anything else."

Dutifully Dandre put one of the small brown chunks into her mouth and chewed the tough strings slowly and thor-oughly.

"Something must be done," she said simply, when she had swallowed her mouthful.

"Now you know why I am here, why I sought out Richard Oastler and why I offered my services to Mr. Sadler when he made his proposal. I would rather be in Timbrey—" when he mentioned his home there was a deep longing in his voice "—but if I can help change this I must try."

"What are we to do?" she asked.

"We must find out how and when the women and children are mistreated," he said.

"I can tell you," she said quietly.

Chesterton studied her face carefully for a moment but did not pursue the half revelation she had made, perhaps reluctant, as she was, to face the irrefutable actions a full revelation from her would require.

"Your word would carry no more weight than mine," he said, addressing that topic rather than the one she had raised. "You and I would both be considered outsiders, by the workers *and* the owners. The committee members could not accept our testimony as representative of conditions in the mills."

Dandre's brow furrowed.

"What are we supposed to do, then? We can take one small boy out of there, but exhausting all of our combined resources cannot rescue more than a minuscule handful of the children."

Chesterton shook his head. "That is not the purpose of this investigation anyway. We certainly do not want to stop the progress of Britain's textile industry, only keep it from destroying the defenseless in its haste," he said. "My next step is to convince some of the workers themselves to talk to Richard Oastler and to testify for Mr. Sadler."

Now Dandre shook her head as she remembered the taciturn Doll on the machine next to her, who would abandon herself to Mr. Juggs to avoid cleaning her own machine. How could she, and the other girls like her, be expected to put their livelihoods in jeopardy by coming forward with their stories?

"'Ere you go, Mrs. Boyle. Tasty as ever. They don't serve biscuits any lighter than that in Palmerston's House uptown. How much do I owe you, then?"

"Sixpence," Mrs. Boyle said.

Dandre and Chesterton's quiet conversation was interrupted by the exchange between the proprietress and one of her customers.

"'Ere's a shilling. You take what's left and see that it gets to the infirmary. The little Nelson girl caught 'er finger in the wheel this morning."

Mrs. Boyle made a conciliatory sound in her throat.

"It didn't take 'er, thank the good Lord, but she's cut up some. The doctor says she may 'ave a chance if she gets fed on some proper food. You see that she gets some, now."

"'Tis food in the poor girl's stomach, Bill. Her mother thanks ye."

Bill, the generous customer, self-consciously brushed aside the praise that acknowledged the sizable bite out of his weekly wage that he had just donated to the injured girl.

Dandre ducked her head, embarrassed by the ungenerous thoughts that had filled her mind only moments before.

"Have you asked any of them to come forward? To testify?" she asked Chesterton.

"I have talked to some of the men," he said. "But they are unwilling. Most of them are heads of families hanging on to tenuous employment that barely feeds and houses their wives and children now. They cannot risk the loss of that income. Not even for the sake of the children they see mangled and killed every day."

Chesterton looked sorrowfully after the man who had just left the little shop, willing to donate to the injured child's care but only because he was earning money to do so.

"The women and children would perhaps be more willing to risk it," Dandre suggested.

"That is what we are hoping."

She nodded thoughtfully.

"Perhaps I can talk to some of them," she said.

"You?" Vincent exclaimed, just as if Dandre had never suggested such a thing before, just as if he had not witnessed her working at that reeling post all the long day. "I cannot..." he began in protest.

"No, you cannot. That is why I must be the one to approach them."

Chesterton sighed heavily and shook his head. The girl was so damnably right. He did not have the opportunity to talk to the children or the women, either. And he certainly would not witness their abuse for the sake of Sadler's committee hearings.

"I work with them," Dandre continued. "They were cool today, but surely they will become more comfortable with me. Let me try, Vincent. For Danny."

Chesterton winced when she said the child's name, and if Dandre had been a manipulating female she might have elicited any sort of response she wanted from the man by playing on his fondness for the child. But she was considering only her own fondness for Danny when she spoke.

Chesterton sighed again but glumly nodded his head.

"All right," he said. "But if you do, you must do it on the sly, as Danny would say. Do not let Juggs hear you discussing conditions or encouraging the women to come forward. And tell the women they will be able to meet with Mr. Oastler outside the mill."

"Where?" Dandre asked.

"I do not..."

Dandre looked about her. "Here perhaps?"

Chesterton followed her gaze. He had not thought of this place before, but it would be perfect. It was local, filled with friends and people all known to one another, and if he bought supper for some of the girls or children with families here in town, those who were not locked away in stone huts when the evening bell rang, he was sure tongues would be loosened and wariness seen as unnecessary.

"Excellent suggestion," Chesterton said. "I could talk to some of the workers and tell them I have a friend I would like them to meet some Saturday. Saturdays are supposed to be half days, so everyone should be finished by five o'clock. I will get in touch with Oastler, find out when he can be here."

"Mr. Richard Oastler would wish to come here?" Dandre asked, impressed that Vincent could call on the celebrated man so informally.

"Oh, he would insist on it," Vincent assured her. "He has made it his life's mission to better the lot of the factory worker."

By now Chesterton had finished his own stew and Dandre had picked out the few remaining bits of meat in her bowl that the gentleman insisted she eat.

He paid Mrs. Boyle, also contributing to the nourishing food for the little Nelson girl, and purchased two small pots of Mrs. Boyle's highly seasoned lentils for his and Dandre's lunch the next day.

Arm in arm, they returned to the tenement, each swinging one of the earthenware pots in a free hand. They looked like two lovers out for an evening stroll, but the image was jarred on the steps of the tenement, where Chesterton stopped the girl before they entered.

"I have considered the thing from every angle," he said.

"And?" she asked expectantly, smiling up at him.

But he did not return her smile. His expression was very serious.

"I cannot allow you to return to the mill," he said.

"Vincent," she chided him gently, a half smile still on her lips. "We have been through this once before. Then, I am afraid, I was forced to demonstrate that I will not be dictated to by you."

"I am serious, Dandre," he said, putting his hands on her shoulders, the right one holding his pot of lentils rather awkwardly. He ignored the crockery tapping against her shoulder, and for the moment so did she. She was captured by the intensity of his eyes.

"You have not told me what Juggs did to you . . ."

She parted her lips and inhaled to make some sort of denial or explanation, but Chesterton gave his head one small shake, never taking his eyes off hers.

"I do not believe it was serious. If you are standing here with me this evening I know it was absolutely nothing compared to what he could do to you, what he would *like* to do. The man is like a wild beast, Dandre, who has taken his first bite of human flesh. They say that a man-eating lion will never touch other food once it has tasted man. You are Juggs's prey. Today he had his first morsel. He will not quit the hunt until he has consumed every part of you."

"Vincent, I cannot abandon you, and them, now," she said quietly.

Chesterton put his arms around her and crushed her to him, this time with her clay pot pushing against his abdomen.

"Dandre, do not do this to yourself. Do not do this to me," he whispered fiercely.

The note of pleading in his voice touched her deeply, but his plea might have been directed back at himself. She remembered the sheen of perspiration on his face and arms as he carried the heavy reels through the sweltering workroom, how he was called to work everywhere, yet had been there with his rescuing arms for her this morning, with his dried beef for Danny tonight. Though he seemed much more to herself and Danny Fry, the man really *was* mortal and the workload he was carrying was inhuman. How could she send him back there alone?

"We will hurry," she whispered against his cheek. "It will go much faster if I talk to the girls. We will arrange the meeting and then we will leave and take Danny with us."

"Dandre," he began.

"I will be very careful. I will work hard and obey the company rules and stay out of Mr. Juggs's way. You must not worry."

He did not try to dissuade her. Her mind was set, and she was surely the most stubborn woman he had ever met. But he also did not try not to worry.

It would be well if she worried some for herself, too.

Chapter Twelve

Dandre spent an uneasy night. Her muscles ached, her eyes burned, the lint caught in her throat and lungs made her cough every time she began to drift off. And though Mr. Juggs's lashing had been light, occasionally in her thrashings she would lie directly on the fading stripes on her back or the fabric of her nightgown would abrade the tender flesh, causing bright flashes of pain.

But the most unpleasant part of the night was that it was over so soon.

Long before light, long before even the birds would awaken, and certainly long before she was rested at all, Chesterton tapped at her door.

"Dandre?" he called softly.

"What is it?" she answered, sitting up in bed.

"It is time to rise. We must be at the mill by fifteen minutes past five o'clock. You must dress quickly, and remember to wear something very lightweight. I will wait for you at Mrs. Bink's desk."

She heard his tread retreating down the hall in the direction of the desk and the front door.

She pushed the rough woolen blanket aside and struggled to her feet. She had forgotten, amidst her other discomforts, that her feet hurt. Now she remembered.

She went to the washstand and poured a little water into the bowl to splash on her face. How she longed for her Aunt Bea's bathtub, filled with steaming hot water, fragrant and soothing, and about two hours of leisure time to enjoy it.

Instead, she quickly washed her face and neck, arms and hands, and swiped with the washcloth at her breasts and torso and the dried perspiration that had drenched her body the day before.

She dried herself imperfectly with the gauze-thin towel provided by Mrs. Bink and slipped into her summer smock. In Coventry, in the Collin home, this smock was worn over a dress and petticoats as a protective apron. After just one day in the factory Dandre knew she did not want to wear anything constricting and heavy, not even anything as heavy as a skirt and simple shirtwaist. This little, lightweight pinafore, shamefully indecent anywhere else on earth—discounting the villages of naked tribesmen in Darkest Africa, of course—seemed perfect to her that morning.

The smock material was thin, and the short sleeves and raised hem exposed more of her arms and legs than she had exposed in public in all of her young adult life. It was quite a bit more modest than some of the threadbare dresses the other girls had worn inside the mill, though, and public decency had different criteria between Timbrey Hall and Braid's mill.

When she opened the door to join the young man waiting for her, it was Vince Chess, the rough workman, who watched her approach and judged her attire approvingly, rather than Mr. Vincent Chesterton, who would have been as scandalized to see Miss Collin dressed in such a fashion in his drawing room as she would have been unlikely to so appear.

"Here, you will want this," he did say when she drew near to him. He held out a large, bulky overcoat. Dandre looked at it in surprise. "For the walk to the mill," Chesterton explained. "It is cool out-of-doors."

Dandre took the wrap and the two of them left for the mill.

From the office of Braid's mill was a short ladder that led down onto the working floor. A few feet from the door was another ladder that led upward. At the top were a number of meters and gauges that monitored the power source and the machines in the factory. The ladder had been placed there for the convenience of the mechanics whose job it was to keep the boiler and the implements in operation, but the person who used the ladder the most, more often than the mechanics at Braid's ever had, was Eldridge Juggs.

He stood on the second rung from the top, turned out to face the workroom. Gazing down on it like a wicked bird of prey, he scanned its desert territory for any invader, especially the weak and faltering, who would collapse beneath the pitiless sun of toil to lie powerless beneath the vulture's raking talons.

He was perched there, waiting, when Chess and the new girl came in together at ten minutes past five o'clock. His upper lip rose and his brows drew together. She believed she had found a protector, that the man could save her. Unconsciously, Juggs shook his head slightly. There was no defense sure enough to save her from him.

But not yet. Not yet. Still strong, his prey had arrived in time, early in fact, for work. He could have no objection, could take no action . . . yet.

He saw Chess nod to her. He saw her take her place at her station. She smiled at Doll, who did not return the smile, Juggs was certain, though he could not see her averted face. Doll, he knew, had no reason to smile this morning. She would be moving stiffly today, but if her work was not done she knew she could look forward to more of the same treatment tonight.

They liked it, he thought, his upper lip rising again, this time in a smile more malevolent than his angry snarl. And she would, too. She would like it soon. And often. Not yet, but soon.

The dark gleam of his eyes never left Dandre's form as she seized the ends of thread and started them to wind around her reels. Every movement of her body, a body better formed than poor Doll's sack of drooping flesh and jutting bones, was easily definable under the loose covering of the slight dress she had worn today.

His eyes glittered and the muscles of his body tensed as he imagined the feel of that silky skin beneath the rough callus of his hand, beneath the heavy length of his own body. Not yet. But soon. She would like it. They all did.

With barely a thought to what she was doing, Dandre wound the threads around each of her three reels and watched them begin to fill as the workday began.

When she first arrived, as the machines were starting to growl to life, she had smiled at Doll across the space that separated the two worktables. The young woman did not return her smile. In fact, she seemed surprised by it. But Dandre held the girl no ill will for the cleaning of her machine the night before. This morning the girl had a red mark on one cheek, a mark that would doubtless turn into a bruise, reminding Dandre again of the fortune of her lot in only being required to clean two machines.

Vincent's assignment, and therefore *her* assignment, was to talk to some of the women and children working here and convince them to testify before Mr. Sadler's committee. If she could gain Doll's confidence and enlist her aid, she was certain she would have tales of horror to tell. And if she were to lose her job here at Braid's for testifying, it would relieve her from the oppression of Mr. Juggs and could only be looked upon as a boon.

But until the lunch break she could make no other over-
ure besides her smile. Talking was forbidden by the com-
any rules, and Dandre had promised Vincent that she
would obey those rules. She also promised that she would
void Mr. Juggs's attention, but across the length of the
workroom she felt the dark fire of his gaze.

Nevertheless, even with that ominous undertone, the
noise, the rhythm, the hypnotic effect of the spinning reels
and the mindless activity of her job dulled her consciousness to a sort of blur.

She was aware that her feet and back ached. She vaguely
saw the reels fill and roused herself enough to pull them
clumsily off their spools and haul them across the aisle to
the bin against the wall.

Her head ached.

Her eyes burned.

She coughed rawly, disturbing the tiny filaments of cotton stuck in her throat but not expelling them.

Danny Fry was at his post. His eye, like Doll's cheek, was
red, but his injury was fading and hers was just beginning
to blossom. Today Dandre had the leisure to contemplate
the job of the little boy and the rest of the child pieceners.
Her duties, other than the lifting and carrying of the filled
reels and the necessity of being on her feet all day, were not
demanding. The little pieceners worked much harder and
at a much more uncomfortable angle.

When the threads broke the child had to hold the spindle end with his left hand, and then, lifting the left shoulder up and bending the right knee inward, he had to stoop
down to find the other end of the broken thread with his
right hand and fasten the two ends.

Danny, who had been working here less than six months,
could still stand straight, though, thinking back on it, she
realized he did tend to stand with his right knee bent inward.

Other children, those who had worked as pieceners perhaps only a few months, even a few weeks, longer than
Danny, could not stand straight. Their soft bones, still
forming, had risen on the left shoulder and bent inward at
the right knee.

Whack!

"Get your mind on what you're doin', girl."

Dandre jumped, the skin of her back stinging under the
blow of Mr. Juggs's strap. He whirled and brought the
strap down on Penny, the little girl who was working as
Doll's piecener today.

"And what're you lookin' at there? Back to work with
you. With both of you!" He raised his arm again, but Doll
cringed and immediately dropped her eyes to her reels.
Juggs grimaced appreciatively before he turned back to
Dandre.

Dandre stood watching, the pain of her own lashing
dulled, if not forgotten, by her outrage at the overlooker's
assault on the child, who had done nothing more than look
up when Mr. Juggs struck her. Doubtless he would have
lashed the child if she had *not* looked up.

When the man faced her again, his hair bristling on his
round head, the sparks of his eyes shaded by his low brow,
she recalled Vincent's words to her: "The man is a wild
beast. *You* are his prey."

Like a doe brought to bay by a pack of howling hounds,
Dandre stared at him with wide eyes, feeling a strange
quiver under her skin that was the tensing of her muscles.

"Pay more attention to your job and less to other jobs
and we'll all get on better," he said. "Now back to work."
He flicked the strap again and nervously Dandre turned to
her reel.

She understood now what Vincent feared. Here in the
mill she could not take herself out of Mr. Juggs's way. He
would be there with his leather strap whenever the other

nan was not, and Vincent could not stay with her always, ot if he was to complete his assignment.

Her eyes blurred by tears, she knew she could not ask for Vincent's help or rely on his defense. She had placed herelf in this position and refused to let him remove her from t. The consequences were hers to face.

Mr. Juggs finished his pass down her row of machines nd should have moved on to the next row. Instead he urned and started back along the same row again.

Dandre, acutely aware of his every step this time, held her oreath as he neared her station.

His step slowed.

She was forced to exhale.

He stopped beside her and raised his hand. She tensed, vaiting for the blow, but instead he laid his rough, heavy oaw against her back.

The material of the smock she had chosen to wear was ery thin. She had been much more comfortable at her vork today, but when the strap struck her it might have oeen landing on bare flesh, and now the hot meatiness of he overlooker's hand was repellently familiar as his fingers roved across the welts beginning to rise.

"You're not used to the nip of my little pet, are you?" he vhispered near her ear. He raised his other hand and ran he handle of the strap down her cheek. "He likes you. But like you, too. And I'm the only one who can keep him in check. You be good to me, and I'll see if I can't keep you wo apart." He laughed a low laugh that puckered the skin on her arm into gooseflesh.

He left her side and continued his pass. Dandre watched him, turning her head slightly, praying that he would not ee her notice.

Juggs did not turn, but she saw that Doll, surprisingly, aad. Her expression was not one of jealousy or resentment, which Dandre might have expected from her after

Juggs's half caress, regardless of how unwelcome it was. Instead, Doll looked commiserating.

Dandre smiled at her and shrugged her shoulders, indicating that she was all right, the overlooker's treatment no worse than she could endure.

The morning was long. All of the aches she had taken to her room with her last night had found her again and returned with so tight an embrace she could only assume they had missed her. Her neck, her shoulders, her hands and fingers, her back, her hips, her legs—all were sore, each insisting that she give it particular attention. But it was her feet she was afraid were not going to support her until the dinner bell rang.

Yet they did until it finally sounded. Dandre's machine stopped humming. The reels slowed and came to a standstill. She claimed her pot of lentils and slid down against the wall to sit on the floor, too tired to move, almost too tired to remove the lid from her little clay pot.

Danny had joined her before she had removed the lid, and then, before he could speak, they were both surprised by the approach of someone else.

"There's a table over there, on the other side. Most of the girls eat over there." It was Doll. She stood above them both and Dandre smiled up at her wearily.

"I do not feel as if I could get up from here again," she said.

The other girl's lips curved and parted, exposing a yellowish smile with one incisor missing.

"I know," she said. "You just want to sink down by your winder and go to sleep. But you'll get stiff down there and the floor's damp. Makes a body puny."

Doll extended her hand to assist Dandre back onto her feet, and gratefully the young woman accepted the help. She really did not know if she could have risen unassisted.

Once on her feet she reached down in turn and drew Danny up beside them.

"Me, too?" he asked.

Doll nodded and led the way to the end of the aisle and then across the breadth of the room to the other side and the rude table set against that wall. There were three other women seated on the benches attached to the legs of the table. Two of them were girls Dandre judged to be about her age. The other was an older woman, probably in her forties.

"Bett, Nan, this is Danny O'Brien and little Danny Fry. Danny, that's Bett with the red hair and Nan. This lady here is Sophy. She mothers the three of us and all the children, and you, too, if you let her."

The three women greeted the newcomers, and Sophy, the older woman, motioned the girl to sit down.

"Danny Fry I know," she said, patting the little boy's arm. "But you're new here. 'Danny,' too, did Doll say?"

"Danny is short for Dandre. It was my grandfather's name. Danny is more simple and does not require a full family history when I meet someone new. Usually," she said ironically, acknowledging the fact that she had, after all, given the women at the table some of her family history when she introduced herself.

"Well, Danny, you are welcome to join us here, though I'm sorry you had to come to Braid's to do it."

The younger girls nodded in agreement.

"A body has to eat, I suppose," one of the girls—Nan, if she remembered correctly—said.

"Not any too well," Doll complained, dropping onto the other bench across from Dandre. She put a kerchief on the rough board in front of her and unwrapped a lunch of three small potatoes that really did suggest that the wages she earned here were none too generous.

Bett was eyeing the new girl critically, noting her healthy face and figure, rare attributes here in the mill.

"You're new," she said. It was not a question. It did not have to be. Dandre's obvious well-being was sufficient evidence.

"I started here yesterday," Dandre said.

"And what brought you to Braid's?" Bett asked. "Or should I say, what brought you *down* to Braid's?"

Dandre looked at the curious, questioning faces and shrugged.

"As Nan said, one has to eat."

The girls nodded.

"But you can eat without workin' too hard, if you get my meaning. That is, if you've made it up to Mr. Juggs," Bett continued.

Dandre grimaced in disgust, and Nan and Bett laughed loudly and coarsely.

"Don't refuse 'im until you've 'eard Doll tell about 'ow nice 'e can make it," Bett crowed.

But Doll did not join in the hilarity.

"Shut yer yap, Bett," she warned darkly. "Juggs has tried to make it up to her already, but Danny's made it clear she's not interested. Maybe she's got the right idea. Bad as it was before, I think it's worse now. There's no gettin' away now." She took a bite of the cheese that, with the potatoes, constituted her lunch and chewed at it belligerently.

Sophy nodded sagely and patted the little boy's arm again. Danny Fry stood listening to the women with wide-eyed fascination. He had been very careful with the dried beef Vince had given him yesterday and had been able to bring a narrow strip of it to the mill today for lunch. Silently, he worked the unfamiliar treat in his mouth as the women talked around him.

"And was it bad before?" Dandre asked softly.

Nan, sitting beside her, nudged her arm.

"Doll was a doffer before Mr. Juggs put her on the line," she said.

"A doffer?" Dandre asked.

"You *are* new to this, ain't ya?" Bett pronounced.

"Doffing is a terrible cruel job," Sophy said, shaking her head sadly. She lifted her head to look toward the other end of the room. "Back there's where the weavin' is done. On great big frames, tall as you. When they gets full, the doffer has to stop them, take the flyers off, take the full rack down and carry it to the roller. Then she puts an empty rack up and sets the frame goin' again. It's not so hard up here. We just got one station, but there are five or six frames back there and the doffer girls have to be quick, runnin' from one frame to the next all day."

"I couldn't have lasted much longer back there, with or without Mr. Juggs," Doll said. "If he hadn't come along, I suppose I would have keeled over dead one day." She squeezed her thumb and forefinger together, mashing the bit of warm cheese she held. "Sometimes I think it would have been better if I'd stayed," she murmured.

"Aw, whatdaya mean?" Sophy cajoled. "You got a nice job, friends here." She looked at Nan and Bett, who both nodded dutifully. "Two or three bob to take home on Saturdays..."

"Not after Mr. Juggs and Mr. Donner take off their fines," Bett reminded her.

"Fines?" Dandre asked.

"They call it bad work," Nan said.

Bett snorted. "'Bad work' my arse. Work's the same, day in, day out, every day of the week. Mr. Braid just expects Donner to dock so much a week. I lost sixpence last week. It'll be Sophy's turn this. Doesn't matter. At least they don't dock the same one every week, unless they're after somebody's hide. And some they don't dock at all," she finished, looking pointedly at Doll, who colored miserably under her workmate's charge.

"I gets docked, same as the rest," she protested.

"Maybe less, maybe more," Sophy interjected. "My point being that Doll has to make a payment the rest of us don't. At least not now."

Again the girls nodded and murmured their reluctant ceding of Sophy's point. Dandre glanced uncomfortably at Doll, this time her own face coloring at Sophy's words.

"That goes around, too, don't it?" Nan asked. "We all takes our turn same as with the pay cut."

Bett laughed again. "It won't be my turn anytime soon. Not with Danny here now."

Danny Fry, who had been attending to a little square of bread Sophy had slipped to him, looked up surprised. But Dandre knew to which "Danny" Bett was referring. And to what she was referring.

"I will not," she denied vehemently.

"Oh, luv, it's what they all promise. But like the song says,

> A pretty lass through the factory door
> Finds her favors sold and boughten,
> For we are from dear Lancashire,
> And thank the Lord for cotton."

Sophy sang in a thin, nasal voice but Dandre recognized the tune as the one Mr. Jeremy Redding had introduced into the Woodley sitting room so long ago. She remembered Vincent said then that he did not like the song, and now she began to understand him.

"You make the mill sound like some sort of—brothel." Dandre spoke the whole sentence softly and dropped the final word to a barely audible whisper.

Bett chuckled and nodded her head, though Sophy tried to deny the allegation.

"That's not so. Not at all. It's entirely different. If certain—*services* are exchanged, it's between friends."

"If services are rendered, no money is exchanged. *That's* the difference," Bett said, or rather cried, for that young woman spoke in a naturally amplified voice that carried remarkably well. All of the workers catching a quick cat-nap against the mill wall opened their eyes and looked at the women gathered at the table.

"How horrible!" Dandre protested after most of the eyes had closed again.

Nan giggled. "'Orrible? I wouldn't call it 'orrible, luv. I'd call it right good fun."

Sophy smiled indulgently, then, patting Dandre's hand, she tried to calm the girl's obvious disgust.

"It's a break from all this, at least," the woman said, looking around the room.

"But Mr. Juggs?" Dandre asked disbelievingly.

"Oh, we're not talking about Mr. Juggs," Sophy said. "Nan meant some of the men here in the mill and other factory workers around the quarters."

"And as for Mr. Juggs," Bett began, then stopped. After a moment's pause she shrugged. "You do what you 'ave to, don't you? Ain't that so, Doll?"

Everyone turned to Doll, who hesitated for a moment herself and then nodded resignedly.

"And we're not as bad off as the mill children. Broken and twisted before they've lost their baby teeth. How does that next verse go, Sophy?" Nan asked, directing everyone's attention to the other end of the table and the older woman.

Sophy began to chant.

"That wee babe lost a hand or foot,
This one's bent and misbegotten,
But we are from dear Lancashire,
And thank the Lord for cotton."

"Ain't it the truth, though?" Bett said, finally dropping

the volume of her voice and looking around her sadly at the exhausted children, one or two of them not yet six years old, seated on the floor around the little table.

"How can you let it go on?" Dandre asked fiercely, forgetting for a moment the role she was assuming of being one of these working people.

"And just how are we supposed to change it?" Doll returned.

Dandre leaned across the table and whispered conspiratorially.

"Have you heard of a Mr. Richard Oastler?" she asked.

"You mean King Richard." Bett grinned. "Aye, we've 'eard of 'im. Who 'asn't? Sophy there claims she met the man once."

"I heard him in Leeds, five, maybe six years ago," Sophy said. "He was speaking for the Poor Act then. A darlin' of a man, he is. Broad shoulders, rosy cheeks, stands six foot or better. Better, I would say." The woman smiled and sighed softly, a faraway look of retrospection in her eyes. "And talk? The man could charm the stars down from the heavens! If he says it's about to rain, by gor, ye'd taken yer rain bonnet with you into that Seehara desert."

"You know he has turned his attention to the factory abuses, do you not?" Dandre asked, keeping her voice low.

"Well, of course we know that," Bett said, not being so careful. "And who workin' in a factory doesn't know that? But 'e's just one man—" she glanced at Sophy "—be he ever so fine a talker. What can one man do about this?" Now she looked around her at the rows of worktables and overhead at the confusing network of machinery.

"Maybe nothing, alone," Dandre said. "Obviously he will need help. He needs to know what goes on in here, and he needs witnesses who are willing to tell the country the cost in lives of their Sunday apparel."

As if suddenly recognizing a curious object of interest to be a live explosive, the four women drew back from Dandre and sat up straight in their chairs.

"I don't..." Bett began, but her words were cut short by the loud whistle that signaled the end of the lunch break.

Before the whistle had stopped sounding there was a rush of air and the leather thongs of Mr. Juggs's strap snapped against the tabletop between the women.

"Up and at 'em, ladies," he bellowed, then, lifting the strap off the table, he lashed it through the air again and brought it down on Danny Fry's back as he struggled to get up from the floor where he had been leaning against the table leg. "I said everybody back to work, boy!"

Doll was the one sitting closest to the boy when the blow of the lash drove him to his knees. The woman reached down to assist the child, shooting a venomous glance at Juggs.

The overlooker bent forward, pulling the boy's thin arm out of Doll's grasp and jerking him to his feet.

"Everybody!" he snarled, a note of genuine pleasure in his voice. The man enjoyed his work. He pushed Danny and another little boy and girl along in front of him in the direction of the machines beginning to wake from their short slumber.

When the overlooker's back was turned, Dandre leaned forward and spoke, but only loudly enough for the women to hear her.

"Think about it," she said.

Surprisingly, they looked as if they would.

Like the day before, the second half of the workday was longer than the endless first half. Mr. Juggs made frequent passes along Dandre's row, keeping the women nervously alert as his strap fell on the little pieceners, unable, as afternoon turned to evening and the bobbins never slowed, to be kept awake by fear or even pain.

Juggs did not strike her, but occasionally he stopped beside her, putting his rough hand against her back, across her shoulders, cupping her buttocks with the slab of his hand in a way that made her feel violated and unclean, always dangling the thongs of his strap against her legs as coercion.

Dandre would have gladly preferred one of the overlooker's vicious lashings.

Chesterton might have been back at Timbrey Hall. She had not seen him since she entered the factory with him that morning. She kept looking for him, glancing up eagerly whenever her peripheral vision detected a movement, often meeting the beady glitter of Mr. Juggs's eyes but never Vincent's clear blue ones.

And always and forever, the thread spun onto her reels. Around and around and around.

After one day Dandre could not imagine how anyone could bear the monotonous grind of that labor. As her second day of employment ended it was a struggle to recall anything else in her world but the thread and the reels, any other activity than tightening and smoothing and lifting the filled reels. Her life seemed to have nothing in it but cotton and machines. And Mr. Juggs.

"D'ya see how much better this is when I keep my friend here under control?"

Dandre cringed away from the grating whisper at her ear.

Once again the overlooker stood beside her, this time the fingers of his hand inching across her back and around her waist.

"Leave me alone," she said between gritted teeth.

The rumble of his laughter made the dark birthmark on his cheek jump.

"Or what?" he taunted. "What is it you think you can do to old Juggs?" Now his hand moved up her side and nudged against the underside of her thinly covered breast.

Dandre jerked away but was unable to free herself from his hand. One of her reels had filled and she was forced to lean forward, onto his disgusting hand, to pull it off its spindle.

"I have to put this in the bin," she said in what she meant to be a warning voice. But the lascivious leer on his face changed it to a cringing plea for which she hated herself.

He withdrew his hand and motioned to the bin with a mocking sweep of his arm.

"By all means," he said. "I like a girl who does her duty. Ask Doll there if I don't."

Without a word, Dandre pulled the heavy reel into her arms and turned to the bin. She raised her eyes and met Doll's pitying look. Pitying, but with a glimmer of relief.

Juggs suddenly pulled away from her workstation.

"We'll talk about this later," he said, and then turned away from her. Curious, Dandre sought for the source of his alarm and for the first time in all of that long day saw Chesterton two aisles over. His form rose above the work frames, which almost reached his shoulders, making him clearly visible and most of the room clearly visible to him.

At last. She felt a catch in her throat as the nearly hysterical thought formed in her mind: he has come to save me!

And with Chesterton there, it was true that Juggs left her and took himself to another part of the room. But Vincent's passage through the room had been purely coincidental. He had warned her that he could not always be there "to save her."

And if he could not, who would?

Chapter Thirteen

"*Now* do you believe me?" he whispered fiercely.

The long day was over and Dandre and Chesterton were once again seated at a table in Mrs. Boyle's homey establishment.

Mrs. Boyle had been cooking a mammoth roast all day, which was now being cut and diced and served in small amounts, with every combination of boiled, fried and baked vegetables Mrs. Boyle had at her command.

Vincent had asked for the potato, carrot and onion dish, while Dandre tried the corn chowder. The gentleman ordered bread to accompany the meal. When Mrs. Boyle brought the bowls of vegetables and meat, she also placed on the table two slices of coarse brown bread, two slices that together would have made a complete loaf. A loaf of bread so large as to make little Danny Fry's eyes open wide with wonder. Dandre did break her slice in two and wrapped half of it in her kerchief to give to the boy when she saw him the next day.

The tables in Mrs. Boyle's were small, and with no difficulty Chesterton was able to make her hear him, along with the nuances of justified anger, even when he lowered his voice.

"It does not matter what I believe," she whispered back to him. "I have to return. You see that now."

Chesterton extended his hand across the short distance between them and seized her hand in a grip as fierce as his whisper.

Dandre marveled at the difference between his touch and that other she had been forced to endure earlier. What was it, she wondered, that made her skin crawl beneath Mr. Juggs's repulsive touch and yet take pleasure in this hand, even though it was holding hers in anger? She ached for Vincent's touch, thrilled to the feel of his callused hand on hers, would have welcomed him touching every part of her body.

She had not been able to dismiss the unpleasant incident with Mr. Juggs for Vincent's sake tonight. For one thing, Vincent had been witness to part of it. And for another, Juggs's unwelcome familiarity had offended her more deeply than his physical abuse of her could. She had been shaken and had the distasteful feeling that she was dirty, that his hands had left some sort of filthy, oily, ineradicable vestige on her clothes and skin. Two hours later her face was still pale.

"What do you mean, you have to return?" Vincent demanded.

She nodded wearily. "I told you what Sophy and Nan said. I told you what Mr. Juggs did to Doll and her disgust with the situation. They talked to me, and they listened. You know I have to return."

Unhappily, Chesterton lowered his eyes and seemed to be concentrating on Dandre's hand as he rubbed his thumb back and forth across the soft white knuckles of her fingers.

The girl had made it infuriatingly clear that forbidding her to go into the mill was useless. And after her report of her discussion with the other women today, he was forced to admit that she had made more progress in two days than he had in two months.

He cringed to think of her putting herself within the sphere of Juggs's authority again, but his passage through the spinning room this afternoon had not been as purely coincidental as Dandre had supposed. If—*if*—the girl returned to the mill, he could arrange for a greater lack of equipment, more tool breakages, more useless conferences with Mr. Donner so that he could pass through the spinning room often, regardless of what distant post Mr. Juggs sent him to.

He had been set to work outside all day today and was even sent to the Exchange once with a communication for Mr. Braid. He knew full well that Mr. Donner usually sent one of the piecener boys with messages for the Exchange. Allowing the lads out into the open air to run and exercise their legs was one of the minuscule acts of charity Mr. Donner was able to perform within the parameters of his job.

But Mr. Juggs insisted he send Chess this afternoon, and though ostensibly the overlooker's superior, Donner was frankly intimidated by the man.

Not only did Vincent hate to leave Danny and Dandre alone in the mill, but he hesitated to make an appearance at the Manchester Exchange as mill worker Vince Chess. Mr. Vincent Chesterton of Timbrey Hall was not an unknown presence at the commerce center. He did not know Mr. Braid himself, but there was every possibility that men there would recognize him, perhaps even someone to whom Mr. Braid would be talking when Vincent delivered his message.

Nevertheless, the assignment was his. When he found the mill owner at last, in a tavern outside the Exchange, Vincent had recognized several erstwhile colleagues, but no one at all had seen the impeccable, wealthy, young and handsome Mr. Chesterton beneath the poor clothes and dirty face of the mill worker.

After the Exchange there were other outside duties, other errands, and Vincent was occupied all day, worrying at the restraints that kept him away from the spinning room. It did not occur to him until the day was nearly finished to drop his hammer. Actually, it took several smashes against the cobblestones that surrounded the mill to break the head off the tool.

"Damn!" he roared when the thing finally fell apart. "Broke my hammer!" he called to the carding room overlooker, who guarded the back entrance of the mill.

"That'll come out of your pay," the overlooker warned.

"I know it. But I can't do anything without a hammer."

"See Mr. Donner," the man said.

"That's where I'm headed," Vincent called over his shoulder, holding the broken pieces of the hammer for the overlooker to see.

It was on that pass through the spinning room that he had seen Juggs with his arm around Dandre. She told him it had not been the first time he had touched her that day, but she did say the overlooker had not harmed Danny at all. Somehow that assurance did not give him any comfort. To see that man with his hands on the girl, on this woman, had made him—and he had not thought such things really happened—see red for a moment.

But now, having discovered a way out of Juggs's noose, he would not leave Dandre alone in there for another entire day. If she would not allow him to do anything else, at least he could do that. The company rules decreed that any tool lost or broken was to be paid for by the worker who had been using it, but it was a very small price to pay for Dandre's safety. Chesterton was prepared to buy a new implement every hour, to retool the entire factory, if need be.

"Do you believe the women would be willing to talk to Oastler?" he asked at last. He had evidently smoothed her hand to perfection and now raised his eyes to hers again.

But he did not release her hand, nor did Dandre pull her fingers away.

"I believe so. Eventually they will. Soon," she quickly added, seeing the light of impatience in his eyes. "They are not ready to see him today, perhaps. But I will talk to them again tomorrow. I will not let the subject rest. If I could tell them when he will be here, if the day were actually approaching, I am sure that would help."

"I shall write to Mr. Oastler again and request he be here at the end of the month. Is that soon enough?"

Dandre nodded, but the trauma of the day's grueling labors and Mr. Juggs's nauseating familiarity were weighing heavily on her, and suddenly the effort of speaking seemed too great.

Chesterton lifted his hand from the back of hers and leaned across the table. Delicately he touched her face. She smiled and raised her hand to hold his fingers. She turned her head and kissed them.

"He only put his arm around me. It was nothing. It is over now." But the way she rested her soft cheek in the palm of his hand suggested it had been more than nothing.

He stood and pulled her to her feet, unwilling to leave her even long enough to pay Mrs. Boyle's modest fee. Together they walked back to the apartment building. They walked very slowly. Chesterton holding her to him, Dandre resting her head on his shoulder as they went.

"Danny was very good and brave today," she said.

"Did he see Juggs...?"

She shook her head. "I do not think so. He was working several stations down from me, out of direct line of sight."

"Good," Chesterton said.

"Yes, he would have found it embarrassing and degrading."

"More than that, he might very well have drawn injury to himself in trying to defend you."

She patted his arm. "Do not worry. Danny Fry is wise enough not to challenge Mr. Juggs and invite his wrath."

Now Chesterton shook his head. "I think Danny is the sort of lad whose self-interest is no interest at all when someone he loves is threatened."

"I think he is trying to grow up to be just like his hero," the girl said, smiling.

Chesterton did not respond to the flattery he found embarrassing, but in a moment he quietly murmured, "He is a good boy."

"I understand now why you could not desert him," Dandre said. "Do you understand why I cannot?"

Chesterton nodded in defeat.

They walked in silence for a few minutes.

"When this is over, I should like to take Danny into our home," Chesterton said.

Dandre caught her breath and pulled the man beside her to a stop.

"Into *our* home?" she whispered.

Chesterton lightly kissed the matted strands of hair on top of her head, still damp from the humidity of the mill and her own perspiration.

"Into Timbrey Hall, where you shall reign as queen," he whispered.

He had not knelt upon a silken cushion, she had not blushed and murmured faint refusals before daintily offering him the back of her hand, but it was the sweetest proposal Dandre could possibly imagine.

"I should like that very much," she told him. "With my husband and my son beside me."

Softly, tenderly, he held her in his arms and bent his head to kiss her lips this time, sealing their engagement.

She sighed and rested her head against his shoulder. Slowly they walked along the boardwalk, as if strolling under the scented lilacs along a riverbank instead of through the busy, noisy, stinking thoroughfare of an industrial city.

At last they reached the stone steps, and then Mrs. Bink's desk, and then the door to her room.

Mrs. Bink peeked curiously around her doorframe and saw the two young people talking together in hushed tones for a few moments, and then Vince kissed the girl. With more fervor and passion the girl returned his kiss.

Oh, my dear boy, the landlady said to herself, an invitation engraved on a white card could be no plainer. What are you waiting for?

Vince pulled himself away at last, though, and opened the door behind the girl. He said something else and she nodded. Then she went into the room and shut the door.

Hastily Mrs. Bink pulled her head into her own room before the young man could see her, but her lip was curled contemptuously.

Who *do* they think they are fooling? she asked herself.

At Dandre's door, Vincent told her he would rise early and go around to Mrs. Boyle's for some bread and boiled eggs for their lunches. He reminded her at what time they would have to leave in the morning. She agreed, and perhaps to escape the utter exhaustion in her eyes as much as anything else, he kissed her. The kiss she returned was not exhausted at all. It was full of longing and the offer of sweet pleasures, suggesting that Vincent's proposal earned him special privileges and Dandre did not want to wait for Timbrey Hall. It threatened to start a fire that neither one of them had the strength to extinguish—or enjoy. Reluctantly he pulled himself away.

"*Can* you return tomorrow?" he asked again, searching her eyes.

"I can if you will be there for me," she said.

"Always," he promised.

It was a promise they both prayed he could keep.

* * *

Much to Mrs. Bink's disgust, and occasionally, quite frankly, to Dandre's disgust, as well, Vincent left her alone in her room every evening and knocked on her door every morning to rouse her. When she opened her door he was always dressed, even shaven most mornings, with something for their breakfast and lunch in the mill that he had purchased the night before or been out to get that morning.

Dandre really did not know how he was able to do it. Every morning it became more of a struggle to drag her consciousness from the blessed recesses of sleep, to pull her aching body from the bed, to slip into her smock, which had become soiled and torn on the sleeve and skirt.

Yet every morning she did it. And when she was dressed she would join Vincent in the hall and together they trudged to the mill.

Mr. Juggs did not cease his unwelcome attentions, but with the regular sabotage of his work implements, Chesterton was able to interrupt the overlooker before his groping hands could have been defined as molesting.

Somehow Dandre endured it. At noon every day she would join Doll and Nan and Bett and Sophy at the rough lunch table. They were soon joined by the youths and older children who worked in the mill, and Dandre was afforded a close study of the effects of long-term factory employment.

The boys and girls were all undersize, with sallow skin, bloodshot, red-rimmed eyes and hacking coughs that would never again clear their lungs. Most of the children suffered from rickets brought on by insufficient exposure to sunlight. Some of those young people who had been subject to conditions in the mill for an extended period of time had a weakness in their lungs that signaled the onset of consumption.

In addition, most of the mill workers, beginning at eleven or twelve or even younger, found their only relief from their labor and the pain it occasioned in alcohol or laudanum, which they purchased instead of food with their weekly wages.

She noted the misshaping of thigh bones, the inward bending of knees, the curvature of the spine, which she could tell was Danny Fry's tendency after his short employment.

When the children became pubescent they also, almost universally, became promiscuous. England was producing an entire generation of ill-formed, unhealthy, illiterate, immoral young people. Young people not so much living as barely existing in a world that had been thrust upon them.

The workers, the young ones especially, were interested in what Dandre had to say. They loved to hear her denounce the working conditions and tell them that they should demand better. They wondered, perhaps, how she could afford to put her livelihood at risk like this, but it was gratifying to hear her say the words out loud that they all said to themselves.

"These machines ought to have fences or rails around them," she exclaimed. "Of course hands get caught in the belts and wheels if they are left open like that."

"Mate of ours—you remember old Charlie?—'e was taken by that wheel over there," one of the older boys told her. "It was 'is sleeve what did it. The sleeve of 'is shirt. Charlie was walkin' by, wheel grabs 'is shirt, shirt pulls old Charlie in, and that was it. 'E was all mashed and broken, poor bloke. Died right then, of course. Good thing, too, says I."

"It's not the machines, as bad as they are, that are the real devils," Nan said.

Everyone who heard her nodded in agreement.

"Once I run away," another of the boys said. "Got past the overlooker and took off. 'Course, I couldn't run very fast because of my legs, and they caught me in, oh, no more'n 'alf an hour. The overlooker, not Juggs then but another fiend as black as 'ell, took me into the back room, tied a rope across my mouth and flogged me with a hazel stick till the skin was flayed off my back.''

"And you came back?" Dandre gasped.

"Not right away," the boy said, shaking his head. "But as soon as I was able. I 'ad to, so's my mum could eat, and my little sister. I wasn't goin' to send '*er* in 'ere! I'd kill 'er myself before I sent 'er in 'ere.''

They all sat around the lunch table, telling Dandre chilling stories, but so far no one was willing to lay his job on the line and agree to testify before Mr. Sadler's committee. As the lad who had been beaten so eloquently expressed it, the loss of his job might mean that his mother or sister would have to come to the mills to work. And he was not the only one who would rather see his sister dead than put to work in the factories.

Dandre kept them talking, though, and by the end of the week they were all anxious to meet the famous Richard Oastler, anyway. Hearing "King Richard" talk was not too dangerous, as long as word did not get back to Mr. Braid. What was the harm in just listening to the man?

Saturday was a half day, which meant they began at five o'clock, worked until noon and then stayed to clean the mill thoroughly before they were allowed to leave.

It was then that Vince washed and shaved himself, trimming his own hair, brushing his own clothes, transforming himself back into Mr. Vincent Chesterton.

Not allowing a single word of protest, he took Dandre with him as far as a fine hotel in the center of Manchester.

"Now you stay here and sleep until I return. Anything you want you may have a boy bring for you." He pushed a large handful of bank notes into her hand. *"Anything,"* he reiterated.

She smiled up at him.

"Why do I need these?" she asked. "I was paid today. I am a woman of independent means now."

She held out the three bits of silver that were recompense for five and a half days of slave labor.

He curved her fingers around the coins.

"Save them for your trousseau," he said, then put his lips next to her ear and whispered, "If what you are wearing costs no more than that, it will ease my conscience when I tear it from your body."

Dandre giggled. It was wonderful to see Vincent assume his rightful place as the very handsome, debonair, very *proper* Mr. Chesterton, but she was guiltily pleased to discover part of him was still the coarse and earthy Vince Chess.

After the moment's levity, Chesterton grew very serious again.

"You can come back with me," he said. "In fact, you know I want you to."

"I know."

"The interview with Oastler is arranged. And as persuasive as you have been, my dear, he is a mesmerist and will instantly charm them, instantly lay their doubts to rest, instantly convince them that for their good and the good of their children they *must* testify."

"I do not doubt it. But I would like to meet him myself..."

"I would be able to arrange a private meeting anytime..."

"And more than that, I want to witness the denouement of what we have started here."

He took her hands, the one clutching the coins and the other the bank notes.

"You and I did not begin this movement, and even the passage of Mr. Sadler's undiluted bill would not be its denouement. The changes may take time, but eventually they will come, though you and I may not even *live* to see its final denouement.''

''I will not leave Danny alone in there.''

At last she had presented an inarguable reason for her continued employment in the factory.

''Very well,'' he said. ''But you can rest for the next day and a half, at least.''

She touched his cheek.

''I wish you could, too.''

''Soon.''

''And I wish Danny could be here with us.''

''He will be.''

Reluctantly, Chesterton left her, making certain her accommodations were the most luxurious that all of Manchester offered.

As the door closed behind him, Dandre sank to the mattress of the bed. She could imagine no cloud being fluffier. She closed her eyes to rest them for a moment and opened them six hours later in a perfectly dark room. For a panicked moment she was afraid that she had fallen asleep after Vince's call and they would both be late for the mill. But the moment she put her hand against the cool, silky sheets, she knew she was not in Mrs. Bink's rooming house, and the next moment she remembered where she was.

On the heels of that realization came the one that she was very hungry. A week ago she might have said she was famished, but in the week since she had seen what ''famished'' meant.

It was at least ten o'clock by now, perhaps closer to midnight, but on a Saturday evening in the lively metropolis of Manchester there were still sounds of full activity outside her door. Dandre struck one of the lucifer matches supplied to the hotel guests and lighted the lamp on the table in the middle of the room. In the soft light of a single lamp Dandre studied the walls of the room until she found the bell that would bring one of the hotel runners to her room.

"Yes'm?" the boy asked not three minutes later, touching the red cap he wore as she opened her door a crack.

Dandre ordered one of the deluxe hotel dinners, complete with a cut of beef, gravy, roasted potatoes, flaky rolls that rivaled Mrs. Boyle's in size and a cream-filled pastry that was the dessert specialty of the hotel.

When the boy returned with the order he was unable to carry the tray jauntily on one upraised hand but supported it, with some effort, with both hands and appeared relieved to set it down on the table.

Dandre paid with one of Chesterton's bank notes, pausing to consider that this meal cost more than she could earn in a month at the mill. Her pause was very short, though. Almost before the lad had closed the door behind him, the girl was seated and busily employing the knife and fork.

She cleaned every crumb off the laden tray, then set the tray outside her door, washed her face, put on her nightgown and went to bed again, where she slept for another ten hours.

Though Dandre had imagined she might attend a church service and receive food for her soul as well as her body, when she awoke and stretched the next morning she admitted she did not want to leave the room. She was not sure she would even change out of her nightgown.

Six days shalt thou labor, but on the seventh day thou shalt rest. Wasn't that what the Lord had commanded Moses?

She rang the service bell again and ordered a breakfast almost as large as the dinner she'd eaten the night before, salving her conscience, as she returned to the bed and gathered the pillows around her, with the thought that she was strictly obeying the word of the Lord.

After breakfast she had a hot bath drawn and felt as if she had never experienced a bath before. A week's worth of fatigue and grime and even the clinging film of Mr. Juggs's touch finally floated away on the scented steam.

It was almost ten o'clock that night when a soft tap sounded on her door. The delicate vision who opened the door took Chesterton's breath away. Her smile was warm, her eyes dark, half-shadowed; the outline of the auburn tresses surrounding her face was softly indistinct as strands floated past her eyes, around her cheeks and came to an uneasy rest against her neck.

"I have missed you," she said. Her voice was low and throaty. She rested her head against the hand that held the door open and allowed herself the luxury of simply looking at Vincent's dark brown hair, his strong chin, the breadth of his chest. She remembered the muscles of his arms, of his legs, from that very first day when he pulled her from harm's way and held her to him.

The memory brought a glow to her cheeks and eyes that Chesterton recognized as an unmistakable signal.

"You have taken my advice, I see," he said, smiling.

"I have," she replied, pushing the door open for him to enter, following him into the room.

"And you are completely rested?" he asked.

Dandre took a moment to shut the door behind them before she answered.

"Completely," she said.

"The bed was comfortable?"

"Why don't you try it for yourself?" she invited.

"May I?" he asked.

"It was your money that paid for it. I certainly believe you have the right to test it."

Vincent sat on the edge, bouncing lightly to test the spring of the mattress.

"Very nice," he said approvingly. "Especially after my hard ride, yesterday and again this evening."

"Was it very difficult?" she asked him.

"Oh, well, not difficult, I suppose. It is not difficult to sit in a saddle, but despite what imaginative tales of romance may suggest, a long ride on a horse is just a long ride on a horse. And I was anxious to get back, so I pushed old Bandit harder than I should have, I suppose. He worked up quite a lather. We are both exhausted, and both emit a rather strong odor, I am afraid."

"Not at all," Dandre said.

Without another word, she knelt directly in front of him and took hold of one of his shod feet.

"What are you doing?" he asked.

"You suggested that you are tired after your ride. I am trying to help you relax," she said.

She pulled back on the heel of his boot and felt the foot give a little inside. She eased her effort a bit to make the procedure as lengthy as possible.

"Actually, this is not relaxing me at all," he warned, but his warning was unnecessary. She was very well aware of what she was doing.

"How did you find things at Timbrey Hall?" she asked.

"Jeremy sprained his ankle in the stable on Wednesday. He was forced to spend all of Thursday in the library with his foot up on the ottoman."

"How unfortunate," Dandre murmured.

They were both more interested in the steady pull she was exerting that was slowly unsheathing his foot. When one boot was off she took his other foot in her hands.

"My Aunt and Uncle Woodley?" she asked.

"I did not see them. Neither my sister nor my brother-in-law mentioned them, and if they told me the Misses Humphries have decided to renew their piano studies and Rawley Cooper fired his foreman for stealing a bale of hay, surely they would have told me any news from the Woodley home."

Now both of Vincent's boots lay on their sides almost under the bed. Dandre began to roll down the top of his stocking over one ankle. When both stockings were off, she crumpled them together and tossed them beside the tipped traveling boots. The topics of Oldham neighbors and Timbrey Hall had been forgotten. The room was filled now with a heavy silence, accented rather than disturbed by their steady breathing.

She put her slim hands flat against his bare feet, rubbing them lightly, concentrating on the soft skin and the bones she could distinguish under her fingertips.

With a hand on either leg now, she caressed his calves, able to feel the tenseness of his muscles through the dense fabric of his trousers.

The gown that covered her, more or less, was of a diaphanous, flimsy material, opaque only because of its several layers—in some alluring places not as many layers as elsewhere.

Vincent was entranced by the floating material, as he had been by the loose strands of her hair when she opened the door. He reached down and took a single layer of the material that formed the ruffle about her throat. He held the film between thumb and forefinger and stroked it lightly.

"This is a beautiful gown," he said. "I do not believe I have seen it before."

She smiled. "It is a peignoir," she whispered. "It is hardly the sort of thing I would wear in public."

"I am not the public, then?" he asked teasingly.

"Oh no, Vinnie Chess. Like Danny, I have made you my personal hero. My personal and very *private* hero." Her hands had come to a rest on his knees and she looked up into his eyes.

"*You* are beautiful," he said. It was the sort of comment that usually precedes a kiss, but Vincent did not lower his head or draw her to him. Instead, he sat quietly and carefully studying every part of her face and form. She allowed him the same liberty she had taken with him when she first answered his knock.

At last his eyes returned to her face.

"I think you should take off your coat," Dandre told him.

"I should?"

"Well, it is warm in here and we want to make you comfortable." She spoke very seriously and matter-of-factly, defending a perfectly mundane, logical suggestion.

Vincent smiled. "And should I take off anything else?" he asked.

"We will see," she said.

As he pulled his jacket off his arms, Dandre saw a twinge of pain cross his face.

"Something?" she asked.

"Oh, my shoulder. It is a little stiff," he said.

Dandre stood and went around to the other side of the bed, where she crawled up onto the mattress herself to kneel behind him. She put her hands onto his shoulders on either side of his neck and began to press and coax the tense muscles to relax.

Vincent made small, appreciative sounds as her fingers and the palms of her hands found and loosened some of the tight knots of muscles.

After a few minutes of her ministrations, Dandre put her lips next to his ear.

"Perhaps you ought to take off your shirt and lie down," she suggested.

"That sounds like a wonderful idea."

In almost less time than it took her to suggest it, his shirt was on the floor beside his boots and stockings. At Dandre's instructions, he turned onto his stomach, and she continued to rub his back, pushing the heels of her hands into the flesh of his shoulder blades, her two thumbs caressing his spine.

In the silence of the room, Dandre considered the difference this man had made in her life, the part of her life he had become. When she was with him, she was willing to trudge to the mill every morning, would stand on her feet in the heat and the haze of cotton puffs all day for the reward of glimpsing him, could bear Mr. Juggs's lashes and his more noxious familiarities, was willing, in fact, to enter the very jaws of hell itself with him beside her.

Yet in the thirty hours he had been away, she had had no desire even to rise from her bed or dress herself.

"Vincent, do you not find it interesting . . ." she began.

There was no break in the rhythm of his breathing, no acknowledgment that she had spoken. There was, however, a very soft snore.

"Vincent?" she asked softly, stopping her gentle massage and putting her face down close to his.

His eyes remained closed.

She smiled. It was not a happy smile, but it was forgiving. When this was over they would have a lifetime together and she would see to it that they were not always tired when they retired for the evening. But tonight he needed his sleep.

She rose and kissed his cheek lightly, then, pulling one of the fluffy comforters over his bare shoulders and taking the other one for herself, she sat in the upholstered chair beside the window and closed her eyes.

She would rest herself, but from this chair she could hear the bell in the Manchester tower as it struck the hours and would wake Vincent when three *bongs* shook the air.

Chapter Fourteen

The summer shipments of baled cotton had begun to arrive at the Liverpool docks. The mighty sailing vessels, some combining the new steam engines with their canvas rigging and some not, were crowding into the Liverpool harbor. Huge pyramids of the tightly packed cotton filled the warehouses, rose in the open air of the shipyards, greeted the incoming ships at the water's edge.

The massive accumulation of raw cotton was represented on small slips of paper, which were traded in the Manchester Exchange for other small slips of paper representing massive accumulations of gold and silver.

Traders and mill owners in swallow-tailed coats and tall hats were at the Exchange from ten o'clock in the morning until five o'clock every evening, furiously passing the slips of paper back and forth until the air appeared to be filled with a cloud of fluttering white butterflies.

Mr. Braid, owner of Braid's Cotton Mill, returned to his fine home on Cheetham Hill in the evening simply exhausted. If he had to slap one more shipper on the back or buy one more fellow mill owner a drink, he knew he would simply collapse.

As he entered his home after such a day, Leonard, the serving man, would take his coat from him and his wife would greet him with a consoling peck on the cheek.

"Oh, my poor darling," she would say. "Come sit down. You look all done in. How was it today?"

"Beastly, Mrs. Braid. Perfectly beastly. Have Millie bring me a Scotch and soda, will you? I need something to revive me."

Mrs. Braid would summon the maid, order the drink and then escort her husband to his favorite chair in the sitting room.

"Did you buy any cotton?" she asked.

Mr. Braid snorted rather uncouthly into the crystal tumbler that held his Scotch.

"Oh yes, my dear. I bought some cotton. I bought a great deal of cotton."

He finished his drink and then allowed a smile to settle on his lips. It was exhausting, certainly, but it always did a man good to get out and work hard sometimes.

Sylvia Braid smiled a silken smile to herself as she watched her husband's eyes close for a well-deserved nap.

Production at the mill had been stepped up owing to the season of the year and the purchases of large orders of raw cotton Braid had made.

The workers were required to be at the mill by four o'clock in the morning now, which made it necessary for Dandre to wake Vincent from his heavy sleep at three o'clock.

She had changed from the alluring dressing gown to the little white pinafore, which was hardly more concealing. She did not like to think of the comments that must have been made in the laundry room of the Sheffington Hotel when she sent the filthy work dress down with the bellhop to be cleaned, but the garment had been returned to her smelling fresh and looking clean except for the stains that would not wash out. She had requested no starch—heaven forbid, it made her skin chafe just to think of the starched material clinging to her trunk and legs in the hot, damp air of the mill—and that the two holes she knew about and any others they might find of which she was unaware be patched and mended. Both requests had been met and Dandre felt as if she could face another day at the mill. Which proved how refreshed she was. She had not felt as if she could face the mill again since the second morning here in Manchester.

"Vincent?" she whispered, touching his hand. "Vincent, it is time we left."

"What? Where? Dandre?" He woke with confusion but quickly oriented himself. "I did not mean to doze. Will you not join me?" He held his hand out toward her, inviting her to his bed.

"You did more than doze. You have slept the night away. What there was of it. It is three o'clock now, and we must be at the mill by four o'clock this morning. Remember?"

Chesterton groaned. Evidently he did remember.

He rolled to his side and then sat up. As much as he loved the woman who stood in front of him, as much as he desired her, he had enjoyed that sleep. And his neck and shoulders felt wonderful.

Hastily he pulled his shirt and footwear back on and the two of them scurried from the hotel.

They had to go to his room at Mrs. Bink's first so Vincent could change to his mill clothes, but he accomplished that in less than three minutes. They stopped at the bakery for meat pies and at the fruit seller's stall for some early plums. Not only the mill but the merchants that served the workers were required to open earlier and earlier because of the incoming cotton.

By now the hour of four o'clock was fast approaching and Chesterton took the girl's hand in his as they sprinted toward the mill on Withing Grove Street. Feet pattered quickly before and behind them, impetus being added as they neared the factory and saw the steam and smoke already boiling from the tall stacks.

Bleary-eyed children, roused from their beds by fretful mothers at two-thirty, pushed through the factory entrance. Nan's dress was not fastened at the back, and Bett had failed to remove the scrap of material she wore as a nightcap over her hair.

But no matter what the hour, early or late, Mr. Juggs was there before them, his evil appearance unchanged.

"Get down here!" he roared, cracking his strap once in the air and once against the back of one of the sleepy children. "Machines are going. Spindles are turning. You're docked tuppence if you're not at your stations in half a minute!"

He grabbed a little girl as she climbed down the short ladder to the workroom floor. As if she were no more than a dried autumn leaf caught in an October gale, Juggs tore the child from the ladder and threw her onto the floor. She stumbled and fell, knocking her head against one of the metal supports of a workstation.

In her haste, Sophy stumbled over her and landed heavily on her knee. The pain was excruciating. The woman wanted to howl in agony, but there was no time for that now. She pushed herself to her feet and limped to her post. Mr. Juggs would not fine her today, not for being late, anyway.

Dandre and Doll watched the older woman compassionately as she took her place, but no one paid any attention to the tiny piecener girl Juggs had thrown down. Penny Braugh's head had struck the pole with a crack that was not heard above the woman's heavier fall.

Dazed, the child rose from the floor, turning from side to side and then completely around, trying to find her workstation, which was directly in front of her.

To say that no one noticed the little girl was to say that none of the adults or older children saw her hit her head, but at the girl's level, Danny Fry saw the injury and was puzzled by her confusion. As she began to wander from her spot, the boy grabbed her arm and led her to the small bobbin already flapping a broken thread against the steel post underneath Sophy's workstation.

He received a stinging blow from Mr. Juggs's strap for his trouble when he returned to his own bobbins.

"Mind your work, boy. If you haven't got enough to do we can set up another spool or two."

"Yes, sir. I mean, no, sir," the boy hurriedly replied. "I was only..."

"No talking!" the overlooker warned angrily. The strap he held twitched impatiently, but he did not crack it again.

With no more attempted explanations, Danny turned to his work, but he afforded a worried glance at Penny now and then. Her eyes still had not cleared to alert attention. This was different from the glaze of sleep, with which Danny was very well acquainted. He had the uneasy feeling that Penny was going further away than sleep.

Juggs continued his slow progress past the women and children and spinning threads. Doll stood next to Sophy. Juggs grimaced, though it was hard to make so fine a distinction just by looking at his face.

Doll, there, had hurried away between Nan and Bett last Saturday. He had gone to the little boarding place where they all stayed as soon as Donner let him go, but she wasn't there. None of them were. He'd had to pay for his pleasures this weekend, and judging by the uncomfortable itching at his crotch that he was beginning to suffer, his merchandise had not been clean. She better not have passed on anything that would necessitate a visit to the shop infirmary or he'd find the slut and teach her a thing or two. *Another* thing or two. For free.

He laid the strap across Doll's back as he passed, in partial payment for what she had put him through. But no lashing he could deliver would be full payment. That he would deliver later, when he could feel her skin and bones beneath his fists.

He barely noticed Doll's flinch and outcry. By then he was focused on the real source of his discomfort and frustration.

Dandre stood putting tension on a lax thread, acutely aware that the overlooker had come to a halt behind her. His unwarranted lashings of Danny and Doll were not so unusual as to alert her to his dangerous humor. She was steeling herself for his malignant touch when the strap came down across her shoulders, and then, before she could draw in the breath that had been surprised from her, the strap fell against her back.

"What . . . ?" she cried, half-turning in protest.

She saw the thongs descending again and turned away enough to save her eyes. The strap left three stinging welts against her cheek and a fourth open cut next to her ear, which immediately began to bleed.

"No talking! Watch your line there. You know the rules. Now get back to work!" He whirled around to find all the reelers and pieceners stopped and staring at the blood. Juggs and his strap were customary evils, but blood was something of a novelty, even in Braid's factory. "Back to work all of you!" he cried, raising the strap threateningly.

Dandre, hurt and frightened, took up the slack in her thread again, wiping the blood from her ear with the short sleeve of her dress. The blood had stopped flowing and now was drying against her cheek.

Juggs moved along the row of spinners, a furious snarl twisting his lips.

Dandre took a breath and became aware that her hands were shaking badly. She glanced sideways to try to locate Mr. Juggs and found Doll's eyes on her.

The other girl raised her brows questioningly, but Dandre shook her head slightly, indicating that she was not so badly hurt that she could not continue.

Danny had been horrified at the episode, and as Chesterton had suggested, he was not willing to be a silent wit-

ness to such treatment of the woman who claimed so much
of his affection. All of his affection except that which he
lavished upon Vince. And little Danny Fry had a great deal
of affection to distribute.

At Juggs's first blow he had taken a half step forward,
but Nan laid a hand on his shoulder. He looked up questioningly and missed the overlooker's second blow. Nan
shook her head slightly, warning the boy against taking action that would only bring harm to himself without easing
the situation for Dandre.

He cried out softly when he saw the cut that the strap left
on her face and strained against Nan's hand. But the young
woman held his shoulder tightly, and with the rest of the
pieceners and reelers he was forced to watch Dandre meekly
turn to her work again, her cheek and the white sleeve of
her dress red with smeared blood.

An uneasy atmosphere filled the room as each of the
workers watched Mr. Juggs under lowered brow, tensing as
the overlooker drew near, releasing their breath as he
passed, then stiffening again whenever he drew near
Dandre, each one waiting for the strap —or worse.

Attached to the billy-spinner was an iron-ended rod
called the billy-roller. Juggs had been known, in fits of rage,
to use the billy-roller. It had been some time since the last
beating. Then he had broken a girl's arm, one of the spinners. Her name was Molly Toolson and Mr. Donner spon-
sored her at the infirmary, but she did not return to the
factory and the report was eventually circulated that all had
not gone as it should with the setting of the bone and eventually she lost the arm. Some said she was in the poor-
house now, others that she had been granted transport to
Botany Bay with a rough lad she had taken up with. Some
said she had died.

Juggs was not remorseful, but Mr. Donner reported the
incident to Mr. Braid and returned with a warning from the
mill owner that another such occurrence would mean the

loss of Juggs's job and Mr. Donner was to personally no-tify the police, going so far as to sign a complaint and ask that a warrant be issued if necessary. Mr. Donner's ac-tions, naturally, had not endeared the overlooker to him, and Mr. Donner had separated himself even further from the workroom, but the incident had checked Juggs's homicidal rages—until today.

Molly Toolson had been another pretty girl—though not as pretty as Dandre—who had resisted Juggs's familiari-ties. That additional bit of information, not available to Dandre herself, was what made spines tense and knuckles whiten each time the overlooker paced by the girl.

It was the drama and the universal attention being paid Dandre that allowed the weakening condition of little Penny Braugh to go unnoticed for so long. Even Danny became intent on Dandre and her blood-streaked face and the murderous light that was beginning to gleam in the darkness under Mr. Juggs's overhanging brow.

But the evil light filling Juggs seemed to be draining the light from the little girl. Sophy, only paying haphazard at-tention to her reels, did not notice that her piecener was no longer working, that the small bobbin under her table was spinning, the thread soiled and broken.

The girl slumped forward, her hands dangling heavily at her sides. Her eyes were unfocused and a stream of saliva inched from the corner of her mouth. Her face had be-come chalky white and her breathing very slow and shal-low.

Mr. Juggs, at the other end of the line, was just turning to make his return pass when Penny gasped suddenly and sank to her knees.

Danny, working at the next station, saw her fall and left his bobbin to help her, forgetting his fear of Mr. Juggs in the deeper fear of what was claiming Penny. He dropped to his knees next to her and peered into her face, trying to find the little girl he knew there.

"Penny?" he whispered.

So frightened was he by her lifeless eyes that he did not hear the overlooker's heavy step approaching. The blow fell on the boy's back, driving him to the floor. It was not the billy-roller he held, but he had turned his strap and now swung the wooden handle.

"I said see to your own work! Are your ears not working, boy? What will it take to mend them, d'ya think?" Each sentence was punctuated by a blow from the strap handle.

Danny lay cowering under the attack. The handle struck his shoulder, his side and the upper part of his leg, but miraculously there was no snapping of bones or tearing of flesh.

Attention turned from Dandre to the children underneath Sophy's workstation. Nan and Bett stood watching, fearful that if they stepped forward to save the boy their lives would be forfeit. Sophy, who had managed to survive factory work longer than any of them, even took a step back from her post to allow Mr. Juggs more room.

But one of the reelers was willing to brave the overlooker's frenzy of rage. Dandre knew, though she had never been witness to the horror before, that she was about to witness a cold-blooded murder. The overlooker was going to beat the child until Danny was dead, and perhaps he would continue to beat the boy's flesh long after he was dead. She also knew that Danny Fry was not the focus of Juggs's rage; that in fact, it had no focus, but would concentrate itself on anyone at hand. She knew Juggs would turn on her, would strike her with the handle of the strap, doubtless until she was senseless. Probably until it was she who lay dead beneath his blows.

Without hesitation the young woman dropped her thread, ran around Sophy as she stepped backward and flung herself at the overlooker, clutching his upraised arm, deflecting the fourth blow from the child.

The unexpected attack knocked Mr. Juggs off balance. He lost his footing, but he did not fall. He stumbled, caught himself and whirled around. In the process of finding his footing and identifying his assailant, he loosened Dandre's hold on his arm and threw her onto the floor. On hands and knees she scrambled to put herself between the overlooker and the children. Roaring like a maddened beast, Juggs turned, hunting for the fool who had stopped him. Someone was going to die here.

The handle of his strap cracked against the stone floor. The reelers and pieceners had all stepped back now, forming a horrified half circle around the man, the woman and the two children underneath Sophy's worktable.

At last Juggs located his attacker. When he recognized Dandre, his eyebrows rose so far in surprise as to almost unhood his eyes. Then the scowl and his snarl deepened.

"You!" he shouted. It was less a word than a cry of bloody victory.

He turned the strap, gripping the handle, cracking the thongs as he stepped toward her. He wanted to hurt her, but he did not want to beat her senseless. Not yet. Not to begin with. He wanted her conscious and screaming for as long as possible.

She huddled over the children, exposing her back to the lash. She was relieved to hear Danny groan against her bosom even as the leather thongs struck her. Juggs swung his arm in a continuous motion so the blows rained upon her back hard and fast. In moments the thin material of her dress was shredded and the leather nipped at the naked flesh beneath. The next blow drew blood. Droplets sprang to the surface in two thin lines along her back. Juggs licked his heavy, purple-hued lips.

Dandre had cried out once or twice, but she had not screamed. Juggs wanted to hear her scream, wanted to hear her beg him for mercy, which he would not grant. As the blows continued to fall, though, he realized she was not going to scream; she was going to die beneath his hand before he heard her plead for mercy.

So be it.

He raised the strap, pausing for a moment to grasp the thongs and turn the handle out again. If she did not want mercy, then she would receive none.

Vincent had been set unloading bales of cotton, he and one of the frame stretchers. The other man was a product of factory life. He stood only five feet five inches, if that tall. He was scrawny and pale. He squinted shortsightedly and addressed his task with little interest and less energy. The red of his eyes suggested habitual drinking, a habit that was universal with the factory workers. In short, when Vincent and Roberts were set to a task, it was Vincent who performed the labor.

His heart sank when Mr. Donner summoned him to the office that morning and commissioned him. This probably was not even of Juggs's orchestration, since Vince was the logical workman to assign to the heavy task.

The job kept him outside all morning, pulling the heavy bales from the wagon onto the loading dolly and then stacking them inside the warehouse attached to the factory. The task was gratifyingly physical and let him breathe the air of Manchester's city center. By no standard could it be termed "fresh air," but after the tropical heat of the mill itself, the Manchester air seemed to Vincent to be a breath of the open country.

He would have very nearly been enjoying himself, but his labors prevented any pass through the spinning room. There was no tool to break or lose, nothing he could finish quickly, repair quickly or put out of order quickly. Only bales of cotton to load and unload, load and unload, load and unload.

It was almost noon before the wagon was emptied and the bales had been pushed and pulled and even lifted into an orderly mass in the wide, echoing storage room. Roberts sat on one of the canvas-wrapped bales, panting heavily, wiping the sweat flowing from his forehead. Vincent jumped from the last bale he had pulled into place to stand on the floor next to his workmate.

"That it?" Roberts asked.

"That is it, my friend," Vincent told him, taking out his own handkerchief to wipe his face.

"What time do you think it is?" Roberts asked.

"Noon, if not later, I would say."

"We'd hear the bell from here, wouldn't we?" Roberts asked.

"Not necessarily," Vincent said. "We had best go in."

The other man sighed heavily and remained sitting where he was.

"They don't know we're done. No one's 'ere to tell us what to do. To get up and get busy. To go 'ere or go there. To lift this and pull on that and carry the other to 'ell and back. No one knows we're finished. No one'd *believe* we're finished if we went in now. I say we just sit for a while. In fact, we could sit for the rest of the day if we felt like it." Roberts fell back to lie the length of the cotton bale. "And believe me, I feel like it."

Vincent smiled sympathetically but shook his head.

"As inviting as that sounds, I'm afraid I can't join you. I need to go in to...check things."

"What 'things?'" Roberts asked contemptuously.

"Just things," Vincent replied vaguely.

"There's nothing in there you can do anything about, Vince. Who do you think you are? One of the overlookers?"

"No," Vincent replied, "but I hate to leave Juggs alone in the spinning room with the women and children."

"Better in there than out 'ere with us, says I." Roberts was still lying on his back, now with his eyes closed, but when he heard Vince's departing footsteps he opened them curiously. "You goin' in, then?" he called.

"I'll tell them you are finishing up a few things. Hide yourself behind some bales so you can hear anyone coming who may be sent to check on you. That way you can get up and look busy by the time they find you." Vincent's parting words of advice were proffered over his shoulder as he left the warehouse to go around the mill to the front entrance.

When he entered the spinning room, he saw the disturbance over by Dandre's station from atop the platform before he climbed down the ladder.

He noted the semicircle of workers standing around watching something. Across the room he could even make out the expressions of fear and disgust on the faces of the crowd.

He started as he heard the crack of Juggs's whip and then, as one of the workers stepped back in alarm, he caught a glimpse of light material.

It was enough.

He did not climb down the ladder. He leapt to the workroom floor and raced down the length of the aisle that separated him from the tragedy being enacted at the other end.

"You'll beg me now, you bitch!" Juggs screamed, grasping the thongs to strike the semiconscious girl with the strap handle.

Suddenly his arm was grabbed from behind, the strap pulled from his hand and his wrist twisted sharply.

Roaring with pain, the overlooker whirled to face this new attacker. Juggs had very seldom been frustrated in his sadism. His victims were always the weak and defenseless, who could offer no resistance. But twice in a single morning his attacks had been obstructed. Once by this girl, when he had meant to beat young Danny Fry until his rage was dissipated, and now by Vince, when he had turned his rage on the source of his maddening sexual frustration. Eldridge Juggs had a weak mind and acted on base instinct. The roar that issued from him when he turned was that of a crazed man.

With lowered head he rushed toward his assailant. His eyes glowed with an eerie red gleam from under his bushy brows. His lip was raised, exposing his upper canines like a mad dog.

His attack was so sudden and so furious it caught Vincent unprepared. Juggs's rocklike head hit him in the abdomen, forcing the air from the younger man's lungs, paralyzing his diaphragm momentarily and making it impossible for him to catch his breath again. He stumbled back and bent over, gasping wildly.

Not allowing him time to recover, Juggs leapt on his shoulders, pounding his arms, back and stomach with a maelstrom of blows. Vincent managed to ward most of them off, and then, his breath restored, he twisted and turned, forcing the smaller man from his back to a position where he was able to land some of his own blows.

He finally dislodged the overlooker with a cut to the jaw. Now Juggs fell back. Vincent followed him, pressing his advantage. He hit Juggs's shoulder, dodged his flailing fist, hit him again in the face.

Juggs went down on one knee. Vincent stood over him, waiting for him to get up.

Juggs had fallen against one of the spinning frames. While Chesterton waited for him to rise, panting, the deranged man ran his fingers frantically over the work post behind him in search of something he could use as a weapon. His hand finally encountered a loose iron rod. It was one of the metal posts that held extra bobbins for the pieceners. Juggs yanked it from its socket and swung it before him. Instead of a defeated opponent, Vincent found himself facing an armed lunatic.

With another blood-chilling scream, Juggs rose to his feet, knocking the steel rod against the worktable and the

reels with resounding *clangs*. In surprise, Vincent stepped
back. The end of the pole was rusty and jagged, and it was
that end Juggs was swinging, missing Vincent by a frac-
tion of an inch as he backed away. Juggs took a step forward, forcing Vincent to retreat another step. Fanning the
air murderously, the overlooker advanced.

The spectators parted and closed ranks to allow the op-
ponents' space. The noise of the factory machinery cam-
ouflaged the eerie silence of the onlookers. The children
were frightened and confused by Juggs's rage and terrified
now for Vince's safety, for Vince's life. The women had
been stunned and sickened by the overlooker's battering of
Danny and Dandre, but none of them were willing to call
Juggs's fury down on themselves.

They had been hopeful when Vince had stopped the terrible beating, but now they saw that Juggs would require
somebody's life today. Perhaps not only one. As soon as he
had dispatched Vinnie, there was no doubt that he would
return to finish his work on Dandre. And if he was not satisfied by then, who would be next? The women watched in
silence, and in silence each prayed it would not be her.

Juggs swung the iron shaft again and Vincent felt the wall
of the factory meet his shoulder blade. Juggs smiled wick-
edly, the red gleam still in his eyes. He grasped the pole like
a spear and paused just long enough to take aim at the
man's chest.

A shot rang out. It echoed thunderously through the big
open room.

"Drop the rod, Mr. Juggs, or an iron ball through your
shoulder will drop it for you."

It was Mr. Donner who had come down onto the work
floor and now stood behind the workers, pistol in hand.

The women and children quickly parted, leaving a clear
path to Juggs and the young man pinned against the wall.
Juggs did not drop the poised metal. Instead, his muscles
tightened and Vincent drew in his breath. The man before

him had clearly lost his reason and would kill him regardless of the consequences.

"I assure you, Mr. Juggs, I am an excellent shot. Now put the pole on the floor at your feet."

A moment more Juggs hesitated, and then Vincent was relieved to see the fire dull in his eyes, returning them to their coallike opaqueness. He knew, as Mr. Donner was steeling himself to shoot a man, that Juggs would put the jagged piece of metal down.

Slowly the man lowered his arm and dropped the length of steel onto the floor.

"Now get out," Mr. Donner warned. "And do not return. You may apply to Mr. Braid himself for any money you believe to be owing you, but you are not to enter this building again. I will see that Roberts and Mr. Chess there are armed to prevent any such attempt."

Juggs turned to the mill manager. Considering the ghastly appearance of his face, it was a tribute to the manager that he did not take a step back or even blanch. He kept his place, the gun aimed levelly at the overlooker's chest. Their eyes had locked as Juggs backed away toward the platform and the office, and Mr. Donner turned to watch him go.

The air in the factory was breathlessly still. There was no guarantee that Juggs would respect the manager's firearm. There was the definite possibility that the man would snap and attack again, and unless Mr. Donner was every bit as good a shot as he claimed, there was the danger of Juggs being loose in the room of women and children like a wounded animal, more furious and deadly than ever.

But in the end Juggs backed down. With a final dangerous nod of his head, he turned, climbed the ladder, crossed the platform and entered the outer office.

Only then, only when the door was closed behind him and sufficient time had elapsed for the man to have left the building and enter the traffic on the street, did Mr. Donner lower his gun.

Vincent had not waited that long to go to Dandre.

During his fight with the overlooker he had seen clearly that the girl Juggs had been beating was indeed Dandre. He had seen the torn cloth of her dress and the blood that stained it. She was slumped forward, but as the fight progressed he had seen her head turn to watch its progress.

She was not dead. She was even conscious.

As soon as he was released from the threat of Juggs's deadly spear, he rushed to the figures huddled under Sophy's workstation.

First he confirmed that Dandre was conscious and in her right senses. He could see that she was disoriented, but as he dropped to his knees beside her, he could tell that, thank God, with proper care her condition would not be life threatening. He sighed a sigh of relief.

"Dandre?" he whispered tenderly.

"He is gone?" she asked.

"Yes, he is gone. He will not return."

"Danny?" she asked.

Now, with a struggle, she raised herself on her hands and knees to reveal the two little bodies beneath her. The boy moaned.

Already portions of his exposed skin were beginning to puff and turn purple, but as Vincent carefully turned him over he could not see that any bones had been broken. If even one more blow had landed, the child doubtless would have sustained irreparable internal as well as external damage. His injuries, though, also appeared treatable. He would have to be taken to a doctor, of course, a genuine doctor, but Vincent determined that the child would live.

Dandre, sitting now and watching Vincent examine the boy with fear-filled eyes, held out her hands. Vincent looked into her eyes skeptically, but she appeared to be serious about her invitation, so he put the little boy into her arms.

That left one more small body.

The little girl did not move. She did not moan. The pearly whiteness of her skin showed no signs of maltreatment, not like Dandre's bleeding back or Danny's swelling injuries, yet Vincent's heart ached painfully when he touched the fragile little cheek.

Dandre watched his long fingers as they rested against her cheek, against her neck, moved softly down her arm and held the little wrist between thumb and forefinger. Then carefully he put her hand down, laying it across her chest. With both hands he turned her head to reveal all of her face. Placing the palm of his hand against her forehead, he pushed back the dirty, matted fringe of blond hair to reveal one bruise above her temple.

"Is she...?" Dandre whispered.

Vincent turned to her and nodded slightly. Tears sprang to the young woman's eyes as she quickly looked down at the child. Little Penny Braugh had never known a day without hunger, without pain, without sorrow in her six short years, yet in death her face was now serenely beautiful.

"Mr. Juggs pulled her from the ladder and threw her onto the floor, but I did not know she was hurt so badly," Dandre said, self-blame in her voice as she assumed responsibility for a tragedy she felt she surely could have prevented if she had been more attentive.

Vincent shook his head. "It looks as if something struck her head."

"Is that what...?"

Again the man nodded.

By then the standoff between Mr. Donner and the overlooker had ended, and the factory manager came to stand over the injured group.

"How are they?" he asked.

"The young woman and the boy have been shamefully beaten, but they will recover," Vincent replied. He did not qualify his statement by saying they would recover with the proper care and nutrition if no work was required of them and they were allowed to rest, as such statements usually had to be qualified here in the mill. If it meant constant care and spoon-feeding both patients for months, he would personally assume those tasks. The young woman and the boy *would* recover. "I am afraid the little girl is dead."

Mr. Donner took a startled step backward. He had, for the most part, been able to put enough distance between himself and the shop floor to avoid contact with the grim realities here.

"Did Juggs do it?" he asked.

"It looks like something struck her head," Vincent said.

"She fell against my post when Mr. Juggs knocked her to the floor."

Both men looked up, surprised to see Sophy standing nearby. She had broken from the line of silent onlookers to confirm the girl's identity and offer her explanation.

"Fell against your post?" Donner asked.

"And I . . . I tripped over her trying to get to my station," Sophy said, ending the sentence on a sob.

Now another of the observers, Nan, broke rank and came to stand by Sophy, putting an arm comfortingly around her shoulders.

"There now, it's all right. Nothin' you could've done. It wasn't your fault. Juggs threw 'er down, and you couldn't 'elp falling over 'er."

Sophy turned her head and sobbed loudly.

"'Ere now, Soph, don't cry. The blame is on ol' Juggs's black soul, and as for li'l Penny, why just take a look at her there. Tell me if you've ever seen the child lookin' so peaceful? She looks 'appier now than she ever was in her whole sad little life." There was a quiver in Nan's voice, too, and together the two women stood looking on as the tears rolled down their cheeks.

"Who is she?" Donner asked uncomfortably.

"She's a piecener." Nan told him. "Just started a month or two ago."

"Is she one of the orphanage children?" Donner asked.

The two women looked at each other and Sophy shook her head.

"I don't think so, sir," Nan Said. "She's from 'ere in Manchester."

"What is her name?"

"Penny."

"Penny who?"

Nan looked at Sophy again. The older woman shrugged. Nan raised her eyebrows and shook her head. Evidently the women had exhausted their knowledge of the girl. Donner turned to face the line of workers.

"Did any of you know this girl . . . Penny?" he asked. It was easier for him to speak of her in the past tense, since he had never known the frightened, shy little soul in the present. "Does anyone know her family's name?"

A little boy, standing behind one of the older girls, answered. "'Er name's Penny Braugh."

"Penny Braugh?"

"Yes, sir."

A girl in the front row took a half step sideways, putting the speaker, a small boy, in clear view. He did not look pleased by his exposure, but his assistance appeared to be committed now.

Vincent stood up and spoke quietly to Mr. Donner.

"The girl's body will have to be taken to her home."

Mr. Donner took another step back.

"That is rather hard, isn't it? To arrive on the home doorstep with a dead child?"

"Not that way," Vincent argued quietly. "The girl's people will take her, but someone needs to notify them.

And, of course, the child cannot remain here on the mill floor until they arrive. She will have to be taken somewhere."

"The infirmary?" Donner asked.

Vincent nodded.

"But how will we get word to the parents?"

"Someone will have to go," Vincent said.

Donner looked even less pleased by this responsibility than the small boy who had supplied the girl's name had been by his. The manager considered the problem for a moment, his eyes darting about the room. They came to rest on the man in front of him.

"You want me to go," Vincent supplied as the manager tried to form the request on his tongue.

"I do," Donner confirmed.

"I am taking the young woman and the boy with me," Vincent said.

"We can see they get to the infirmary," Donner offered. "I can write out the order now."

"I am taking the young woman and the boy with me," the young man repeated firmly.

Donner made no further attempt to dissuade him; the mill manager could see that the man would not be moved. Donner turned toward the crowd of workers, who had, finally, begun to talk quietly among themselves. He singled out the boy again and spoke directly to him.

"Where did she live?" he asked.

The boy glanced to either side to see if any one of his neighbors was going to reply. When he looked back at the manager the man's eyes were still on him.

"'Er mother lives in Irish Town," the boy finally responded.

"Her mother? Does she not have a father?"

"She did once, I guess. I don't know if 'e's around these days. I know she 'as a brother or sister or something. Too young to work in the mill, she said."

Both Mr. Donner and Vincent gazed down in surprise at the lifeless child. As they looked at her innocent face, it did not appear to them that the girl's parent had considered any age too young to work in the mill.

"Do you know *where* she lives?" Vincent asked kindly.

"Irish Town," the boy repeated.

"I believe Mr. Chess would like to know in which house she lived in Irish Town," Mr. Donner said in an attempt to clarify the request.

"Lor', mister," the boy chided, "there ain't no 'ouses in Irish Town, just boxes and blankets."

"Could you go with Mr. Chess to find her mother, then?" Mr. Donner continued.

Now it was the boy who took a step backward in alarm.

"Into Irish Town?" He turned to look imploringly at Vincent. "I don't think so, Vince. You wouldn't want me to go down there with you, now would you?"

"No, do not worry. Someone will give me directions once I get there." Vince lowered his voice to speak quietly to the manager once more. "Do you have anything with which I can cover her face?"

Mr. Donner nodded.

"Everyone back to your machines," the manager called. "Get them cleaned and we will call a short day today." Mr. Braid would not like it, not with those bales of cotton sitting out in the warehouse, but Mr. Braid was not a heartless man, and in the end, reluctantly, he would approve of the half day.

Mr. Donner's announcement did not signal the holiday air that such an announcement would usually have sparked. The workers melted back to their stations, but less in accordance with Mr. Donner's order than in relief to leave the lifeless little body to someone else's care.

Mr. Donner also left, to return in a few minutes with a small woolen blanket.

While he waited, Vincent went to Dandre's side. The young woman appeared to be somewhat recovered, but he suspected she was revived by the energy of her emotions and that the physical strain of the beating would soon catch up with her.

"How do you feel?" he asked. He ached to hold her, to give her some of his strength, but he did not know where he could touch her that would not give her more pain than comfort.

"I feel relieved. And angry. And frightened. And very worried."

Vincent had meant how did she feel physically, but looking at the little boy in her arms, he could understand her concern. Nor was he surprised that she gave more thought to the child and his pain than to her own.

"He will be all right, Dandre. He is bruised, but I do not believe anything is broken."

Just then Danny moaned and twisted painfully in the young woman's arms.

"Ow," he sighed in protest.

"Danny? Danny? Try not to move. Lie still. Everything is fine," Dandre cooed.

"Is he gone? Are you all right?" the little boy whispered, opening his eyes a crack.

"I am going to be perfectly all right, and so are you," she said, producing, from somewhere, a little smile.

"But he hit you," the boy protested. "He hurt you."

"He hurt us both, Danny. But I will promise to get better if you will."

Danny nodded weakly.

"It's a deal," he said, closing his eyes against the pain. "What about Penny?"

Dandre glanced quickly at Vincent, trying to find in his sorrowful expression some gentle way to tell the boy the truth.

"She bumped her head," she began carefully. "She was injured worse than we knew."

The boy cracked his eyes open again to look at her face, fearful of the purport of her solemn tone.

"Will she be all right?" he whispered.

Dandre shook her head but could not speak as tears filled her eyes.

"She's dead, isn't she?" Danny asked.

Vincent extended his hand, uncertain of touching the boy without causing him pain, too. Gently he laid his hand on the child's forehead.

"I am afraid she is, Danny," he said.

The boy was quiet and thoughtful for a few moments.

"She'll be better off now," he said at last. "It's hard on the girls here, you know." He spoke seriously, suggesting that little boys are much better suited for abuse and physical deprivation. "I don't even think it was too bad for her, really. Her eyes just got dimmer and dimmer, like she was fading away. Like she was going away, but to a nice place. Don't you think she's gone to a nice place, Danny?" the boy asked, looking back at the woman who held him.

"Yes, I do, Danny," Dandre said quietly. "I believe Penny's pure little soul has gone to someplace glorious, a place filled with light and love, a place where there are countless other pure souls to care for her. I believe there are wonderful things for her to see there, and marvelous things for her to do. And I believe the moment she arrived, the dear Lord Jesus took her in his arms to comfort and to hold her and made every bit of pain and suffering she ever experienced vanish completely."

Danny sighed and closed his eyes again, a small smile on his lips.

"That's what I believe, too," he murmured. Then he opened his eyes to study Dandre's face again. "Do you believe I'll go there?" he asked.

"Someday, perhaps," Vincent said. "If you are very good. But not today. Today you are going to come with us and get all better."

Danny's eyes opened wider as he looked back and forth between the two grown-ups who had come to fill his empty world.

"Really?" he asked.

Dandre and Vincent both nodded.

The little boy's face was suffused with the light of sublime happiness for a moment, but then a shadow of sadness fell across his eyes.

"What about...her...Penny...her, you know..." He fumbled for the delicate phrase that would designate the shell his workmate had left behind her when she was released to find her place of rest.

"Vincent is going down to Irish Town to try and find her mother," Dandre said.

Danny clutched the material of her dress where it sagged loosely at her waist.

"Don't leave me alone," he whispered frantically.

"I will not...I will stay with you," Dandre crooned, rocking slightly as she held the boy to comfort his fears.

"Before I do anything else, I am going to take you both to Mrs. Bink's, where I want *you*—" Vincent looked pointedly at Dandre "—to pack your things. We will be leaving here as soon as I get back." He paused for a moment without releasing his breath, ready to meet any argument the girl might lodge. Dandre did not say anything, only inclined her head wearily. She was ready to leave this place as far behind her as possible.

Vincent stood. He took Danny into his arms and then helped Dandre get to her feet.

As the young woman was struggling painfully to rise, Nan, who had finished cleaning her machine, came to stand before the three of them.

and Godfrey's Cordial, so as far as the mill workers could tell, he was a medicine man of the first degree.

Danny and Dandre had accompanied Vincent to the infirmary, but it was small wonder that he would not trust their well-being to the man.

"A bit of a reprimand, I see," Dr. Fisher said when he saw the young woman's tattered dress and the stripes and blood on her back.

Her "bit of a reprimand" had very nearly leveled her. Vincent refused the proffered medicine—"Good for what ails you"—and merely left Penny's body with the "doctor" while he hurried his two living charges out of the infirmary before more harm could be done them there.

At the building where Mrs. Bink acted as landlady, Vincent took them to Dandre's room. By then he was more or less carrying both of them, and he could tell the young lady was not up to packing her things or doing anything else. He knew she would be able to sleep, though, for several hours, but that was as much as she would be capable of.

Danny had moaned a time or two as he was being carried to the tenement building, but Vincent thought he was unconscious. When he laid the child on the bed, he was surprised to see the boy's eyes open.

"You're going down to Little Ireland now?" he asked in a very small voice.

"Yes, I am," Vincent replied.

"You're taking Penny?"

"No, I will leave her with Dr. Fisher while I go to find her mother," Vincent said.

"Be careful," Danny warned.

"I will be very careful," the man promised.

"And tell her mama that I don't think it hurt her very much. I think in the end she just went to sleep."

"I will tell her. She will want to know that. Now you rest. And you see that Dandre rests, too. You are both hurt and tired and need to sleep. As soon as I get back I will send uptown for a real doctor, and if he says it is all right, we will leave here tonight.''

"We'll be together? Like you promised?" the little boy asked.

"Just like I promised."

"Hurry back," Danny said.

"I will," Vincent replied, but he was not sure the boy heard him. The child's eyes were closed and he was breathing deeply by the time the words were spoken.

Carefully the gentleman stepped around the bed and helped Dandre lift her feet onto the mattress. He supported her head and shoulders as she turned herself onto her side, being careful of her stinging back.

"You heard what I told Danny?" Vincent asked her, his lips very close to the pale pink of her cheek.

Dandre nodded.

"Those same instructions apply to you. Lie here and sleep. That is all you are to do. I will be back as soon as I can."

"I will be here," she said.

It was all he asked for the rest of his life. He put his lips tenderly against hers, then pushed himself to his feet. He was pleased to see that she was asleep, as well, by the time he got to the door.

In two hours or less he would return, gather his little family to his bosom, and they would leave this place forever. But before then he had one last duty to perform.

The mill towns of Dewsbury, Huddersfield, Oldham, Stockport, Wiggan, Bury, all villages of central Lancashire, had, like the city of Manchester itself, grown up around the rivers and streams that provided the power to run the machinery. Every waterway, every inch of every waterway, powered a mill. The Irk, the Irwell, the Ribble, the Meresy and the Medlock.

The vegetable-dealer looked up, absently scratching at an insect bite on his neck.

"Mrs. Braugh now is it you're lookin' for? Which Mrs. Braugh would that be? Liza Braugh who works in the tannery? Or Mrs. Jamey Braugh, goodwife of the pig man?"

"It is the Mrs. Braugh whose child works in the mill," Vincent offered.

The man roared with laughter, releasing a blast of fetid air into Vincent's face. Chesterton raised his head in an attempt to rise above the stench of the man's breath.

"Saints be praised, man," the seller said, still chuckling, "there's not a child down here who can walk on two feet who isn't sent to the mills to work."

Vincent glanced about him at the grizzled adults, infants in arms and toddlers clinging to their mothers' skirts and could see for himself that there were no children here in Little Ireland running and playing and sporting about in the middle of the day.

"The child's name was Penny," he said.

"*Was?*" the man asked, raising his eyebrows.

"There has been an accident."

The merchant shook his head. "Accidents happen," he said philosophically.

"When little children with little sleep and rotten food—" Vincent glanced down at the poor wares on the man's cart "—are set to work for fourteen or sixteen hours without rest, among huge machines, with cruel taskmasters watching them who whip them and kick them and beat them senseless, yes, accidents do happen." Vincent spoke bitterly, blaming himself and the man in front of him and Juggs and Mr. Braid and King William himself, blaming everyone and everything in the present system of life that let little girls suffer and die on spinning room floors.

He rubbed his eyes wearily and the vegetable-man cleared his throat self-consciously.

"You say the girl's name was Penny?" he asked.

"Yes. Penny Braugh. From Irish Town. That is as much as I know about her."

"Penny Braugh. Penny Braugh." The man spoke slowly, considering the countless faces he saw pass his cart every day, going in and out of Little Ireland. The community was like a teeming anthill, but Vincent had made his inquiry of one of the few people here who could offer him some practical aid. "Little girl. Blond hair. Blue eyes, if I remember rightly."

Vincent nodded.

"I think she belongs to Jenny Braugh. Has another little baby, if I'm not mistaken. You threw me with your 'Missus' Braugh. The lass has no husband. She's the sort who takes whatever Providence sends her way, and so far that's been several gentleman friends and two bairns, but no man willing to take on a wife *and* a family."

"Where does she live?"

"With her sister Kate and her husband."

"And where is that?"

The seller looked behind him and then back at the man making his inquiries.

"You ever been down there?" he asked.

Now Vincent shook his head. "No," he said. "I have had no call before today."

The seller wagged his own head. "You can't really give directions. It's not like there are roads and house numbers. Folks who live here can find their way around, but strangers..." His voice faded hopelessly.

"Can *you* show me the way?" Vincent asked.

The man looked down at his cart.

"I've got my things..." he began, but Chesterton jingled the handful of coins he had pulled from his pocket. One of the coins alone would have purchased all of the sorry vegetables on the man's cart, and the handful would buy him a new cart, stocked with better vegetables, and leave enough for a bottle or two of good Irish whiskey to cheer his heart for days to come.

"Righto," the seller cried, turning from his cart and wares and plunging into the roadway—or more nearly "pathway"—behind him.

Vincent was forced to push the cart aside and hurry a grunting pig from his path with his boot before he could follow his guide. By then two other people, an old man in a torn brown coat and a woman in a torn brown skirt, had come between him and the vegetable-dealer. But Vincent sidestepped the two Irish Town locals and rushed after the man, catching up with him just as he turned a corner that would have hidden him from view and lost him to Vincent just as surely as if he had fallen off the face of the earth.

They entered a covered passage between two of the old, tumbledown houses. It was dark, even in the daylight hours, and only wide enough to admit one at a time. Vincent put his foot down on something that gave. It was not exactly soft, not soft enough to be mud or fresh excrement, but was more like a pile of rags or a dead animal. He did not look down to determine which.

The lane into which they emerged was faced on either side by a solid row of the misshapen black houses. Here a stream of water from the Medlock had been diverted. It ran sluggishly down the side of the lane, coal black, thick with solid waste thrown into it from the kitchens and privies of the houses. In places the water formed little puddles that shimmered greasily or bubbled with trapped gases.

And there were people. People wandering the lanes, sitting in front of the houses, poking with sticks through the piles of debris found everywhere one turned. But there were even more people. People who were not seen. Masses of people packed behind the walls of the houses. Vincent could hear men and women shouting at each other through broken windows, could hear the business of living going on behind thin walls, could almost feel the throb of crowded, diseased humanity.

The air was dim with smoke from the factories. For ten months of the year the wind drove the smoke directly into Little Ireland.

Vincent coughed heavily. He would not have believed it possible, but this was worse than the lint-filled air of the factory.

His guide glanced over his shoulder.

"Not much further," he offered encouragingly.

But he led the young gentleman through a winding maze of cottages built back-to-back with no ventilation, no access to the stream, no floors and no drains. There was no air and no water. It was inconceivable that there could be life here.

At last the erstwhile vegetable-seller came to a stop in front of one of the cottages. With balled fist he pounded on the door. It gave beneath his onslaught and the merchant yelled through the opening.

"Mick O'Rork! Katey! Jenny! Anybody in there?"

Dogs barked up and down the lane, and behind the door, in the recesses of the dark room, a baby began to cry.

"Wha' d'ya want?" came the female scream.

The door was pulled open to reveal a short, dumpy girl. Seventeen or eighteen years old, Vincent would have guessed. He recognized the deformity of her humped shoulders and rightly guessed her to be a factory girl. Two filthy little children clung to the tattered hem of her skirt or crawled around her feet. Behind her the baby still cried.

"You Jenny Braugh?" the man asked boldly.

"And who is it wants to know?" the girl challenged.

The merchant turned to Vincent and nodded.

"This one's Jenny, all right. Those two I'd take to be Kate's," he said, pointing to the children at her feet. "Or mebbe neighbor ladies' brats. Aye! You watch the bairns of the gals hereabouts?" the man called in to the girl.

"Mine and others," she answered warily.

"Well, this gen'l'man has news 'bout yours."

The vegetable-seller stepped back from the door to allow Vincent to come forward. The baby's cries had become fretful, exhausted mewls, and Vincent knew the girl quieted her charges with numbing doses of laudanum to ease her task during the long day when the children were hers to watch but not hers to feed.

"Is Penny your little girl?" he asked carefully. "She works up in Braid's mill?"

The young woman nodded her head hesitantly.

"I am afraid there has been an accident . . ."

"Penny? Is Penny hurt? Where's my little girl?" the mother cried.

Mothers know. Vincent could tell she had known from the moment the seller pounded on her door. She looked fearfully into Vincent's eyes, but she knew.

"Let me get my shawl," she called, turning back into the dark room. "My Penny needs me. Clara! Clara! Come watch the children. Penny's been hurt. I have to hurry!"

"Jenny?" Vincent called after her softly. "Jenny?" The gentleness of his voice cut through the air like a rapier.

The girl turned to him, her eyes wide and filling with tears.

"Penny is gone," he said. "She fell and hurt her head."

"'Er 'ead's been 'urt? They can fix that, can't they?"

"No one knew how bad it was, Jenny."

"She wouldna cry . . . she never cried at all when she was a babe," Jenny sobbed.

"And then she just slipped away. She was gone before anyone knew she had been injured."

Another woman had come to the cottage door. This was evidently Clara, the woman Jenny had called for. She stepped around Vincent and put her arm across the girl's shoulders.

"You go with the gentleman, Jen. I'll watch the children. You go get your little girl."

"When Kate and Mick come..." Jenny began, but stopped, her mind too filled with sorrow to remember details.

"I'll send them up to Braid's. Mick'll help bring 'er down. But you go be with 'er now." The woman pushed the girl's misshapen shoulder slightly and Jenny Braugh stumbled through the door. She pulled the shawl over her head, and without a word the vegetable-seller led them back the way the two men had come.

The girl sobbed softly now and then. Vincent offered his arm, but she did not try to take it, since often the way necessitated travel in single file.

When they reached the open ground that led up the bank and out of Irish Town, they found the vegetable-dealer's cart still there, though it had been emptied of wares. With the coins now jingling in his pocket, the man had no cares for the poor vegetables, and as soon as he could get a bottle in his hands he would have no cares for anything. Vincent pulled the girl behind him up the steep bank and then he led the way to Braid's mill and the shop infirmary.

Dr. Fisher was waiting impatiently. With the declared half day at the mill he should have been allowed a holiday, too. But the body of the child on the table in the inner room and Mr. Chess's ominous-sounding instructions that he stay until the child's mother came had kept the doctor in the infirmary. He might have been even more fretful and impatient if he had not administered a dose or two of Godfrey's Cordial to himself while he waited. He found Godfrey's always soothed his nerves, and Mr. Braid supplied it to the infirmary for medicinal purposes. What was more medicinal a purpose than soothing the doctor's taut nerves?

He raised his slumped head when the infirmary door opened.

"Chess?" he called, blinking to clear his vision. "And you must be the girl's mother. Sad business. Sad, sad business. Well, come on in and collect her. I'm going now, Mr. Chess. Please close the door when you leave. No need to lock it. I'm taking the medicine home with me." He was swaying on his feet and patted his coat pocket two or three times.

Vincent would have argued with him, claiming that he could not stay, but looking at the man he could see he was not fit to be with the grieving mother. Dandre and Danny should both be asleep, but if they woke, he had left a loaf of bread and another piece of the dried beef the boy had so enjoyed to break their fast. Neither one would feel lively enough to go anywhere, and he supposed they would not mind an entire day of rest.

"Go ahead," he told the doctor.

But the doctor had been "going ahead" with or without the other man's permission and was halfway out the door by the time Vincent spoke.

Jenny had been standing speechless since she entered the infirmary. As the door shut behind the doctor she pulled the shawl from over her head and raised her eyes to the messenger who had brought death to her door that day.

"Where is she?" she whispered.

"In here," he said, going to the office door and pushing it open.

A few flies buzzed unhealthily in the room, but there was no other hint of what was under the dark blanket.

"Has she been washed?" the mother asked.

Vincent sounded confused and surprised when he answered, having no knowledge of the rituals of death.

"No," he said. "I wrapped the blanket around her and brought her in here. It does not look like Fisher has touched her."

"She has to be washed . . . we have to get her ready," the young woman said woodenly.

She looked around the room and in a moment found a relatively clean rag, which she tore in two. The water in the basin had a skin of dirt and soap across it, but there was more water in the pitcher.

Vincent emptied the fouled water from the basin and Jenny Braugh filled it with fresh. Together they stood before the bundle on the low table. The young mother looked up at him.

"Will you unwrap her?" she asked.

Tenderly, as if it were his own little Danny, bruised and whimpering in pain, Vincent took the blanket from around the body. The girl's mother caught her breath on a sob when she saw her child's face.

"Oh," she crooned. "Oh, she looks so beautiful. I swear she never looked so pretty in her life. Oh, my baby."

Vincent put his arm around the girl's slumped shoulders.

"A little boy named Danny Fry worked with your daughter," he said. "He saw that Penny was hurt and tried to help her when she collapsed, but it was too late then. He told me to tell you that she did not appear to be in pain. He said at the end she just went to sleep. To a peaceful sleep."

The young mother cried softly for a few minutes while Vincent held her shoulders, but finally she wiped at her eyes and nodded her head to signal that she could go on.

The woman handed him one of the cloths and showed him what was to be done. They washed the frail body, smoothing soot from her cheeks and limbs, which had perhaps never been washed clean before. She *was* a pretty little girl, as her mother had no doubt once been herself.

Like Mary Magdalene washing the Savior's feet, Jenny shed tears onto her cloth and onto her child's skin, so that, conceived and born in tears, Penny Braugh was now prepared for burial with tears.

After the child's body was washed, Jenny asked Vincent to put the blanket around her again. Vincent suggested she wait for her sister and brother-in-law in the next room, and Jenny asked that he stay with her until they arrived.

Side by side, in silence, they sat in the outer room of the office. Vincent held the girl's hand. As shadows began to fill the room it seemed to him that the mother's hand was no larger than her child's. She was little more than a child herself. Tears dimmed his own eyes, and not for the first time, at the thought of what this child had been forced to do today, and of the grief and hardship of her entire life.

One man is powerless to change everything, but one man can change some things, he thought to himself.

Finally, when it had become quite dark in the little room, Mick and Katey O'Rork arrived, tapping timidly at the door.

"Jenny?" her sister called softly.

Crying, the girl rushed to her sister's arms.

Vincent took a few moments to find and light a lamp, then he and Mick O'Rork, who had entered behind his wife, stood apart to discuss arrangements for getting the body down to Little Ireland and the interment that would follow immediately in the pauper's cemetery, which was too close to the dwellings in Irish Town to be healthy.

Mick, also a product of the mills and so undersized and underdeveloped himself, lifted the bundle, struggling awkwardly with the child's stiffening limbs. But Penny Braugh had never been one to give trouble, and now, having been a very small child, even her Uncle Mick could carry her back home.

Vincent left them at the infirmary door. He closed it tightly behind him in accordance with the good doctor's instructions. Then, at last, with night making full claim of the sky, he was free to return to his own loved ones.

One man is powerless to change everything, but one man *can* change some things.

Chapter Sixteen

The pain flowed through her. It was all around her. She rose and sank into sleep on its swells.

The boy whimpered next to her, his boat of sleep rocked by the same turbulent sea.

Like Vincent, she knew their injuries were not mortal or even so painful they could not be escaped in sleep. Almost.

In a natural motion she turned to her back. Her eyes flew open and she gasped sharply. Why were the wounds on her back still open and exposed? Where was Vincent with the doctor?

The shadows that filled the room were late afternoon shadows; Vincent had been gone longer than the two hours he promised.

With that thought came the recollection of where the man, her hero, her love, had gone; the duty he had accepted. She realized that any number of complications might have arisen to prevent his quick return and she should not be alarmed or anxious. She should not even be impatient, but that she could not help.

She heaved herself painfully to her side and then swung her legs off the bed and pushed herself to a sitting position. For just a moment the room swam before her eyes, but then her vision cleared and the pounding in her head lessened.

She glanced behind her at the little boy still asleep. The bruises from the strap handle had darkened, yet his dear little face was relaxed in sleep.

Dandre rose carefully, both to save herself pain and to keep the look on the boy's face from changing. Once up, she limped to the small mirror above her dresser to inspect the visible damage.

The four red stripes along the side of her face worried her. Carefully she studied them. The three outside ones were angry welts, but the skin had not been broken, so eventually, probably soon, they would fade and completely disappear. The fourth stripe, the one closest to her ear, was marked by a hardened crust of blood that ran its length. There would be a scar there. She sighed. She supposed she could wear her hair in a style that would hide it.

Next she turned to peer over her shoulder, trying to get a look at her back. It hurt far worse than the cut on her face and she hated to think what the permanent marks there would be.

The glass was very small, though, and the room was filled with shadows. She could see no more than a few shreds of material stained red.

Straightening, she sighed again, a sigh that nearly turned into a groan. She would have to change clothes either before or after the doctor looked at her injuries, and it would be simpler if she changed and cleaned herself as best as she could now.

She glanced quickly at the little boy, sleeping more or less peacefully. If she tried to change and wash herself in here, it would certainly waken him. But he would be well enough here while she slipped into Vincent's room to wash and put on one of her soft, loose nightgowns. Not the dressing gown she had been wearing when Vincent returned to her at the Sheffington, of course. There were a number of reasons why she did not want to put that on right now. For one thing, the material was so thin it would cling to any open

wound on her back. For another, she hated to stain the
snowy frills of the gown with her blood. And there was another, private reason she did not articulate to herself. She
had worn that gown on the night she had planned to give
herself to Vincent. She still wanted to wear it for that occasion.

But she had other nightgowns. Old, worn, comfortable
flannel gowns that would not bind and would not cling, and
which she could see stained without the slightest twinge of
conscience.

She turned from the mirror to limp painfully to the
dresser. Carefully she opened it, glancing at the bed at every
squeak and groan of the old wood.

The boy slept on.

She pulled a nightgown and some underthings from the
drawer, then, with fresh clothes in hand, she softly opened
the door of her room.

When the door opened, Mrs. Bink stood at her desk, but
by the time the girl had emerged into the hall and closed the
door behind her, the landlady had retreated to her quarters. Mrs. Bink had learned long ago that tenants always
had demands of the landlady when she was standing at the
front desk, but the demands did not often survive the
lengthy process of summoning the landlady and waiting for
her to arrive at the desk.

But Dandre did not go to the front desk. Walking close
to the wall, putting her hand against it occasionally for
support, she made her way slowly down the dark passage-
way and stopped at Vincent's door.

With an appearance of familiarity she really did not feel
in entering a man's room, even Vincent's, even after all they
had been through, she pushed the door open and slipped
through the dark space.

As she closed the door behind her and crossed the room,
she began to pull the skirt of the torn smock over her head.
Gently she worked the threads loose that were caught in the

dried drops of blood on her back. Much as she loved Vincent Chesterton, as ideal a hero as he was in her eyes—handsome, strong, brave—still, with a pained smile, she had to admit he was not a very good nurse. He should not have allowed her to go to sleep in this filthy rag. If he scrupled to help her out of it, he could have asked Mrs. Bink to perform the service.

She knew, of course, why he had not put her through that. It was out of consideration for her. She had been in pain and fatigued, and surely he believed he was doing the best thing for her by letting her go directly to bed. But allowing this dress to dry on her back had *not* been the best thing for her. She pulled another few inches of fabric free, biting her lip to keep from crying out.

At last the dress and all of its loose threads came free. In relief she dropped it to lie in a clump at her feet. Her underclothing had also undergone a radical change since her employment at Braid's. It had become much less restricting and formal than the elaborate underpinnings worn by women of fashion. Without her dress, she stood in only her chemise, which had also been shredded by the lash, her pantaloons and a pair of long gray woolen stockings.

Studying herself in the mirror, she smiled another small, exasperated smile. He might at least have taken her stockings off.

She sat on the edge of the bed and rolled the rude woolen leggings down her calves and pulled them off at the toes.

Taking off the dress had loosened the chemise, and with only a twinge or two she managed to remove that scant undergarment. Breathing heavily, feeling as exhausted as if she had run a race, Dandre sat down on the bed again for a moment to recoup her shallow reservoir of strength.

In a minute, perhaps two, she rose to complete her task, which was becoming more and more arduous for the worn girl. She poured water, lukewarm by now after sitting in the hot room all day, from the pitcher into the large washbowl. With a ragged little sponge she washed her face, cleaning the torn flesh near her ear and rinsing the hair matted with dried blood. She dabbed at her arms and her neck, the mounds of her breasts, her legs and feet. Then, squeezing the sponge several times in the cloudy water and once above the bowl to drain out most of the moisture, she reached behind her and began the excruciating operation of washing her back.

Gently she began, concentrating on the places that hurt the most, since she was unable to see what she was doing. The sponge came back red but not drenched with blood, and was lighter after each rinsing and the next washing.

So painful was the washing, so intent was she on her labors, so distracted by her efforts not to cry out or groan foolishly, she did not hear the door open behind her. Mrs. Bink's hallway was as close as the rooms, so the opening door did not allow a breath of cool air that might have alerted her.

Now, with only a pair of pantaloons on, her hair floating loosely about her face and shoulders, she bent and arched and contorted her trunk and arms, attempting to wash the unattended wounds on her back.

Click.

It was the sound of the door closing. Her eyes flew to the mirror above Vincent's dresser to meet the shadowed gaze she had come to hate and fear. A shadowed gaze she had believed she would never encounter again.

But there it was. There *he* was. Staring at her. Like this.

In a reflexive motion she pulled the coverlet off the bed, dragging it from the thin, sagging mattress and holding it in front of her before she turned.

The black glimmer of his eyes seemed to see right through the material, as if she still stood as bare, as exposed as she had been when he entered. How long had he been standing there?

Still, she clasped the coverlet to her like an enchanted breastplate that could protect her from the evil of Mr. Juggs's eyes.

"What are you doing here?" she whispered.

"I see your Mr. Chess isn't here. Gone down to Irish Town, I hear. Had a piece of bad news to deliver. When I heard he was gone, it came to me that you and me have some unfinished business. Business better completed without Vinnie's interrupting. In fact, it came to me, as I thought on it, that since Chess and Donner have made a fugitive of me, they owe me something. *He* owes me something. He owes me a going-away present. I've come to claim it."

"What do you mean, 'fugitive'?" she asked, avoiding the more obvious question for fear of the answer she would receive.

"There have been other—misfortunes. Other mills, other lazy women and children. I just do my job." He raised his eyes to look into the mirror behind her at the reflection of her torn back. His lips curled in a bone-chilling smile. "I *enjoy* doing my job."

They heard a faint sound outside in the hallway. It was probably Mrs. Bink at her desk. Juggs started, though, aware of how late it was, how long he had been here, wondering how long Chess had been gone and when he would return. Suddenly he came to the conclusion that Dandre had reached when first she woke, that Chess had been gone long enough to reach Irish Town and get back again, that at any moment he could be returning.

"Put something on," he snarled. "We're going."

"Going?"

"Don't ask any questions. I haven't got time for explanations. If you don't come now, I'll leave you dead right here."

Juggs's tone was completely lifeless when he made his threat, and Dandre knew he would have no compunction

whatsoever about killing her here and now. She also knew
it was only a question of "here and now" or "someplace
else, later," but like the rest of the human race, "someplace else, later," always sounds better, even though the
time between now and later may be filled with degradation
and agony.

Still holding the coverlet from Vincent's bed in front of
her chest, keeping her eyes on Juggs's face, Dandre felt
around on the bed for the chemise and nightgown she had
dropped there. When her fingers encountered the little undershirt, she grabbed it, and then, because she had no other
choice, she turned her back, dropped the blanket and
scrambled into the brief garment. It did not cover much,
but it covered her bare breasts and gave Dandre the wholly
unfounded feeling of assurance that what Mr. Juggs could
not see he could not violate.

The only other thing she had to wear was the old nightgown she brought in here with her, but when she reached
down to the bed for it, Juggs stopped her.

"Not that," he warned.

Dandre looked over her shoulder fearfully at the man.

"It is the only thing I have in here," she said.
"This . . . this is not my room."

Juggs's eyebrows rose and he smiled his terrible smile
again.

"Oh? And whose . . . ?" His eyes wandered to the blanket hanging in front of the closet nook. Taking a step to
bring him to the cubbyhole, he pulled the blanket from its
slight support to reveal Vincent's clothes. Three pairs of
dark trousers and two or three light shirts. "So you've set
up housekeeping in Vinnie's room? Easier than going down
to your room every night, I suppose." He nodded his approval of the arrangement, seeming to be quite pleased.
"That's good," he said. "This way he'll miss you soon, and
a lot. Couldn't be better."

During this brief soliloquy, Dandre had once again pulled the blanket up around her. She was cold. Her scant attire could not account completely for the deep chill she felt, and the blanket, though it covered her, could not warm her, could not stop the quivering of her flesh or slow the beating of her heart.

Juggs returned his attention to the girl and then pulled a pair of the trousers and one of the shirts from the closet. He threw them at her and surprised her into catching them and releasing the blanket. Now she held Vincent's clothes in front of her.

"Put those on. It's unusual but won't draw the attention that my dragging you through the streets in your underthings would. Well, put 'em on. Hurry up. Or do I have to show you how? You know how to take off a man's pants, I'll wager, but maybe not how to get them on."

He took a half-step toward the girl, who hurriedly dropped the pants and began fumbling into the big shirt. It might have almost wrapped around her twice. The tail of the shirt fell almost to her knees, and the ends of the sleeves brushed the knuckles on the back of her hand, but with Juggs watching her dress, Dandre did not stop to consider the ill fit of the garments. With the shirt on, she reached for the trousers and awkwardly pulled on the completely unfamiliar article of clothing. The man's shirt was voluminous, the shoulders alone nearly drowning her in a sea of cambric. The trousers, on the other hand, fit snugly across her hips and buttocks and then gathered loosely around her ankles in still more folds of thick fustian.

"Let's go," Juggs barked.

"Go where?" she asked.

In answer, Juggs grabbed her wrist and struck her cheek with the back of his hand.

Roughly he pulled her behind him, out of the room and down the hall, past Mrs. Bink's desk, which was vacant as usual.

At the door he twisted her wrist behind her back, holding the girl so close to him that her nostrils were filled with the heavy smell of the man. It brought to mind dark, dirty cellars, damp air foul with disease and decay.

"Not a word," he spat into her ear. "Not a sound. At the least noise from you, I'll snap this arm like a matchstick. Do you understand?"

She nodded.

Juggs opened the door, looked up and down the street outside, then pushed her through ahead of him.

Dandre did not struggle. That was useless. But neither did she lead the way to pull him along. They did not speak, but both of them were breathing heavily. Their passage from the tenement building onto the street outside was not noisy enough to call undue attention to themselves, but it did cover the sound of a door opening and a pair of small feet following them.

Juggs led her along the street that had become so familiar to her, as familiar as the houses and shops of the Coventry neighborhood where she had grown up. Mr. Sibb's bakery, the housewares store on the corner where she made the first turn. She even recognized one or two of the faces they passed, but these people did not seem to recognize her in her foreign attire or else they did not recognize her companion, or perhaps they did not think it strange that she should be with Mr. Juggs. Two weeks ago she might have believed that they simply did not care, but now she knew that was not true. These people cared a great deal and were willing to do what they could to help.

But now, no one recognized her moment of peril. No one interfered, no one offered to help her. Juggs pushed her down the street, passersby afforded them a single glance or ignored them altogether, and a small form hurried from shadow to shadow, following after them.

He was taking her to Braid's mill. Mr. Donner, she was sure, had, as he promised, notified the local constabulary.

From the dark comment Juggs had made when first he surprised her in Vincent's room, she surmised that he had been in hiding from the arm of the law for other cruelties, perhaps other deaths in mills where he had been overlooker before. Therefore he was no doubt being hunted at this very moment, and if he was, the last place they would look for him was the scene of his latest crime.

The mill would be dark and deserted. No one would be there to stop this very dangerous man who had her in his power, no one would hear her cries of fear and pain.

In the time it took them to reach the darkened factory, the sun sank below the horizon and the shadows of late afternoon became the gloom of dusk.

Once at the building, Juggs took her to a small door on the far side. Still holding her arm behind her back with one hand, he tried the latch of the door. It was locked, but it was not a sturdy lock. Juggs put his shoulder against the panel and increased the pressure of his meaty hand; in a moment she heard the mechanism give and the door popped open. Juggs stumbled through the entryway, pulling her painfully behind him.

He kicked the door shut with his foot. Never, since the moment he grabbed her wrist in Vincent's room at Mrs. Bink's, had he released his hold on her. She had not had a breath of opportunity to free herself from the man, to dart away into traffic or some shop they might have passed. It was with a dim, nebulous plan to do something of that sort to save herself along the way that she had donned the clothes he threw at her and left the apartment building so docilely with him. Now, as the door swung shut behind them in this deserted, echoing building, the hopeless feeling came over her that she had erred terribly to choose "someplace else, later," when given the option for her death.

The room had become pitch-black when the door swung shut, and Dandre had no idea where she was, what part of the inside of the factory corresponded with the outside entrance Juggs had forced. But the man seemed familiar with his surroundings. He pushed her forward. She hesitated. He applied additional pressure to her already aching arm. She gasped and stumbled forward as he propelled her thoughtlessly, using her body and legs as a shield against any obstacles in front of them.

Once again they did not hear the door open behind them, and they were too far into the building to notice any change in the quality of the darkness.

Juggs had not spoken since they left Mrs. Bink's, maintaining a suspicious silence in the open air of the street.

He distrusted the freedom of open space. It was too uncontrolled, it made him feel unprotected and powerless. Openness was like innocence or truth, it left him no handhold of power. Now, though, he began to speak.

"Do you remember that first day? When I found you at Donner's door, a quaking, fearful foundling?" He asked his questions in a low, familiar tone next to her ear. His voice was warm and intimate, as if the two of them were lovers speaking to each other with heads propped on the same pillow.

"I knew then that you would be mine. I knew I would have you someday, in a dark place like this. In a place where you could scream until your throat was raw, until the blood ran from the gouges your fingernails made in the palms of your hands."

"What are you going to do with me?" she whispered, regretful that she should give him the satisfaction of hearing the quiver of tears and terror in her voice.

"Oh," he sighed, "many things. Many things."

Dandre had believed the spinning room *was* the factory. She had never been beyond it to the carding room or the stretching room, or seen the mammoth looms that wove into huge sheets of material the threads she wound onto her heavy reels.

In common with the other factories that had sprung up like midnight mushrooms after the invention of James Watt's steam engine, Braid's mill was situated near a water source, specifically a branch of the Medlock that ran through Manchester, supplying power to countless other factories. The steam engine provided power for Cartwright's power loom, for Crompton's mule and the carding engine and spinning throstle invented by Richard Arkwright.

Juggs took the girl into the very heart of the factory, where the huge shaft was located that generated the power to run all of the separate machines and marvels of invention in the textile mill.

He pushed Dandre against a steel post. Her eyes had adjusted to the darkness and she was now able to make out the towering forms of the giant mechanisms. She saw that Juggs was busy with his free hand, but she could not tell what he was doing until he raised his hand to grab her other arm and she felt the cracked leather of his belt.

Clumsily he pulled the strap tight around her wrists and the pole behind her, then looped it over, then under, then around again, repeating the process a time or two. The leather had already begun to bite into her wrists and she refused to imagine what it would be like when she began to strain against her bonds, writhing in pain.

"This is my favorite room in Braid's," the man said, turning from her when she was completely secured. "It's a room of power. Limitless power. When the shaft begins pumping, when the strap starts to spin, the whole place throbs to its rhythm, and anything in its way is crushed out of existence." He turned back to the girl sagging against the post. "Don't you love it? Don't you feel it?" He came to stand next to her, pushing his body suffocatingly against hers. "Don't you feel the throb?" he whispered against her cheek. In disgust she turned her face away.

He stepped back and studied her for a moment, then looked behind him at the dim room.

"You can't see it. That's why you can't feel it. Here, let me show you the workings of Mr. Juggs's mill."

He fumbled in the pockets of his pants and from some hidden recess was able to extract a match. A lantern was hanging from a nearby post, and he pulled it down and lit it. Then, holding the lantern above his head, he turned to show her the room. The shadows jumped in the uncertain light, so Dandre could not be sure that the shadow she saw move among the handles and wheels and wooden crates was not caused by Juggs's motions, even though it had seemed to move independently. Juggs did not notice it and Dandre was too frightened to divert her attention to the consideration of one strange shadow.

Juggs replaced the lantern on its hook.

"Magnificent, isn't it?" he asked her. The beams of light bounced off the maze of metal machinery. In the center was the huge shaft of steel, and attached to it was a broad conveyer belt. "Imagine that shaft going up and down, up and down, increasing in force, generating untold power. Imagine it. Imagine the light rising and falling along its gleaming length. Imagine it." He spoke hypnotically. He was standing away from her, slowly circling the machine, fascinated by the image he had evoked. He sought her eyes and found them, wide with fear, not on the cold idol in front of them but on him.

It was like a magnet. He walked toward her, pleased to see her sink back against the metal post. Pleased to feel her fear deepen as he approached.

"Don't you think it's fascinating?" he whispered.

He had come to stand directly in front of her and now raised his hand to her face. He touched the red marks on her cheek, smiling when she drew in her breath sharply and tried to jerk away from his fingers and the rough calluses that irritated the torn skin.

In a heavy caress he moved his hand from her cheek to her jaw and then around to the back of her neck.

"Don't you think it's fascinating?" he asked again.

She nodded, steeling herself for the unpleasantness of his kiss. But he did not force her lips against his. A meeting of their lips would have given her too much humanity. Juggs was not interested in the young woman as a person, only in the machinery of her body, the mechanism of her pain.

He moved his hand from the back of her neck and laid it, like a slab of raw beef, against her chest. He rubbed his palm across the mounds of her breast under the fine-twilled cambric of Vincent's shirt, then, impatiently, he hooked his fingers in the vee of the collar and tore the shirt open, baring her shoulders, revealing the heaving of her bosom under the thin chemise.

"Machines have always interested me...fascinated me," he said in a thoughtful, distracted voice, watching his dark fingers moving over her white flesh. "Not the machines so much as the power they possess. Power. Ah." He sighed softly, releasing his rancid breath into her face.

She pulled her head back to escape the vapor but was stopped by the pole behind her. She watched him fearfully under half-lowered lids.

"Do you know what it's like, Miss O'Brien, to have absolute power? To hold someone else's life or death in the palm of your hand? Oh, it's a heady feeling." Now he laughed, the sound low and soft, like the lover turning on the pillow to the woman he adored. But it was not a woman Juggs adored.

He ran his hand down her side, his fingers brushing one of the welts on her back. She gasped. His smile deepened. He hooked his fingers in the waistband of the trousers and with one violent motion jerked the buttons free and pushed the trousers to the floor around her ankles.

"Power. It's a wonderful thing. To see people cringe when you pass, to feel their fearful eyes on you when you walk away. To hear someone scream for mercy. Scream from pain. Scream for death.''

Now, with both hands, he grasped the swell of her hips and pulled her toward him.

''You will never know what that kind of power means, but you can share mine. Do you want to share mine? Do you want to give me that power and feel it surge through both of us in the heat of passion? Then, afterward, as the life flows from your body, don't you want to know what the ultimate power is like?''

He stopped and raised his shadowy eyes to meet hers, and she was filled with a fear she had never imagined before. He drank it in, and then, surprisingly, he released her and turned back to the room.

''But we don't have to hurry. We have plenty of time, and I want you to feel the power of that shaft. *I* want to feel the power.''

He walked across the room to a large box against the wall. When he opened the door, dozens of switches and buttons were revealed. He turned some of the wheels and then pulled down on a handlebar. A deafening roar came up from the shaft and the deep well in the middle of the room. Dandre started.

In the glimmer of the lantern, she saw the metal shaft shiver as the fire of life began to fill its length. Slowly it began to rise. Higher and higher. The top of it disappeared into the blackness overhead. Then, when it reached its full ascension, it plunged into the opening in the floor below. Faster this time, it rose again, then fell again.

The belt attached to it began to turn, conveying motive power to all the rest of the machines in the factory. Juggs stood with his back to her, watching the process, feeling the vibrations as they encompassed the figures in the room, filling him as the gleaming shaft had been filled.

''Do you know what they call that?'' he shouted back at her, pointing to the belt attached to the shaft. ''They call that—" he turned to her "—the Strap." In his hand he held the strap he wielded as overlooker. She had not seen him get it. It must have been hidden inside his clothes the whole time. He cracked it loudly. She jumped. He laughed.

"Don't you find that interesting? I would think a bright girl like yourself would even call that poetic. My strap—" he cracked it again "—was named for that Strap. It is the center of the factory. It harnesses all of the power of that mighty shaft of steel. And it is the most deadly piece of equipment in the entire mill. Anyone caught in its spin is seized and carried up with blinding speed, then thrown against the ceiling above and the floor below. Too fast to stop, almost too fast to see. You cannot be saved from it. It breaks every bone in your body, dashes your brains out onto the floor. Your body is pulled from it utterly mangled."

He paused for a moment and moved slightly to the side so she could clearly view the speed and feel the power of the Strap.

"My strap may seem weak by comparison. And true enough, it can't break bones or smash a skull—" he sounded regretful of its limitations "—but its bite is wicked and its appetite is insatiable. It may not break bones, but it can strip every ounce of flesh off those bones."

He took a step toward her. He cracked his leather strap sharply, then gathered the lashes into his big hand. Slowly, he pulled the thongs through his fingers, savoring the texture and strength of the leather. He shook his head.

"No, my friend here won't break bones in the wink of an eye. He works at a slower pace, at a finer pace. I can work him like an artist works his brush. Oh, that big old Strap there can smash bones, but then what do you have? A mangled lump of flesh that can't feel a thing. Not even much blood, unless the brains have been knocked out." He smiled at the look of revulsion on the girl's face. "I know it sounds ghastly, but I think you'll find that would actually have been preferable.''

He drew back his arm.

"But there is no hurry, is there? Let's do this nice and slow. How about if we start with your legs there?''

He whipped the strap across her bare thighs, exposed when he had torn the trousers down from her hips. Dandre cried out in pain and Juggs smiled appreciatively. He even stood back to admire his handiwork for a moment.

"Shall we see how long those pretty legs will hold you up? Longer than if the bones were thoughtlessly broken, I'll wager.''

He drew back his arm again.

"No!"

In a blur, the small figure flew from the dark shadows around the perimeter of the room into the center, lighted by the lantern. The boy's gait was awkward, a sort of limping gallop, but he was fast and unexpected. Juggs was surprised, caught off guard. He did not even have time enough to raise the strap he held in his hand before the cannonball of Danny's head hit him in the stomach.

With a *whoosh,* the air was forced from the overlooker's lungs. He staggered backward, gasping for breath.

The little boy was half-dazed himself with the force of his blow. He stumbled and fell to his knees. Juggs staggered back another step or two before he regained his equilibrium, and then he located his assailant. Drawing back his foot, he kicked the child heavily in the side, sending him rolling across the floor. Rather than pursue the small bundle, though, Juggs straightened and snapped the leather strap, which he had managed to hold the whole while.

"You little bastard!'' he snarled. "You don't want to see your pretty little friend whipped to death? Very well, she can watch you being whipped to death first!''

He cracked the strap again and then flicked it over his head to enable him to gain as much force as possible when he brought the thongs down onto the boy's back. But in a breath, in a heartbeat, in the wink of an eye Juggs had spoken of himself, one of the thongs was caught in the whirling Strap attached to the shaft.

Before Juggs could release the handle, the thong was pulled into the whirling belt, and then Juggs's hand and the man himself.

It happened as quickly as Juggs had suggested. The belt never slowed, the driving force of the shaft was inexorable. Like an insubstantial rag doll, the overlooker was pulled into the Strap and thrown, screaming, to the ceiling above. The belt spun, and seconds later he was smashed onto the floor below, when his screams abruptly stopped.

Ten or fifteen more times, the nauseating *thud* sounded above and below as the body was whirled around by the Strap. The power the man had so admired was faceless and friendless. The shaft and strap that had excited the deranged overlooker to a frenzy of passion beat the body that had been Eldridge Juggs into a sloppy sack of bones and tissue.

Finally, the broken form was thrown loose to land across the room, where a pool of blood immediately began to gather around the mass of flesh that was no longer recognizable as the overlooker. It was no longer even recognizable as a human body.

Dandre had closed her eyes when Juggs was dragged into the Strap screaming. She kept them closed as his body was thrown around the belt, but when she heard the *thump* as the body landed on the other side of the room, she carefully opened them again.

Juggs was long past help, and Dandre could not spare another thought for him.

"Danny?" she called, shouting to be heard over the noise of the machinery, tears streaming from her eyes in the fear that she could not be heard, no matter how loudly she cried.

But the little boy stirred. Slowly, oh so slowly, he rolled over and then managed to raise himself to his hands and knees. Like an innocent, injured puppy, he crawled to Dandre's side before he collapsed, whimpering, at her feet.

"Sh . . . it is all right now, everything will be all right now," the girl crooned above him, nearly insensible herself from pain and fear and horror and blessed, blessed relief.

"Dandre! Danny! Dandre! Are you in here?"

She could hear Vincent's frantic shouts even before the door burst open. The man rushed into the room, ran toward the light, saw the half-clad form against the pole and caught his breath in his own sob of relief when the girl raised her head.

"Danny," she said.

He could not hear what she said, but he saw her lips and then followed the direction of her gaze to the little body at her feet.

Supporting the boy's head with his hand, Vincent rolled him to his back, away from Dandre and the pole. Quickly, he checked his pulse, put his ear to the boy's chest, heard his heartbeat and felt the rise and fall of his abdomen. The boy was alive.

Gently he rested the little head on the floor and then turned to the woman tied to the post. He held her face in his hands. She opened her eyes, to have them fill with tears when she saw the man before her.

Juggs had fastened the belt very securely and Vincent could not unravel it quickly enough. But eventually it yielded, the worn leather loosened, and Dandre was able to pull her hands free and fall into his arms.

"How did you know where we were?" she whispered.

"Mrs. Bink. She heard Juggs take you and I thought, I *prayed*, he would bring you back here. I did not know where else to look."

He rocked her gently in his arms and kissed her forehead.

"Where is Juggs?" he asked at last.

"There," Dandre said.

Vincent looked where she indicated and saw the pile of flesh and torn clothing in the pool of blood. He did not release his hold on the woman to verify the obvious fact that the mass was lifeless.

He did not ever want to release the woman he was holding, or the boy who lay beside them.

And in that, at least, he and Dandre Collin were of the same mind.

Epilogue

On April 12, 1832, the committee considering the Ten-hour Bill met. Michael Thomas Sadler chaired the committee. It met forty-three times and examined eighty-nine witnesses. Half of the witnesses were mill workers, who incurred the resentment of their employers when they testified.

Nevertheless, bearding the storm of anger and retaliation that threatened, they stood before the committee and answered its questions.

The Factory Act was finally passed in 1834. It forbade the employment of children under nine years of age and limited the working hours for children nine to thirteen years old to nine hours a day; youths from fourteen to eighteen years old were limited to twelve hours a day. It provided one and a half hours for meals, prohibited night work for anyone under eighteen years of age and provided for two hours of schooling a day for children under fourteen. But perhaps most important, surgeons and inspectors were appointed to visit the factories to make certain the law was being obeyed.

As hard won as the victory was, as sweeping a change as it signaled, Mr. Richard Oastler saw an even grander vision.

"I have no doubt that a much more extensive measure will be adopted before many years are passed; and though, at present, the idea of working infants *only* ten hours a day may appear ignorant, ridiculous, extravagant, idle, delusive and impossible to the legislators of this country, I cannot doubt that, in a very short time, our legislators will hardly believe it was ever possible for a Christian parliament to refuse such an act."

Mr. Michael Thomas Sadler's failing health did not allow him to see the realization of that broader vista. He was not returned to Parliament and he retired to Belfast. On July 29, 1835, he died at the age of fifty-five.

The leadership for legislative factory reform was passed on to Lord Anthony Ashley, the seventh Earl of Shaftesbury, and finally, in 1847, a comprehensive Factory Act was passed and became part of English law.

Vincent Chesterton and Dandre Collin did not wait so long to make the sweeping changes in their lives. Vincent took the young woman and the child to a private and very expensive physician and clinic in the city, where their injuries were attended to and they were nursed back to health.

At the beginning of their lengthy convalescence, Vincent insisted Dandre write to her parents in Coventry and her Aunt and Uncle Woodley and give them a full report of the past fortnight. She insisted he perform the same act of courtesy for his sister and her husband. Within the week, Dandre's private room was filled with flowers and beautiful cards and parents, family and friends, all agog over the danger and excitement she had endured and, more surprisingly, survived.

Her mother and father were appalled but well able to believe their daughter's derring-do.

Her aunt and uncle were frankly stunned. Her uncle, incidentally, upon hearing her story, immediately sold his share of the textile mill in which he had invested.

Little Danny Fry was not forgotten in all of this and, though shy at first, very soon learned to revel in the attention and admiration that were lavished on him.

Vincent gracefully took a place behind the bright light of family notice, but it was he who arranged for Nan and the other mill workers to meet with Mr. Richard Oastler in Mrs. Boyle's homey café. Oastler was able to cast his powerful spell of oration, and not long afterward, he introduced several of the workers to Mr. Sadler, who took their testimony and helped turn it into law.

As soon as Dandre and Danny were fully recovered, Vincent and Dandre were married and made the legal arrangements to adopt Danny as their son. Their first son.

All together the three of them rode up the lane to Timbrey Hall in the fine coach the restored Mr. Vincent Chesterton had hired for the occasion.

It was nearly winter by then, and many of the trees that lined the lane had lost their leaves. The countryside could be glimpsed through the bare gray limbs. So could Timbrey Hall.

Danny's eyes grew as large as shilling pieces and his jaw slowly dropped. Dandre—Mrs. Chesterton—glanced down at the small boy at her side and smiled at his expression of amazement.

"How do you like your new home, Danny?" she asked.

He turned his wide, wondering eyes on his new mama.

"*That's* our house?" he whispered.

Danny's face did not lose its expression of awe when Vincent helped the two of them down from the coach and the boy saw the lawn that stretched up to the stone courtyard and the fairy tale castle "Mama" had called their new home.

He spoke in reverent whispers when the white-haired Stanis threw open the front doors and Vincent herded them into the portals.

"Jackie! Jeremy!" Vincent cried gladly, greeting his sister and brother-in-law, who had come to welcome them home and for the pheasant shooting, and would remain until well after the first of the new year. "Danny, you remember your Aunt Jacqueline and Uncle Jeremy, do you not?"

That was asking a great deal of the lad. In this wonderland he was not even sure that he remembered who *he* was.

The dazzle of Timbrey Hall did not dim for Danny that day, or the next, or the next week or several months. When "Daddy" brought home the terrier puppy for his very own, the child was touchingly grateful, but he was grateful still a year later when he was presented with his own pony, and several years after that, when his father and mother sent him to a prestigious boys' school.

In the meantime he became the darling of the neighborhood. The Woodleys adored the child, just as Grandma and Grandpa Collin did in the more distant Coventry. Henry Biggins was convinced the boy was the brightest lad in the kingdom, and, just coincidentally, Danny would listen to the caretaker of the Woodley home with mouth agape for hours on end as Henry discoursed at length on every possible subject that presented itself. Mildred spoiled him shamelessly.

In a development not foreseen by any of them, the Misses Humphries abandoned their orchids and Siamese cats and took the little Chesterton boy to their capacious bosoms. By the time spring returned, Danny was calling them "Aunt Bobby" and "Aunt Willy," which never ceased to amaze and amuse Dandre.

Dandre did wear the alluring cloud-white dressing gown she had worn in the Sheffington on her wedding night—at the beginning of her wedding night, anyway—and on many other nights during the long course of her marriage to Vincent. Danny was their first son, but not their only son. And though other children followed, none of the beautiful Chesterton offspring was more loved than Danny.

Vincent Chesterton refused any other confidential government assignments, choosing to devote himself to his family. And his property. He seized the reins as head of the household and assumed the responsibility of bringing Timbrey Hall and the Chesterton lands up to full production.

When his wife and son were comfortably settled in Timbrey Hall, he made a trip into Manchester and one last time went down to Little Ireland.

His vegetable-dealer guide was no longer stationed at the entrance to the slum dwellings, and Chesterton had a difficult time finding his way. But eventually he came to a place that looked familiar.

"Jenny? Jenny Braugh?" he called through the open door of the little shanty.

The girl came out of the shadows, squinting against the light.

"Hello, Jenny, perhaps you do not remember me," he started, but the girl quickly stepped up directly in front of him and seized his hands.

"Oh, you have been my friend," she said fondly. "I'm so glad to see you again."

"Jenny, I have taken a home out in the country since last I saw you, and if you think your sister could get along without you, I was hoping you could come and help take care of my wife and me and our son? The wages will be generous and there will be quarters for you and your child."

The young woman sobbed and threw her arms around his neck. It was reminiscent of the hug Dandre had given him when he suggested the idea to her.

Now, laughing, he extricated himself from the girl's clasp and with some embarrassment accepted her emotional gratitude.

As he told Dandre, as he believed and as he lived his life, one man may be powerless to change everything, but one man, with a good woman beside him, can change some things.

* * * * *

Harlequin® Historical

HARLEQUIN HISTORICALS
ARE GETTING BIGGER!

This fall, Harlequin Historicals will bring you bigger books. Along with our traditional high-quality historicals, we will be including selected reissues of favorite titles, as well as longer originals.

Reissues from popular authors like Elizabeth Lowell, Veronica Sattler and Marianne Willman.

Originals like ACROSS TIME—an historical time-travel by Nina Beaumont, UNICORN BRIDE—a medieval tale by Claire Delacroix, and SUSPICION—a title by Judith McWilliams set during Regency times.

Leave it to Harlequin Historicals to deliver enduring love stories, larger-than-life characters, and history as you've never before experienced it.

And now, leave it to Harlequin Historicals, to deliver even more!

Look for *The Bargain* by Veronica Sattler in October, *Pieces of Sky* by Marianne Willman in November, and *Reckless Love* by Elizabeth Lowell in December.

HHEXP